November 9

November 9

Colleen Hoover

THORNDIKE PRESS
A part of Gale, a Cengage Company

Thorndike Press, a part of Gale, a Cengage Company.

Thorndike Press® Large Print Softcover Romance and Women's Fiction.
The text of this Large Print edition is unabridged.
Other aspects of the book may vary from the original edition.
Set in 16 pt. Plantin.

LIBRARY OF CONGRESS CIP DATA ON FILE.
CATALOGUING IN PUBLICATION FOR THIS BOOK
IS AVAILABLE FROM THE LIBRARY OF CONGRESS.

ISBN-13: 978-1-4328-9729-1 (softcover alk. paper)

Published in 2022 by arrangement with Atria Books, a Division of Simon & Schuster, Inc.

Printed in the USA
2 3 4 5 6   26 25 24 23 22

To Levi —
You have great taste in music
and your hugs are awkward.
Never change.

■ ■ ■ ■

First November 9th

■ ■ ■ ■

I am translucent, aquatic.
Drifting, aimless.
She is an anchor, sinking in my sea.
— Benton James Kessler

Fallon

I wonder what kind of sound it would make if I were to smash this glass against the side of his head.

It's a thick glass. His head is hard. The potential for a nice big THUD is there.

I wonder if he would bleed. There are napkins on the table, but not the good kind that could soak up a lot of blood.

"So, yeah. I'm a little shocked, but it's happening," he says.

His voice causes my grip to tighten around the glass in hopes that it stays in my hand and doesn't actually end up against the side of his skull.

"Fallon?" He clears his throat and tries to soften his words, but they still come at me like knives. "Are you going to say anything?"

I stab the hollow part of an ice cube with my straw, imagining that it's his head.

"What am I supposed to say?" I mumble, resembling a bratty child, rather than the eighteen-year-old adult that I am. "Do you want me to *congratulate* you?"

My back meets the booth behind me and I fold my arms across my chest. I look at him and wonder if the regret I see in his eyes is a result of disappointing me or if he's simply acting again. It's only been five minutes since he sat down, and he's already turned his side of the booth into his stage. And once again, I'm forced to be his audience.

His fingers drum the sides of his coffee cup as he watches me silently for several beats.

Taptaptap.

Taptaptap.

Taptaptap.

He thinks I'll eventually give in and tell him what he wants to hear, but he hasn't been around me enough in the last two years to know that I'm not that girl anymore.

When I refuse to acknowledge his performance, he eventually sighs and drops his elbows to the table. "Well, I thought you'd be happy for me."

I force a quick shake of my head. "*Happy* for you?"

He can't be serious.

He shrugs, and a smug smile takes over

his already irritating expression. "I didn't know I had it in me to become a father again."

A loud burst of disbelieving laughter escapes my mouth. "Releasing sperm into the vagina of a twenty-four-year-old does not a father make," I say, somewhat bitterly.

His smug smile disappears, and he leans back and cocks his head to the side. The head-cock was always his go-to move when he wasn't sure how to react onscreen. *"Just look like you're contemplating something deep and it'll pass for almost any emotion. Sad, introspective, apologetic, sympathetic."* He must not recall that he was my acting coach for most of my life, and this look was one of the first he taught me.

"You don't think I have the right to call myself a father?" He sounds offended by my response. "What does that make me to you, then?"

I treat his question as rhetorical and stab at another piece of ice. I skillfully slip it up my straw and then slide the piece of ice into my mouth. I bite into it with a loud, uncaring crunch. Surely he doesn't expect me to answer that question. He hasn't been a "father" since the night my acting career came to a standstill when I was just sixteen. And if I'm being honest with myself, I'm not even sure he was much of a father *before* that night, either. We were more like acting coach and student.

One of his hands finds its way through the expensive implanted follicles of hair that line his forehead. "Why are you doing this?" He's becoming increasingly annoyed with my attitude by the second. "Are you still pissed that I didn't show up for your graduation? I already told you, I had a scheduling conflict."

"No," I reply evenly. "I didn't *invite* you to my graduation."

He pulls back, looking at me incredulously. "Why not?"

"I only had four tickets."

"And?" he says. "I'm your *father.* Why the hell wouldn't you invite me to your high school graduation?"

"You wouldn't have come."

"You don't know that," he fires back.

"You *didn't* come."

He rolls his eyes. "Well of course I didn't, Fallon. I wasn't *invited.*"

I sigh heavily. "You're impossible. Now I understand why Mom left you."

He gives his head a slight shake. "Your mother left me because I slept with her best friend. My personality had nothing to do with it."

I don't even know what to say to that. The man has absolutely zero remorse. I both hate and envy it. In a way, I wish I were more like him and less like my mother. He's oblivious to his many flaws, whereas mine are the focal point of my life. My flaws are what wake me up in the morning and what keep me awake every night.

"Who had the salmon?" the waiter asks. Impeccable timing.

I lift my hand, and he sets my plate in front of me. I don't even have an appetite anymore, so I scoot the rice around with my fork.

"Hey, wait a second." I look up at the waiter, but he isn't addressing his comment at me. He's staring intently at my father. "Are you . . ."

Oh, God. Here we go.

The waiter slaps his hand on the table and I flinch. "You *are*! You're Donovan O'Neil! You played Max Epcott!"

My father shrugs modestly, but I know there isn't a modest thing about this man. Even though he hasn't played the role of Max Epcott since the show went off the air ten years ago, he still acts like it's the biggest thing on television. And people who recognize him are the reason he still responds this way. They act like they've never seen an actor in real life before. This is L.A., for Christ's sake! Everyone here is an actor!

My stabbing mood continues as I spear at my salmon with my fork, but then the waiter interrupts to ask if I'll take a picture of the two of them.

Sigh.

I begrudgingly slide out of the booth. He tries to hand me his phone for the picture, but I hold up my hand in protest and proceed to walk around him.

"I need to use the restroom," I mutter, walking away from the booth. "Just take a selfie with him. He loves selfies."

I rush toward the restroom to find a moment of reprieve from my father. I don't know why I asked him to meet me today. It could be because I'm moving and I won't see him for God knows how long, but that's not even a good enough excuse to put myself through this.

I swing open the door to the first stall. I lock it behind me and pull a protective seat cover out of the dispenser and place it over the toilet seat.

I read a study on bacteria in public restrooms once. The first stall in every bathroom studied was found to have the least amount of bacteria. People assume the first stall is the most utilized, so most people skip over it. Not me. It's the only one I'll use. I haven't always been a germaphobe, but spending two months in the hospital when I was sixteen left me a bit obsessive-compulsive when it comes to hygiene.

Once I'm finished using the restroom, I take at least a full minute to wash my hands. I stare down at them the entire time, refusing to look in the mirror. Avoiding my reflection becomes easier by the day, but I still catch a glimpse of myself while reaching for a paper towel. No matter how many times I've looked in a mirror, I still haven't grown used to what I see.

I bring my left hand up and touch the scars that run across the left side of my face, over my jaw and down my neck. They disappear beneath the collar of my shirt, but underneath my clothing, the scars run down the entire left side of my torso, stopping just below my waistline. I run my fingers over the areas of skin that now resemble puckered leather. Scars that constantly remind me that the fire was real and not just a nightmare I can force myself awake from with a pinch on the arm.

I was bandaged up for months after the fire, unable to touch most of my body. Now that the burns are healed and I'm left with the scars, I catch myself touching them obsessively. The scars feel like stretched velvet, and it would be normal to be as revolted by their feel as I am by their appearance. But instead, I actually like the way they feel. I'm always absentmindedly running my fingers up and down my neck or arm, reading the braille on my skin, until I realize what I'm doing and stop. I shouldn't like any aspect of the one thing that ripped my life out from under me, even if it is simply the way it feels beneath my fingertips.

The way it *looks* is something else. Like each of my flaws has been blanketed in pink highlights, put on display for the entire world to see. No matter how hard I try to hide them with my hair and clothes, they're there. They'll always be there. A permanent reminder of the night that destroyed all the best parts of me.

I'm not one to really focus on dates or anniversaries, but when I woke up this morning, today's date was the first thought that popped into my head. Probably because it was the last thought I had before falling asleep last night. It's been two years to the day since my father's home was engulfed by the fire that almost claimed my life. Maybe that's why I wanted to see my father today. Maybe I hoped he would remember — say something to comfort me. I know he's apologized enough, but how much can I actually forgive him for forgetting about me?

I only stayed at his house once a week on average. But I had texted him that morning to let him know I would be staying the night. So one would think that when my father accidentally catches his own house on fire, he would come rescue me from my sleep.

But not only did that not happen — he forgot I was there. No one knew anyone was in the house until they heard me scream from the second floor. I know he holds a lot of guilt for that. He apologized every time he saw me for weeks, but the apologies became as scarce as his visits and phone calls. The resentment I hold is still very much there, even though I wish it wasn't. The fire was an accident. I survived. Those are the two things I try to focus on, but it's hard when I think about it every time I look at myself.

I think about it every time someone *else* looks at me.

The bathroom door swings open, and a woman walks in, glances at me and then quickly looks away as she heads toward the last stall.

Should have picked the first one, lady.

I look myself over one more time in the mirror. I used to wear my hair above the shoulders with edgy bangs, but it's grown a lot in the last couple of years. And not without reason. I brush my fingers through the long, dark strands of hair that I've trained to cover most of the left side of my face. I pull the sleeve of my left arm down to my wrist and then pull the collar up to cover most of my neck. The scars are barely visible like this, and I can actually stomach looking at myself in the mirror.

I used to think I was pretty. But hair and clothes can only cover up so much now.

I hear a toilet flush, so I turn quickly and make my way to the door before the woman can exit the stall. I do what I can to avoid people most of the time, and not because I'm afraid they'll stare at my scars. I avoid them because they *don't* stare. The second people notice me, they look away just as fast, because they're afraid to appear rude or judgmental. Just once it would be nice if someone looked me in the eyes and held my stare. It's been so long since that's happened. I hate to admit that I miss the attention I used to get, but I do.

I exit the bathroom and head back toward the booth, disappointed to still see the back of my father's head. I was hoping he would have had some kind of emergency and been required to leave while I was in the restroom.

It's sad that I'd rather be greeted by an empty booth than by my own father. The thought almost makes me frown, but I'm suddenly sidetracked by the guy seated in the booth I'm about to walk past.

I don't usually notice people, considering they do everything in their power to avoid eye contact with me. However, this guy's eyes are intense, curious and staring straight at me.

My first thought when I see him is, *"If only this were two years ago."*

I think that a lot when I come across guys I could possibly be attracted to. And this guy is definitely cute. Not in a typical Hollywood way, much like most of the guys who inhabit this city. Those guys all look the same, as if there's a perfect mold for a successful actor and they're all trying to fit it.

This guy is the complete opposite. His five o'clock shadow isn't a symmetrical, purposeful work of art. Instead, his stubble is splotchy and uneven, like he spent the night working late and actually didn't have time to shave. His hair isn't styled with gel to give him the messy, just-rolled-out-of-bed look. This guy's hair actually *is* messy. Strands of chocolate hair sweep across his forehead, some of them erratic and wild. It's like he woke up late for an appointment and was too hurried to bother with looking in a mirror.

Such an unkempt appearance should be a turnoff, but that's what I find so odd. Despite him looking like he doesn't have one iota of self-absorption, he's one of the most attractive guys I've ever seen.

I *think.*

This could just be a side effect of my obsession with cleanliness. Maybe I so desperately long for the kind of carelessness this guy exhibits that I'm mistaking jealousy for fascination.

I also might think he's cute simply because he's one of the few people in the last two years who doesn't immediately look away the moment my eyes meet his.

I still have to pass his table in order to get to my booth behind him, and I can't decide if I want to break out in a sprint in order to get his eyes off me, or if I should walk in slow motion so I can soak up the attention.

His body shifts as I begin to pass him, and his stare becomes too much all of a sudden. Too invasive. I feel my cheeks flush and my skin tingle, so I look down at my feet and allow my hair to fall in front of my face. I even pull a strand of it into my mouth in order to block more of his view. I don't know why his stare is making me uncomfortable, but it is. Just a few moments ago, I was thinking about how much I miss being stared at, but now that it's happening, I just want him to look away.

Right before he's out of my peripheral vision, I cut my eyes in his direction and catch a ghost of a smile.

He must not have noticed my scars. That's the only reason a guy like him would have smiled at me.

Ugh. It annoys me that I even think this way. I used to not be this girl. I used to be confident, but the fire melted away every ounce of my self-esteem. I've tried getting it back, but it's hard to believe someone could ever find me attractive when I can't even look at myself in the mirror.

"That never gets old," my father says as I slide back into the booth.

I glance up at him, almost having forgotten he was here. "What never gets old?"

He waves his fork toward the waiter, who is now standing at the cash register. "That," he says. "Having fans." He shoves a bite of food in his mouth and begins speaking with a mouthful. "So what did you want to talk to me about?"

"What makes you think I wanted to talk to you about something in particular?"

He gestures over the table. "We're having lunch together. You obviously need to tell me something."

It's sad that this is what our relationship has come to. Knowing that a simple lunch date has to be more than just a daughter wanting to see her father.

"I'm moving to New York tomorrow. Well, tonight, actually. But my flight isn't until late and I don't officially land in New York until the 10th."

He grabs his napkin and covers a cough. At least I think it's a cough. Surely that news didn't make him choke on his food.

"New York?" he sputters.

And then . . . he laughs. *Laughs.* As if me living in New York is a joke. *Stay calm, Fallon. Your father is an asshole. That's old news.*

"What in the world? *Why?* What's in New York?" His questions keep coming as he processes the information. "And please don't tell me you met someone online."

My pulse is raging. Can't he at least *pretend* to support one of my decisions?

"I want a change of pace. I was thinking about auditioning for Broadway."

When I was seven, my father took me to see *Cats* on Broadway. It was the first time I had ever been to New York and it was one of the best trips of my life. Up until that moment, he had always pushed me to be an actress. But it wasn't until I saw that live performance that I knew I *had* to be an actress. I never had the chance to pursue theater because my father dictated each step of my career and he's more fond of film. But it's been two years now since I've done anything with myself. I don't know if I actually have the courage to audition anytime soon, but making the choice to move to New York is one of the most proactive things I've done since the fire.

My father takes a drink and after he sets down his glass, his shoulders drop with a sigh. "Fallon, listen," he says. "I know you miss acting, but don't you think it's time you pursue other options?"

I'm so beyond caring about his motives now, I don't even point out the pile of bullshit he just threw at me. My entire life, all he did was push me to follow in his footsteps. After the fire, his encouragement came to a complete halt. I'm not an idiot. I know he thinks I don't have what it takes to be an actress anymore, and part of me knows he's right. Looks are really important in Hollywood.

Which is precisely why I want to move to New York. If I ever want to act again, theater may be my best hope.

I wish he wasn't so transparent. My mother was ecstatic when I told her I wanted to move. Since graduation and moving in with Amber, I rarely leave my apartment. Mom was sad to find out I would be moving away from her, but happy to see that I was willing to leave the confines of not only my apartment, but the entire state of California.

I wish my father could see what a huge step this is for me.

"What happened with that narrating job?" he asks.

"I'm still with them. Audiobooks are recorded in studios. Studios exist in New York."

He rolls his eyes. "Unfortunately."

"What's wrong with audiobooks?"

He shoots me a look of disbelief. "Aside from the fact that narrating audiobooks is considered the cesspool of acting? You can do better, Fallon. Hell, go to college or something."

My heart sinks. Just when I thought he couldn't be more self-absorbed.

He stops chewing and looks straight at me

when he realizes what he implied. He quickly wipes his mouth with his napkin and points at me. "You know that's not what I meant. I'm not saying you've reduced yourself to audiobooks. What I'm saying is that you can find a better career to fall back on now that you can't act anymore. There isn't enough money in narration. Or Broadway, for that matter."

He says *Broadway* like it's poison in his mouth. "For your information, there are a lot of respectable actors who also narrate audiobooks. And do you need me to name A-list actors on Broadway right now? I have all day."

He yields with a shake of his head, even though I know he doesn't really agree with me. He just feels bad for insulting one of the few acting-related professions I'm able to pursue.

He lifts his empty glass of water to his mouth and tilts his head back far enough to salvage a sip from the melting ice. "Water," he says, shaking his glass in the air until the waiter nods and walks over to refill it.

I stab at my salmon again, which is no longer warm. I hope he finishes his meal soon, because I'm not sure I can stomach much more of this visit. The only sense of relief I feel at this point is from knowing I'll be on the opposite coast from him come this time tomorrow. Even if I am trading sunshine for snow.

"Don't make plans for mid-January," he says, changing the subject. "I'll need you to fly back to L.A. for a week."

"Why? What's happening in January?"

"Your old man is getting hitched."

I squeeze the back of my neck and look down at my lap. "Kill me now."

I feel a pang of guilt, because as much as I wish someone would actually kill me right now, I didn't mean to say those words out loud.

"Fallon, you can't judge whether or not you'll like her until you've met her."

"I don't have to meet her to know I won't like her," I say. "She is marrying you, after all." I try to disguise the truth in my words with a sarcastic smile, but I'm sure he knows I mean every word I say to him.

"In case you've forgotten, your mother also chose to marry me, and you seem to like her just fine," he says in retort.

He has me there.

"Touché. But in my defense, this makes your fifth proposal since I was ten."

"But only the third wife," he clarifies.

I finally sink my fork into the salmon and take a bite. "You make me want to swear off men forever," I say with a mouthful.

He laughs. "That shouldn't be a problem. I've only known you to go on one date, and that was over two years ago."

I swallow the bite of salmon with a gulp. *Seriously?* Where was I when they were assigning decent fathers? Why did I have to get stuck with the obtuse asshole?

I wonder how many times he's put his foot in his mouth during lunch today. He better watch out or his gums are going to get athlete's foot. He honestly has no idea what today is. If he did, he would never have said something so careless.

I can see in the sudden furrow of his brow that he's attempting to construct an apology for what he just said. I'm sure he didn't mean it in the way I took it, but that doesn't stop me from wanting to retaliate with my own words.

I reach up and tuck my hair behind my left ear, putting my scars on full display as I look him square in the eye. "Well, Dad. I don't really get the same attention from guys that I used to get. You know, before *this* happened." I wave my hand across my face, but I already regret the words that just slipped from my mouth.

Why do I always stoop to his level? I'm better than this.

His eyes fall to my cheek and then quickly drop to the table.

He actually looks remorseful, and I contemplate laying off the bitterness and being a little nicer to him. However, before anything nice can come out of my mouth, the guy in the booth behind my father begins to stand up and my attention span is shot to hell. I try to pull my hair back in front of my face before he turns around, but it's too late. He's already staring at me again.

The same smile he shot at me earlier is still affixed to his face, but this time I don't look away from him. In fact, my eyes don't leave his as he makes his way to our booth. Before I can react, he's sliding into the seat with me.

Holy shit. What is he doing?

"Sorry I'm late, babe," he says, wrapping his arm around my shoulders.

He just called me babe. This random dude just put his arm around me and called me babe.

What the hell is going on?

I glance at my father, thinking he's in on this somehow, but he's looking at the stranger next to me with even more confusion than I probably am.

I stiffen beneath the guy's arm when I feel his lips press against the side of my head.

"Damn L.A. traffic," he mutters.

Random Dude just put his lips in my hair.

What.

Is going.

On.

The guy reaches across the table for my father's hand. "I'm Ben," he says. "Benton James Kessler. Your daughter's boyfriend."

Your daughter's . . . *what*?

My father returns the handshake. I'm pretty sure my mouth is hanging open, so I immediately clamp it shut. I don't want my father to know I have no idea who this guy is. I also don't want this Benton guy to think my jaw is touching the floor because I like his attention. I'm only looking at him like this because . . . well . . . because he's obviously a lunatic.

He releases my father's hand and settles against the booth. He gives me a quick wink and leans toward me, bringing his mouth close enough to my ear to warrant being punched.

"Just go with it," he whispers.

He pulls back, still smiling.

Just go with it?

What is this, his improv class assignment?

And then it hits me.

He overheard our entire conversation. He must be pretending to be my boyfriend as some weird way to stick it to my father.

Huh. I think I like my new fake boyfriend.

Now that I know he's toying with my father, I smile at him affectionately. "I didn't think you'd make it." I lean into Ben and look at my father.

"Babe, you know I've been wanting to meet your father. You hardly ever get to see him. No amount of traffic could have kept me from showing up today."

I shoot my new fake boyfriend a satisfied grin for that dig. Ben must have an asshole for a father, too, because he seems to know just what to say.

"Oh, I'm sorry," Ben says, focusing on my father again. "I didn't catch your name."

My father is already eyeing Ben with disapproval. *God, I love it.*

"Donovan O'Neil," my father says. "You've probably heard the name before. I was the star of —"

"Nope," Ben interrupts. "Doesn't ring a bell." He turns to me and winks. "But Fallon here has told me a lot about you." He pinches my chin and looks back at my father. "And speaking of our girl, what do you think of her moving all the way to New York?" He looks back down at me and frowns. "I don't want my ladybug running off to another city, but if it means she's following her dream, I'll be the first to make sure she's on her flight."

Ladybug? He better be glad he's my fake boyfriend, because I feel like punching him in his fake nuts for that cheesy moniker.

My dad clears his throat, obviously uncomfortable with our new lunch guest. "I can think of a few dreams an eighteen-year-old should follow, but Broadway isn't one of them. Especially with the career she's already had. Broadway is a step down, in my opinion."

Ben adjusts his position in his seat. He smells really good. I think. It's been so long since I sat this close to a guy, he may smell completely normal.

"Good thing she's eighteen," Ben says in response. "Parental opinions on what she does with her life don't really matter much at this point."

I know he's only putting on an act, but no one has ever taken up for me like this before. It's making my lungs feel like they're seizing up. *Stupid lungs.*

"It's not an opinion when it comes from an industry professional," my father says. "It's a fact. I've been in this business long enough to know when someone needs to bow out."

I snap my head toward my father at the

same time Ben's arm tenses around my shoulders.

"Bow out?" Ben says. "Did you really just say — *out loud* — that your daughter needs to give up?"

My father rolls his eyes and crosses both arms over his chest as he glares at Ben. Ben removes his arm from around my shoulders and mirrors my father's movements, glaring right back at him.

God, this is so uncomfortable. And so amazing. I've never seen my father act like this. I've never seen him dislike someone instantly.

"Listen, *Ben.*" He says his name with a mouthful of distaste. "Fallon doesn't need you filling her head with nonsense simply because you're excited about the prospect of having a booty-call on the East Coast."

Oh, my God. Did my father just refer to me as this guy's *booty call*? My mouth is agape as he continues.

"My daughter is smart. She's tough. She accepts that the career she worked her whole life for is out of the question now that . . ." He flicks his hand toward me. "Now that she . . ."

He's unable to finish his own sentence, and a look of regret washes over his face. I know exactly what he was about to say. He's been saying everything *but* that for two years now.

I was one of the fastest up-and-coming teen actresses just two years ago, and the moment the fire burned away my looks, the studio pulled my contract. I think he mourns the idea that he's not the father of an actress more than he mourns almost losing his daughter to a fire that was caused by his carelessness.

Once my contract was canceled, we never spoke about the possibility of me acting again. We never really speak at *all* anymore. He's gone from being the father who spent his entire days on set with me for a year and a half, to the father whom I see maybe once a month.

So I'll be damned if he doesn't finish what he was about to say. I've been waiting two years to hear him admit that my looks are why I no longer have a career. Until today, it's always just been a silent assumption. We never talk about *why* I no longer act. We only talk about the fact that I *don't.* And while he's at it, it would also be nice to hear him admit that the fire also destroyed our relationship. He has absolutely no idea how to be a father to me now that he's no longer my acting coach and manager.

I narrow my eyes in his direction. "Finish

your sentence, Dad."

He shakes his head, trying to dismiss the subject entirely. I arch an eyebrow, daring him to continue.

"Do you really want to do this right now?" He glances in the direction of Ben, hoping to use my pretend boyfriend as a buffer.

"As a matter of fact, I do."

My father closes his eyes and sighs heavily. When he opens them again, he leans forward and folds his arms on the table. "You know I think you're beautiful, Fallon. Stop twisting my words. It's this business that has higher standards than a father does, and all we can do is accept it. In fact, I thought we *had* accepted it," he says, cutting his eyes in Ben's direction.

I bite the inside of my cheek in order to refrain from saying something I'll regret. I've always known the truth. When I saw myself in the mirror for the first time in the hospital, I knew everything was over. But hearing my father admit out loud that he also thinks I should stop following my dreams is more than I was prepared for.

"Wow," Ben mutters under his breath. "That was . . ." He looks at my father and shakes his head in disgust. "You're her *father.*"

If I didn't know better, I would say the

grimace on Ben's face is genuine, and he isn't just acting.

"Exactly. I'm her *father.* Not her mother, who feeds her whatever bullshit she thinks will make her little girl feel better. New York and L.A. are filled with thousands of girls following the same dream Fallon has been following her entire life. Girls who are wildly talented. Exceptionally beautiful. Fallon knows I believe she's got more talent than all of them put together, but she's also realistic. Everyone has dreams, but unfortunately, she no longer has the tools it takes to achieve hers. She needs to accept that before she wastes money on a cross-country move that isn't going to do a damn thing for her career."

I close my eyes. Whoever said the truth hurts was being an optimist. The truth is an excruciatingly painful son of a bitch.

"Jesus," Ben says. "You are unbelievable."

"And you're unrealistic," my father replies.

I open my eyes and nudge Ben's arm, letting him know I want out of the booth. I can't do this anymore.

Ben fails to move. Instead, he slides his hand under the table and grips my knee, urging me to stay seated.

My leg stiffens beneath his touch, because my body is sending mixed signals to my brain. I'm pissed at my father right now. *So pissed.* But somehow I feel comforted by this complete stranger who is taking up for me for no apparent reason. I want to scream and I want to smile and I want to cry, but most of all, I just want something to eat. Because now I'm actually hungry and I wish I had *warm salmon,* dammit!

I try to relax my leg so that Ben doesn't feel how tense I am, but he's the first guy in a long time to actually physically touch me. It's a little weird if I'm being honest.

"Let me ask you something, Mr. O'Neil," Ben says. "Did Johnny Cash have a cleft palate?"

My father is quiet. I'm quiet, too, hoping there's an actual point to Ben's random question. He was doing so well until he started talking about country singers.

My father looks at Ben as if he's crazy. "What in the hell does a country singer have to do with this conversation?"

"Everything," Ben quickly replies. "And no, he didn't have one. However, the actor who portrayed him in *Walk the Line* has a very prominent scar on his face. Joaquin Phoenix was actually nominated for an Academy Award for that role."

My pulse quickens when I realize what he's doing.

"What about Idi Amin?" Ben asks.

My father rolls his eyes, bored with this line of questioning. "What about him?"

"He didn't have a lazy eye. However, the actor who played him — Forest Whitaker — *does*. Another Academy Award nominee, funny enough. *And* winner."

This is the first time I've ever seen anyone put my father in his place. And even though this entire conversation is making me uncomfortable, I'm not too uncomfortable to enjoy this rare and beautiful moment.

"Congratulations," my father says to Ben, completely unimpressed. "You listed two successful examples out of millions of failures."

I try not to take my father's words personally, but it's hard not to. I know at this point it's become more of a power struggle between the two of them, and less about him and me. It's just really disappointing that he'd rather win an argument against a complete stranger than defend his own daughter.

"If your daughter is as talented as you claim she is, wouldn't you want to encourage her not to give up on her dreams? Why would you want her to see the world the way you do?"

My father stiffens. "And how, exactly, do

you think I see the world, Mr. Kessler?"

Ben leans back in our booth without breaking eye contact with my father. "Through the closed eyes of an arrogant asshole."

The silence that follows is like the calm before the storm. I wait for one of them to throw the first punch, but instead, my father reaches into his pocket and pulls out his wallet. He tosses cash onto the table and then looks directly at me.

"I may be honest to a fault, but if bullshit is what you prefer to hear, then this prick is perfect for you." He slides out of the booth. "I bet your mother loves him," he mutters.

I wince at his words and want so badly to hurl an insult back at him. One so epic that it would wound his ego for days. The only problem with that is there's nothing anyone could say that would wound a man who has absolutely no heart.

Rather than scream something at him as he walks out the door, I simply sit in silence.

With my fake boyfriend.

This has got to be the most humiliating, awkward moment of my life.

As soon as I feel the first tear begin to escape, I push against Ben's arm. "I need out," I whisper. "Please."

He slides out of the booth, and I keep my

head down as I stand and walk past him. I don't dare look back at him as I head toward the restroom again. The fact that he felt the need to pretend to be my boyfriend is embarrassing enough. But then I had to go and have the worst fight I've ever had with my father right in front of him.

If I were Benton James Kessler, I would have fake-dumped me by now.

Ben

I hang my head in my hands and wait for her to return from the bathroom.

I should leave, actually.

I don't want to leave, though. I feel like I trampled on her day with the stunt I just pulled with her dad. As smooth as I tried to be, I didn't ease into this girl's life with the discreet grace of a fox. I barged into it with the subtlety of a fifteen-thousand-pound elephant.

Why did I feel the need to step in? Why did I think she wasn't capable of handling her father on her own? She's probably pissed at me right now, and we've only been fake-dating for half an hour.

This is why I choose not to have real-life girlfriends. I can't even *pretend* without starting a fight.

But I did just order her a warm plate of salmon, so maybe that'll make up for some of it?

She finally exits the bathroom, but the second she sees me still seated on her side of the booth, she pauses. The confusion on her face makes it apparent she was sure I'd be gone by the time she returned to the table.

I *should* have been gone. I should have left half an hour ago.

Coulda, shoulda, woulda.

I stand up and motion for her to sit. She eyes me suspiciously as she slides into her seat. I reach over to the other booth and collect my laptop, my plate of food and my drink. I set them all on her table and then I occupy the seat her asshole-father was just sitting in minutes before.

She's looking down at the table, probably wondering where her food went.

"It got cold," I tell her. "I told the waiter to bring you another plate."

Her eyes flick up to mine, but her head doesn't move. She doesn't crack a smile or say thank you. She just . . . stares.

I take a bite of my burger and begin to chew.

I know she isn't shy. I could tell by the way she spoke to her father that she has sass, so I'm a little confused by her silence right now. I swallow my bite of food and take a drink of my soda, maintaining silent eye contact with her the whole time. I wish I could say I'm mentally preparing a brilliant apology, but I'm not. I seem to have a one-track mind, and that track leads straight to the two things I shouldn't even be thinking about right now.

Her boobs.

Both of them.

I know. I'm pathetic. But if we're just going to sit here and stare at each other, it'd be nice if she were showing a little cleavage, instead of wearing this long-sleeved shirt that leaves *everything* to the imagination. It's pushing eighty degrees outside. She should be in something a lot less . . . convent-inspired.

A couple seated a few tables over stands up and begins to walk past us, toward the exit. I notice Fallon tilts her head away from them and lets her hair fall in front of her face like a protective shield. I don't even think she realizes she's doing it. It seems like such a natural reaction for her to try and cover up what she sees as flaws.

That's probably why she's wearing the long-sleeved shirt. It shields everyone from seeing what's beneath it.

And of course, this thought leads me to her breasts again. Are they scarred, too? How much of her body is actually affected?

I begin to mentally undress her, and not in a sexual way. I'm just curious. *Really* curious, because I can't stop staring at her, and that's not like me. My mother raised me with more tact than this, but what my mother failed to teach me is that there would be girls like this one who would test those manners merely by existing.

A solid minute passes, maybe two. I eat most of my fries, watching her watch me. She doesn't look angry. She doesn't look scared. At this point, she's not even trying to hide the scars she so desperately tries to cover from everyone else.

Her eyes begin to make a slow descent until they stop at my shirt. She stares at it for a moment, and then moves her gaze over my arms, my shoulders, my face. She stops when she gets to my hair.

"Where did you go this morning?"

Her question is incredibly random and causes me to pause mid-chew. I figured the first question she would ask me would be why I took it upon myself to interfere with her personal life. I take a few seconds to swallow, take a drink, wipe my mouth, and then lean back in my booth.

"What do you mean?"

She motions to my hair. "Your hair is a mess." She motions to my shirt. "You're wearing the same shirt you wore yesterday." Her eyes fall to my fingers. "Your nails are clean."

How does she know I'm wearing the same shirt I wore yesterday?

"So why'd you leave wherever you woke up in such a hurry today?" she asks.

I look down at my shirt and then at my nails. *How in the hell does she know I left in a rush this morning?*

"People who don't take care of themselves don't have nails as clean as yours," she says. "It contradicts the mustard stain on your shirt."

I look down at my shirt. At the mustard stain I hadn't noticed until now.

"Your burger has mayonnaise on it. And since mustard is hardly ever eaten for breakfast, and you're inhaling your food like you haven't eaten since yesterday, then the stain is more than likely from whatever you ate for dinner last night. And you obviously haven't looked in a mirror today or you wouldn't have walked out of your house with your hair looking like that. Did you take a shower and fall asleep without drying your hair?" She touches her long hair and flicks it between her fingers. "Because hair as thick as yours bends when you sleep on it wet. Makes it impossible to fix without rewashing it." She leans forward and eyes me curiously. "How in the heck did the *front* of your hair get so jacked up? Do you sleep on your stomach or something?"

What is she? A detective?

"I . . ." I stare at her in disbelief. "Yeah. I sleep on my stomach. And I was late for class."

She nods like she somehow knew that already.

The waiter appears with a fresh plate of food and refills her water. He opens his mouth like he wants to say something to her, but she's not paying attention to him. She's still staring at me, but she mutters a thank you at him.

He looks like he's about to walk away, but before he does, he pauses and turns back to face her. He wrings his hands together, obviously nervous to ask whatever question is about to leave his mouth. "So . . . um. Donovan O'Neil? Is he your father?"

She looks up at the waiter with an unreadable expression. "Yes," she says flatly.

The waiter smiles and relaxes with her response. "Wow," he says, shaking his head in fascination. "How awesome is that? To have *the* Max Epcott for a father?"

She doesn't smile or flinch. Nothing on her face indicates that this is a question she's heard a million times before. I wait for her sarcastic reply, because based on the way she responded to her father's senseless comments, there's no way this poor waiter is leaving here unscathed.

Just when I think she's about to roll her eyes, she releases a pent-up breath and smiles. "It was absolutely surreal. I'm the luckiest daughter in the world."

The waiter grins. "That's really cool."

When he turns and walks away, she faces me again. "What kind of class?" she asks.

It takes me a moment to process her question because I'm still trying to process the bullshit answer she just fed the waiter. I almost inquire about it, but think better of it. I'm sure it's easier for her to give people the answers they hope to hear, rather than an earful of the truth. That, and she's probably the most loyal person I've ever met, because I'm not sure I could say those things about that man if he were my father.

"Creative writing."

She smiles thoughtfully and picks up her fork. "I knew you weren't an actor." She takes a bite of her salmon, and before she swallows the first bite, she's already cutting into it again. The next several minutes are spent in complete silence while we both finish eating. I clean my entire plate, but she pushes hers away before she even finishes half of it.

"So tell me something," she says, leaning forward. "Why'd you think I needed you to come to my rescue with that fake boyfriend crap?"

And there it is. She's upset with me. I kind of thought she might be.

"I didn't think you needed rescuing. I just sometimes find it difficult to control my indignation in the presence of absurdity."

She raises an eyebrow. "You're definitely a writer, because who the hell talks like that?"

I laugh. "Sorry. I guess what I'm trying to say is that I can be a temperamental idiot and I should have minded my own business."

She pulls the napkin from her lap and sets it on her plate. One of her shoulders rises with a little half-shrug. "I didn't mind," she says with a smile. "It was kind of fun seeing my father so flustered. And I've never had a fake boyfriend before."

"I've never had a *real* boyfriend before," I reply.

Her eyes shift to my hair. "Believe me, that's obvious. No gay man I know would have left the house looking like you do right now."

I kind of get the feeling she doesn't mind

the way I look nearly as much as she's letting on. I'm sure she receives her fair share of physical discrimination, so I find it hard to believe she would be the type to list physical appearance high on her list of priorities in a guy.

But it's not lost on me that she's teasing me. If I didn't know better, I'd say she was flirting.

Yep. Definitely should have walked out of this restaurant a long time ago, but this is one of the few moments I'm actually thankful for the plethora of bad decisions I tend to make.

The waiter brings the check, but before I can pay it, Fallon scoops up the wad of cash her father threw on the table and hands it to him.

"You need change?" he asks.

She waves it off. "Keep it."

The waiter clears off the table and when he steps away, there's nothing left between us. The imminent end to the meal leaves me feeling a little unsettled, because I'm not sure what to say to keep her here longer. The girl is moving to New York and chances are, I'll never see her again. I don't know why the thought of that makes me anxious.

"So," she says. "Should we break up now?"

I laugh, even though I'm still attempting

to discern if she's got an incredible deadpan wit, or absolutely no personality at all. There's a fine line between the two, but I'm betting it's the former. *Hoping* it is, anyway.

"We haven't even been dating an hour yet and you already want to dump me? Am I not very good at this boyfriend thing?"

She smiles. "A little too good. It's weirding me out, to be honest. Is this the moment you break the ultimate boyfriend illusion and tell me you knocked up my cousin while we were on a break?"

I can't help but laugh again. *Definitely deadpan wit.* "I didn't knock her up. She was already seven months pregnant when I slept with her."

An infectious burst of laughter meets my ears, and I've never been more thankful to have a semi-decent sense of humor. I'm not allowing this girl to leave my sight until I get at least three or four more of those laughs out of her.

Her laughter fades, followed by the smile on her face. She glances toward the door. "Is your name really Ben?" she asks, bringing her eyes back to mine.

I nod.

"What's your biggest regret in life, Ben?"

An odd question, but I go with it. Odd seems completely normal with this girl, and never mind the fact that I'd never tell *anyone* my biggest regret. "I don't think I've lived through it yet," I lie.

She stares at me thoughtfully. "So you're a decent human being? You've never killed anyone?"

"So far."

She holds back a smile. "So if we spend more time together today, you aren't going to murder me?"

"Only if it's in self-defense."

She laughs and then reaches for her purse. She wraps it over her shoulder and stands up. "That's a relief. Let's go to Pinkberry and we can break up over dessert."

I hate ice cream. I hate yogurt.

I *especially* hate yogurt pretending to be ice cream.

But I'll be damned if I don't grab my laptop and my keys and follow her wherever the hell she's willing to lead me.

"How have you lived in Los Angeles since you were fourteen without ever stepping foot inside Pinkberry?" She almost sounds offended. She turns away from me to study the choice of toppings again. "Have you at least heard of Starbucks?"

I laugh and point to the gummy bears. The server scoops a spoonful into my container. "I practically live in Starbucks. I'm a writer. It's a rite of passage."

She's standing in front of me in line, waiting for our turn to pay, but she's looking at my container with disgust.

"Oh, my God," she says. "You can't come to Pinkberry and just eat *toppings.*" She looks up at me like I've killed a kitten. "Are you even human?"

I roll my eyes and nudge her shoulder to turn her back around. "Stop berating me or I'll dump you before we even find a table."

I pull a twenty out of my wallet and pay for our dessert. We maneuver our way through the crowded restaurant, but there aren't any free tables. She heads straight for the door, so I follow her outside and down the sidewalk until she finds an empty bench. She takes a seat on it cross-legged and sets her bowl in her lap. It's the first time I take a look at her bowl and realize she didn't get a single topping.

I look down at my bowl — full of nothing *but* toppings.

"I know," she says, laughing. "Jack Sprat could eat no fat . . ."

"His wife could eat no lean," I finish.

She smiles and spoons a bite into her mouth. She pulls the spoon out and licks frozen yogurt off her bottom lip.

I wasn't expecting this today of all days. To be sitting across from this girl, watching her lick ice cream off her lips and having to swallow air just to make sure I'm still breathing.

"So you're a writer?"

Her question gives me the footing I need to pull my mind out of the gutter. I nod. "Hope to be. I've never done it professionally, so I'm not sure I can call myself a writer yet."

She shifts until she's facing me and props her elbow on the back of the bench. "It doesn't take a paycheck to validify that you're a writer."

"*Validify* isn't actually a word."

"See?" she says. "I didn't even know that, so you're obviously a writer. Paycheck or not, I'm calling you a writer. *Ben the Writer.* That's how I'm going to refer to you from this point forward."

I laugh. "And how should I refer to you?"

She chews on the tip of her spoon for a few seconds, her eyes narrowed in contemplation. "Good question," she says. "I'm kind of in transition at this point."

"Fallon the Transient," I offer.

She smiles. "That works."

Her back meets the bench when she faces forward. She uncrosses her legs, allowing her feet to meet the ground. "So what kind of writing do you want to do? Novels? Screenplays?"

"Hopefully everything. I don't really want to put a cap on it yet, I'm only eighteen. I kind of want to try it all, but my passion is definitely novels. And poetry."

A quiet sigh leaves her mouth before she takes another bite. I don't know how, but it feels like my answer just made her sad.

"What about you, Fallon the Transient? What's your life goal?"

She shoots me a sidelong glance. "Are we talking about life goals now or what our passion is?"

"Not much of a difference."

She laughs half-heartedly. "There's a huge difference. My passion is acting, but that's not really my goal in life."

"Why not?"

Her eyes narrow in my direction before she looks back down at her container again. She begins stirring at the frozen yogurt with her spoon. She sighs with her entire body this time, like she's crumbling to the ground.

"You know, Ben. I appreciate how nice you've been since we became a couple, but you can stop with the act. My dad isn't here to witness it."

I was about to take another bite, but my hand freezes before the spoon hits my mouth. "What's that supposed to mean?" I ask, baffled by the nosedive this conversation just took.

She stabs at her yogurt with the spoon before leaning over and tossing it into a trash can beside her. She pulls a leg up and wraps her arms around it, facing me again. "Do you really not know my story or are you just pretending not to know?"

I'm not really sure which story she's referring to, so I give my head a slight shake. "I'm so confused right now."

She sighs. Again. I don't think I've ever made a girl sigh this much in such a short amount of time. And they aren't the kind of sighs that make a guy feel good about his skills. They're the kind of sighs that make him wonder what the hell he's doing wrong.

She picks at a piece of loose wood on the back of the bench with her thumb. She focuses on the wood as if she's talking to it, rather than to me. "I got really lucky when I was fourteen. Landed a role in a cheesy, teenage spin on Sherlock Holmes meets Nancy Drew called *Gumshoe.* I starred in that show for a year and a half and it was starting to do really well. But then *this* happened." She motions to her face. "My contract was pulled. I was replaced and I haven't acted since. So that's what I mean when I say that goals and passions are two separate things. Acting is my passion, but like my father said, I no longer have the tools it takes to achieve my life goal. So I guess I'll be looking for a new one soon, unless a miracle happens in New York."

I don't even know what to say to that. She's looking at me now, waiting for a response, but I can't think of one fast enough. She rests her chin on her arm and stares off behind me.

"I'm not very good with on-the-spot motivational speech," I say to her. "Sometimes at night, I'll rewrite conversations I had during the day, but I'll change them up to reflect everything I wish I could have said in the moment. So I just want you to know that tonight when I write this conversation down on paper, I'll say something really heroic and it'll make you feel really good about your life."

She drops her forehead against her arm and laughs. The sight of it makes me smile. "That is by far the best response I've ever gotten to that story."

I lean forward to toss my container into the trash can behind her. It's the closest I've come to her since we were sitting in the booth together. Her entire body stiffens with my proximity. Rather than pull back right away, I look her directly in the eye before focusing on her mouth.

"That's what boyfriends are for," I say as I slowly back away from her.

Normally, I wouldn't think twice about the fact that I'm deliberately flirting with a girl. I do it all the time. But Fallon is looking at me like I just committed the cardinal sin, and it makes me question if I've been misreading the vibe between us.

I pull back completely, never shying away from the look of annoyance on her face. She points a finger at me. "That," she says. "Right there. That's the shit I'm referring to."

I'm not sure I know what she's referring to, so I proceed with caution. "You think I'm pretending to flirt with you to make you feel better about yourself?"

"Aren't you?"

Does she really think that? Do people really not flirt with her? Is this because of her scars or because of her *insecurities* about her scars? Surely guys aren't as shallow as she's implying. If so, I'm embarrassed on behalf of all men. Because this girl should be fighting off the guys who flirt with her, not questioning their motives.

I squeeze the tension from the center of my jaw and then cover my mouth with my hand while I contemplate how to respond. Of course tonight when I think back on this moment, I'll come up with all kinds of great responses. But right now . . . I can't come up with the perfect response to save my life.

I guess I'll just go with honesty. *Mostly* honest, anyway. That seems to be the best way to respond to this girl, since she reads through bullshit like it's written on transparent paper.

Now I'm the one releasing a heavy sigh.

"You want to know what I thought when I saw you for the first time?"

She tilts her head. "When you saw me for the first time? You mean as in one whole *hour* ago?"

I ignore her cynicism and continue. "The first time you walked past me — before I interrupted your lunch date with your father — I stared at your ass the whole time you were stomping away. And I couldn't help but wonder what kind of panties you had on. That's all I thought about the entire time you were in the restroom. Were you a thong girl? Were you going commando? Because I didn't see an outline in your jeans that hinted you were wearing normal panties.

"Before you returned from the bathroom, I started to get this panicked feeling in my stomach, because I wasn't sure if I wanted to see your face. I had been listening in on your conversation and already knew I was drawn to your personality. But what about your face? People say not to judge a book by its cover, but what if you somehow read the inside of the book without seeing the cover first? And what if you really liked what was inside that book? Of course when you go to close the book and are about to see the cover for the first time, you hope it's something you'll find attractive. Because who wants an incredibly written book sitting on their bookshelf if they have to stare at a shitty cover?"

She quickly glances down at her lap, but I continue talking.

"When you walked out of the bathroom, the first thing I noticed was your hair. It reminded me of the first girl I ever kissed. Her name was Abitha. She had great hair and it always smelled like coconut, so it made me wonder if your hair smelled like coconut. And then it made me wonder if you kissed like Abitha, because even though she was my first kiss, it's still one of the only ones I can remember every detail of. Anyway, so I immediately noticed your eyes after admiring your hair. You were still several feet away, but you were looking straight at me, almost as if you couldn't understand why I was staring.

"But then I grew really uneasy and shifted in my seat, because as you so clearly pointed out already, I hadn't even looked in the mirror yet. I didn't know what you were seeing now that you were looking back at me, and if you even *liked* what you were seeing. My palms started sweating because this was the first impression you were getting of me and I didn't know if it was good enough.

"You were almost to my booth at this point and that's when my eyes fell to your cheek. To your neck. I saw the scars for the first time, and just as I noticed them, you darted your eyes to the floor and let your hair cover most of your face. And you know what I thought in that moment, Fallon?"

Her eyes flick up to meet mine and I can tell she doesn't really want me to say it. She thinks she knows exactly what I thought in that moment, but she has no idea.

"I was so relieved," I tell her. "Because I could tell with that one simple movement that you were really insecure. And I realized — since you obviously had no idea how fucking beautiful you were — that I just might actually have a chance with you. And so I smiled. Because I was hoping if I played my cards right — I might get to find out exactly what kind of panties you were wearing under those jeans."

It's as if the world chooses this moment to go silent. No cars pass by. No birds chirp. The sidewalk around us is completely empty. It's the longest ten seconds of my life, waiting for her to respond. So long, ten seconds is enough time for me to want to take it all back. It's enough time for me to wish I would have just kept my mouth shut, rather than lay it all out there like that.

Fallon clears her throat and looks away from me. She pushes off the bench and stands up.

I don't move. I just watch her, curious if she's chosen this moment to finally fake-dump me.

She inhales a deep breath and then releases it just as her eyes fall back to mine. "I still have a lot of stuff to pack tonight," she says. "Offering to help is the polite thing for a boyfriend to do, you know."

"Do you need help packing?" I blurt out.

She nonchalantly lifts a shoulder. "Okay."

FALLON

My mother is my hero. My role model. The woman I aspire to be. She did put up with my father for seven years. Any woman who could make it that long deserves a medal of honor.

When I was offered the lead role of *Gumshoe* at the age of fourteen, she hesitated to let me take it. She hated the way my dad's career had forced him into the limelight. She absolutely hated the man it turned him into. She said before he became a household name, he was wonderful and charming. But once fame started getting to his head, she couldn't stand to be around him. She said 1993 was the year that led to the demise of their marriage, the rise to his fame, and the birth of their first and last child: *Me.*

So of course she did everything in her power not to let the same thing happen to me when I started acting. Imagine transitioning into the cusp of womanhood while being an up-and-coming actress in Los Angeles. It's pretty damn easy to lose sight of yourself. I saw it happen to a lot of my friends.

But my mother didn't allow it to happen to me. As soon as the director called wrap on set each day, I went home to a list of chores and a firm set of rules. I'm not saying my mother was strict. She just didn't show me any type of special treatment, no matter how popular I was becoming.

She also didn't allow me to date before I turned sixteen. So in the first few months after my sixteenth birthday, I went on three dates with three different guys. And it was fun. Two of them were coworkers I may or may not have already made out with once or twice in a dressing room on set. One of them was the brother of a friend of mine. And no matter who I went out with or how much fun I did or didn't have, my mother would have the same conversation with me every time I came home from a date, about the importance of not falling in love until I'm at an age where I genuinely know myself. She *still* has the same conversation with me, and I don't even *date.*

My mother went on a self-help book binge after she divorced my father. She read every book she could find on parenting, marriage, finding yourself as a woman. Through all of these books, she concluded that girls change more between the ages of sixteen and twenty-three than at any other time in their lives. And it's important to her that I don't spend any of these years in love with some guy, because if I do, she fears I'll never learn how to fall in love with my*self.*

She met my father when she was sixteen and left him when she was twenty-three, so I'm thinking her age range restrictions have a little to do with personal experience. But considering I'm only eighteen and have no plans to settle down anytime soon, I figure it's easy to follow her advice and allow her to take the credit. It's the least I could do.

I do find humor in the fact that she thinks there's this all-magical age when a woman finally has all her shit figured out. But I will admit that one of my favorite quotes is actually one she made up.

"You'll never be able to find yourself if you're lost in someone else."

My mother isn't famous. She doesn't have an incredible career. She isn't even married to the love of her life. But there's one thing she's always been . . .

Right.

And that's why, until I find reason otherwise, I'll listen to every word she says, however absurd it might seem. I've never once known her to give me bad advice, so despite the fact that Benton James Kessler could have walked right off the pages of one of the many romance novels I keep stocked on my bedroom shelf — the guy doesn't have a chance in hell with me for at least five more years.

But that's not to say I didn't want to crawl on his lap and straddle him right there on that park bench while I shoved my tongue down his throat. Because it was really hard to hold myself back after he admitted he thought I was beautiful.

No, wait.

Fucking beautiful were the exact words he used.

And while he does seem a little too good to be true, and he's probably full of flaws and annoying little habits, I'm still just greedy enough to want to spend the rest of the day with him. Because who knows? Even though I'm moving to New York, I might still straddle him tonight and stick my tongue down his throat.

When I woke up this morning, I thought today was going to be one of the toughest days I've had in two years. Who knew the anniversary of the worst day of my life might possibly end on a good note?

"Twelve, thirty-five, pound," I say to Ben, giving him the gate code to my apartment. He rolls down his window and punches in the code. I took a cab to meet my father at the restaurant this morning, so Ben offered to drive me back home.

I point out an empty parking spot, so he turns in that direction and pulls in next to my roommate's car. We both climb out and meet at the front of his car.

"I feel like I should caution you before we walk inside," I say.

He glances at the apartment building and then looks back at me with unease. "You don't live with a *real-life* boyfriend, do you?"

I laugh. "No, not even close. My roommate's name is Amber, and she's probably going to bombard you with a million questions, considering I've never stepped foot through my front door with a guy before." I don't know why it doesn't bother me at all to admit that to him.

He casually drapes his arm around my shoulders and begins walking toward the building with me. "If you're asking me to pretend we're just friends, that's not gonna happen. I'm not downplaying our relationship for your roommate's sake."

I laugh and lead him to the front door of my apartment. I catch myself lifting my hand to knock but turn the doorknob instead. This is still my home for at least ten more hours, so I shouldn't feel the need to knock.

Ben's arm leaves my shoulders in order for me to walk through the door first. I look across the living room to find Amber standing at the kitchen counter with her boyfriend. She and Glenn have been dating for over a year now, and neither of them have come out and said it, but I'm pretty sure he's moving in the second I move out tonight.

She glances up, and her eyes immediately grow wide the second she notices Ben filing in behind me.

"Hey," I say cheerfully, as if there's nothing unusual about me bringing home a very good-looking guy whom I've never once mentioned before.

We make our way across the living room and Amber's eyes never leave Ben the entire time. "Hi," she finally says, still staring at him. "Who are you?" She looks at me and points to Ben. "Who is he?"

Ben steps forward and reaches out his hand. "Benton Kessler," he says, shaking her hand. He reaches over and shakes Glenn's hand next. "Just call me Ben, though." His arm drapes over my shoulders again. "I'm Fallon's boyfriend."

I laugh, but I'm the only one who laughs. Glenn eyes him up and down. "Boyfriend?" he asks, moving his attention back to me. "Does he know you're moving to New York?"

I nod. "He's known since the second we met."

Amber arches an eyebrow. "Which was . . . *when*?"

She's confused, because she knows I tell her everything. And having a boyfriend is definitely considered a part of everything.

"Oh, man," Ben says, looking down at me. "How long has it been now, babe? One . . . two hours?"

"Two at the most."

Amber narrows her eyes in my direction. She already wants to know all the details, and she hates that she has to wait until Ben leaves before she gets them.

"We'll be in my room," I say casually.

Ben gives them a quick wave and then removes his arm from around my shoulders, sliding his fingers through mine. "Nice to meet you both." He points down the hall. "I'm gonna follow Fallon to her room now so I can see what kind of panties she has on."

Amber's mouth falls open and Glenn

laughs. I push Ben's arm, shocked he took the joke that far. "No, you're following me to my room to help me *pack.*"

He pushes out his bottom lip in a pout. I roll my eyes and lead him down the hall to my room.

Amber and I have been best friends for over two years now. As soon as we graduated high school, we moved into this apartment together. Which means I've only lived here for six months, so it feels like I'm packing up all the things I just *un*packed.

When we walk into my room, Ben closes the door behind him. His eyes wander around the room, so I allow him a few minutes to be nosy while I open my suitcase. The apartment I'm moving into in New York is fully furnished, so really, the only things I have to take with me are clothes and toiletries. Everything else is at my mom's house.

"You're a reader?" he asks.

I look over my shoulder and he's fingering the books on my shelves. "I love to read. You should hurry up and write a book, because it's already on my TBR pile."

"Your *TBR pile*?"

"*To be read* pile," I clarify.

He pulls one of the books from the shelf and reads the back of it. "I hate to tell you this, but I don't think you'll like whatever books I end up writing." He slips the book back on the shelf and grabs another one. "You seem to favor romance novels, and that's not up my alley."

I stop perusing the shirts in my closet and stare at him. "No," I say with a groan. "Please don't tell me you're one of those pretentious readers who judge people by the books they like."

He immediately shakes his head. "Not at all. I just don't know anything about writing romance. I'm eighteen. Hardly an expert when it comes to love."

I walk out of the closet and lean against the door. "You've never been in love before?"

He nods. "Of course I have, but not the kind worthy of a romance novel, so I have no business writing about it." He plops down on the bed and leans against the headboard, watching me.

"Do you think Stephen King was actually murdered by a clown in real life?" I ask him. "Did Shakespeare really down a vial of poison? Of course not, Ben. It's called fiction for a reason. You make the shit up."

He smiles at me from his position on the bed, and the sight of him sitting there makes my cheeks feel all hot and bothered. I suddenly want to beg him to roll around on my sheets so I can smell him when I fall asleep tonight. But then I remember I won't be sleeping on them tonight because I'll be on a flight to New York. I turn around and face my closet again so he doesn't see the flushed look on my face.

He laughs quietly. "You were just thinking dirty thoughts."

"Was not," I quip.

"Fallon, we've been dating for two hours now. I can read you like a book, and right now I do believe that book is full of erotica."

I laugh and begin pulling shirts off their hangers. I don't want to bother folding them yet until I figure out how I'm going to pack them, so I just toss them in the middle of the bedroom floor.

I pull down about a quarter of the shirts in my closet before I glance back at Ben again. His hands are propped up behind his head and he's watching me pack. I didn't really expect him to help me once we got here, because he'd probably be more in the way than anything. But Ben acknowledging this, too, makes me feel good that he still seemed excited to spend more time with me.

I decided on our drive over that I wasn't going to question his motives. Of course the insecure side of me still wonders what the hell a guy like him is doing spending time with a girl like me, but every time that thought creeps into my head, I remind myself of the conversation we had on the bench. And I tell myself that everything he said seemed genuine — that he really does find me attractive somehow. And honestly, does it really matter in the grand scheme of things? I'm moving to the opposite end of the country, so it's not like whatever happens in the next few hours will impact my life one way or another. Who cares if the guy just wants to get in my pants? I'd actually *prefer* it if that's all he wanted. It's the first time in two years someone has made me feel desirable, so I'm not going to beat myself up over the fact that I'm enjoying it as much as I am.

I walk to my dresser and hear him dialing a number on his phone. I'm quiet as he makes the call.

"Can I get a reservation for two tonight at seven?"

The silence after that question is palpable as I wait to hear what he says next. My heart has gotten more of a workout in the past two hours than it has in the entire past two months.

"Benton Kessler. K-E-S-S-L-E-R." *More*

silence. "Perfect. Thank you so much." *More silence.*

I'm digging through my top drawer, acting like I'm not praying to the Lord that he intends for me to be his plus one at that dinner. I hear him shift on the bed and stand up, so I turn around to see him walking toward me. He grins and then peeks over my shoulder at the drawer I'm rifling through.

"Is that your panty drawer?" He reaches around and grabs a pair. I pull them out of his hand and toss them toward my suitcase.

"Hands off," I tell him.

He walks around me and leans his elbow against the dresser. "If you're packing underwear, that means you don't go commando. So by process of elimination, I've figured out that you're currently wearing a thong. Now I just have to find out what color it is."

I toss the contents of my drawer toward my suitcase. "It takes a lot more than smooth talk to get me down to my panties, *Ben the Writer.*"

He grins. "Oh yeah? Like what? A fancy dinner?" He pushes off the dresser and stands up straight, shoving his hands in the pockets of his jeans. "Because it just so happens I have reservations at the Chateau

Marmont tonight at seven."

I laugh. "You don't say." I walk around him to my closet again, attempting to hide the huge smile on my face. *Thank you, Jesus. He's taking me to dinner.* As soon as I reach my closet, my smile turns tepid. *What the hell am I going to wear? I haven't been on a date since before my boobs were fully grown!*

"Fallon O'Neil?" he says, this time from the doorway of my closet. "Will you go on a date with me tonight?"

I sigh and look down at my boring clothes. "What the hell am I going to wear to the Chateau?" I look back at him and make a face. "Couldn't we have just gone to Chipotle or something?"

He laughs and then steps into my closet, pushing past me. He sifts through the clothes in the back of my closet. "Too long," he says as he scoots hangers over one by one. "Too ugly. Too casual. Too dressy." He finally stops and pulls something off the rod. He turns around and holds up a black dress I've been meaning to throw away since the day my mother bought it for me.

She's always buying me clothes in hopes I'll actually wear them. Clothes that don't cover up my scars.

I shake my head and grab the dress from

him, hanging it back in its spot. I grab one of the few long-sleeved dresses I own and I pull it off the hanger. "I like this one."

His eyes fall to the dress he initially picked out and he pulls it off the hanger and shoves it at me. "But I want you to wear this one."

I shove the dress back at him. "I don't want to wear that, I want to wear this."

"No," he says. "I'm paying for dinner, so I get to choose what to stare at while we eat."

"Then *I'll* pay for dinner and wear the dress *I* want to wear."

"Then I'll stand you up and go to Chipotle."

I groan. "I think we're having our first fight as a couple."

He smiles and holds out the hand with his dress of choice. "If you agree to wear this dress tonight, we can make up right now in this closet."

He's relentless. But I'm not wearing that damn dress. If I have to play the honesty card, I will.

I release a frustrated sigh. "My mother bought me that dress last year when she was going through her *'Let's fix Fallon'* stage. But she has no idea how uncomfortable it is to be in my skin. So please don't ask me again to wear that dress, because I'm much more relaxed in clothes that don't show too much skin. I don't like making people uncomfortable, and if I wore something like that, they would feel weird looking at me."

Ben's jaw tenses and he looks away from me, down at the dress in his hands. "Okay," he says simply, dropping the dress to the floor.

Finally.

"But it's your own fault people feel uncomfortable looking at you."

I don't even hide my gasp. It's the first thing he's said to me all day that's made me feel like I was being spoken to by my father. I'm not gonna lie. It hurts. My throat feels like it's swelling shut, so I clear it.

"That wasn't very nice," I say quietly.

Ben takes a step closer to me. My closet is small enough as it is. I certainly don't need him standing even closer. Especially after saying something as hurtful as he just did.

"It's the truth," he says.

I close my eyes, because it's either that or stare at the mouth delivering such hateful words.

I exhale a calming breath, but it catches when his fingers brush the hair in front of my face. The unexpected physical contact forces me to squeeze my eyes shut even harder. I feel so stupid for not forcing him to leave, or in the least, pushing him out of the closet. But for some reason, I can't seem to move or speak. Or *breathe* for that matter.

He pushes the hair away from my forehead, running his fingers through it until it's no longer hanging in my face. "You wear your hair like you do because you don't want people to see too much of you. You wear long sleeves and collared shirts because you think it helps. But it doesn't."

It feels like his words are turning into fists and punching me directly in the stomach. I pull my face away from his hand, but I keep my eyes closed. I feel like I might cry again, and I've cried enough for one stupid anniversary.

"People don't feel uncomfortable when they look at you because of your scars, Fallon. They're uncomfortable because you make people feel like looking at you is wrong. And *believe* me — you're the type of person people want to stare at." I feel his fingertips graze my jaw and I flinch. "You have the most incredible bone structure, and I know that's a weird compliment, but it's true." His fingers leave my jaw and trail up my chin until he's touching my mouth. "And your lips. Men stare at them because they want to know what they taste like, and women stare at them out of jealousy because if they had lips the color of yours, they'd never have to buy lipstick again."

I release what might be a cross between a laugh and a cry, but I still don't dare look at him. I'm stiff as a board, wondering where he's going to touch me next. What he's going to *say* next.

"And I've only met one other girl in my life with hair as long and beautiful as yours, but I've already told you about Abitha. And just so you know, she doesn't hold a candle to you, despite being a great kisser."

I feel his hands come up and push my hair behind my shoulders. He's close enough that I know he can see the exaggerated rise and fall of my chest. But my *God,* it suddenly got really hard to breathe, like I'm ten thousand feet higher above sea level than I was five minutes ago.

"Fallon," he says, commanding my attention. His fingers meet my chin, and he tilts my face upward. When I open my eyes, he's a lot closer than I thought he was. He's looking down at me with a pointed stare. "People *want* to stare at you. Believe me, I'm one of them. But when everything about you screams, 'Look away,' then that's exactly what people are going to do. The only person who gives a shit about a few scars on your face is you."

I want so badly to believe him. If I could believe everything he's saying, then maybe my life would mean a whole lot more to me than it does right now. If I believed him, maybe I wouldn't be so nervous about the idea of auditioning again. Maybe I would be doing the exact thing my mother says a girl my age should be doing: finding out who I really am. Not hiding from myself.

Hell, I'm not even *dressing* for myself. I dress in what I think other people would prefer I wear.

Ben's eyes fall to my shirt, and for the first time, I notice his lungs are pulling in air with as much effort as mine are. He lifts his hand and fingers the top button on my shirt, popping it open. I suck in a quick breath. His eyes never leave my shirt and mine never leave his face. When he moves his fingers down to the second button, I could swear he pulls in a shaky breath.

I don't know what he's doing, and I'm terrified he's about to be the first person to see what's beneath this shirt. But for the life of me, I can't find words to stop him.

When the second button is freed, he moves down to the third. Before he flicks that button loose, his eyes lift to mine, and he looks just as scared as I feel right now. Our eyes remain locked until he gets to the last and final button. When it's loose, I look down at my shirt.

Only a sliver of skin is showing over my belly button, so I don't actually feel exposed yet. But I'm about to, because he slowly lifts both of his hands to the top of my shirt. Before he makes his next move, I squeeze my eyes shut again.

I don't want to see the look on his face when he sees just how much of my body was burned. Most of my entire left side, to be exact. What he sees when he looks at my cheek is only a fraction compared to what's beneath my clothes.

I feel my shirt being pulled open, and the more of me that becomes exposed, the harder it is to hold back tears. It's the worst time in the world for me to get emotional, but I guess tears aren't known for their impeccable timing.

His breaths are extremely audible, and so is the gasp I hear him suck in as soon as my shirt is open all the way. I want to shove him out of the closet and close the door and hide, but that's exactly what I've been doing for the last two years. So for reasons I can't explain, I don't ask him to stop.

Ben slips the shirt off my shoulders and slowly slides it down the length of my arms. He works it the rest of the way over my hands until it falls to the floor. I can feel his hands graze both of mine, and I'm too embarrassed to move, knowing exactly what he sees right now as he looks at me.

His fingers begin to rise up my hands and wrists, just as the first tear falls down my cheek. The tear doesn't faze him, though. Chills break out on most of my skin as he continues moving his hands up my forearms. Instead of trailing his fingers all the way to my shoulders, he pauses. I still don't dare open my eyes.

I feel his forehead rest gently against mine and the fact that he's breathing as hard as I am is the only thing that gives me a sense of comfort in this moment.

My stomach clenches when his hands meet the top of my jeans.

This is going too far.

Too far, too far, too far, but all I can do is suck in a wild breath and let his fingers pop open the button on my jeans, because as much as I wish he would stop, I get the feeling he's not undressing me for pleasure. I'm not sure what he's doing, but I'm too immobile to ask.

Breathe, Fallon. Breathe. Your lungs need new air.

His forehead is still resting against mine, and I can feel his breath crashing against my lips. I have a feeling his eyes are wide open, though, and he's staring down between us, watching his hands as they work down my zipper.

When the zipper reaches its destination, he slides his hands between my jeans and hips — casually enough for me to believe it doesn't even bother him that he's touching the scars on my left side. He pushes my jeans down over my hips and then begins to slowly lower himself as he slides them down the length of my legs. The breath from his mouth moves down my body until I feel it stop at my stomach, but his lips never once touch my skin.

When my jeans are at my feet, I step out of them one foot at a time.

I have no idea what happens next. What happens next? What. Happens. Next?

My eyes are still closed, and I have no idea if he's standing or kneeling or walking away.

"Lift your arms," he says.

His voice is rough and close, and it startles me to the point that my eyes flick open involuntarily. He's standing directly in front of me, holding the dress he dropped to the floor earlier.

I look up at him, and I absolutely wasn't expecting to see this look on his face. His eyes are so heated and fierce, it's as if it's taking every last ounce of his restraint not to remove my last two items of clothing.

He clears his throat. "*Please* lift your arms, Fallon."

I lift them, and he raises the dress over my head and slips it down my arms. He pulls it until my head slips through and he keeps pulling it, adjusting it over my curves. When the dress is finally in place, he lifts my hair and lets it fall down my back. He takes a half step back and eyes me up and down. He clears his throat, but his voice still comes out raspy when he speaks.

"Fucking beautiful," he says with a slow grin. "And red."

Red?

I look down at the dress, but it's definitely black.

"Your panties," he says as clarification. "They're red."

I let out a burst of what I thought was going to be laughter, but it sounds more like a warbled cry. That's when I realize tears are still streaming down my cheeks, so I bring my hands to my face and attempt to wipe them away, but they keep coming.

I can't believe he just undressed me to prove a point. I can't believe I *allowed* it. Now I know exactly what Ben meant when he said he finds it difficult to control his indignation in the presence of absurdity. He thinks my insecurities are absurd, and he took it upon himself to prove that to me.

Ben steps forward and wraps his arms around me. Everything about him is comforting and warm and I have no idea how to respond. One of his hands meets the back of my head and he presses my face against his chest. I'm now laughing at the ridiculousness that is my tears, because *who does this? Who cries when a guy undresses her for the first time?*

"That's a record," Ben says, pulling me away from his chest so he can look down at me. "Made my girlfriend cry less than three hours into our relationship."

I laugh again, and then I press my face to his chest and hug him back, because why couldn't he have been there the second I woke up in the hospital two years ago? Why did I have to go two whole years before finally being given the tiniest bit of confidence?

After another minute or two of me trying to rein in my erratic emotions, I'm finally calm enough to realize that he doesn't smell so good when my face is pressed against a shirt he's been wearing for two days.

I take a step back and run my fingers under my eyes again. I'm not crying anymore, but I'm sure mascara is everywhere now.

"I'll wear this stupid dress on one condition," I say. "You have to go home and take a shower first."

His smile widens. "That was already part of my plan."

We stand in silence for a bit longer, and then I can't take being in this closet for another second. I push his shoulders and shove him out into the bedroom. "It's almost four o'clock now," I tell him. "Be back at six and I'll be dressed and ready to go."

He walks toward the door to my bedroom, but faces me again before he exits. "I want you to wear your hair up tonight."

"Don't push your luck."

He laughs. "Why the hell does luck exist if I'm not supposed to push it?"

I point at the door. "Go. Shower. And shave while you're at it."

He opens the door and begins to back out. "Shave, huh? You plan on putting those lips on my face tonight?"

"Go," I say with an exasperated laugh.

He shuts the door, but I can still hear what he says to Amber and Glenn as soon as he walks into the living room. "They're red! Her panties are red!"

Ben

What the hell am I doing?

She's moving to New York. It's dinner. That's it.

But seriously, what the hell am I doing? I shouldn't be doing this.

I pull on a pair of jeans and walk to my closet to find a clean shirt. Right when I get the shirt over my head, the door swings open.

"Hey," Kyle says, leaning against the doorframe. "Nice of you to come home for a change." *Jesus. Not now.* "Want to have dinner with me and Jordyn tonight?"

"Can't. I have a date." I walk to my dresser and grab my cologne. I can't believe Fallon willingly got as close to me as she did with the way I smelled today. It's a little embarrassing.

"Oh yeah? With who?"

I slide my wallet off the dresser and grab my jacket. "My girlfriend."

Kyle laughs as I slip past him and begin walking down the hallway. *"Girlfriend?"* He knows I don't do girlfriends, so he follows after me to drain me for more info. "You know if I tell Jordyn you're on a date with your girlfriend, she'll question me until my head explodes. You better give me something to work with."

I laugh. He's right; his girlfriend likes to know everything about everyone. And for some reason, since she's about to move in with us, she thinks we're already family. And she's *especially* nosy when it comes to family.

Kyle follows me straight out the front door, all the way to my car. He grabs my door before I can shut it. "I know where you were last night."

I stop trying to shut the door and fall against the seat. *Here we go again.* "Your girlfriend has a big mouth, you know that?"

He leans against the door, staring down at me with his arms folded across his chest. "She's worried about you, Ben. We all are."

"I'm fine. You'll see. I'll be fine."

Kyle stares at me silently for a few moments, wanting to believe me this time. But I've promised him I'll be fine so many times, it falls on deaf ears now. And I get it. But he has no idea that this time really *is* different.

He gives up and shuts my door without another word. I know he's only trying to help, but he doesn't need to. Things really are going to change. I knew that for a fact the moment I laid eyes on Fallon today.

I walk up to her front door at approximately 5:05 p.m. I'm early, but like I said . . . she's leaving for New York and I'll never see her again. Fifty-five extra minutes with her isn't nearly as many as I want.

The door opens almost as soon as I knock on it. Amber grins at me and steps aside. "Why hello, Fallon's boyfriend whom I've never heard of." She motions to the couch. "Take a seat. Fallon's in the shower."

I glance at the couch and then at the hallway that leads to Fallon's bedroom. "You don't think she needs my help in the shower?"

Amber laughs, but then just as quick, her face falls flat and serious. "No. Sit."

Glenn is seated on the couch opposite the one I'm being forced to sit on. I give him a nod and he raises an eyebrow in warning. I guess this is the moment Fallon warned me about.

Amber crosses the living room and takes a seat next to Glenn. "Fallon tells me you're a writer?"

I nod. "Ben the Writer. That would be me."

Right before she fires her second question, Fallon suddenly appears in the opening to the hallway. "Hey. Thought I heard you out here."

There are no signs of her actually having just taken a shower. I turn back to Amber and she shrugs. "Can't blame me for trying."

I stand up and walk toward the hallway, pointing at Amber but looking at Fallon. "Your roommate is sneaky-sneaky."

"That she is," Fallon says. "And you're here an hour early."

"Fifty-five minutes."

"Same thing."

"Is not."

She turns around and walks backward through her bedroom door. "I'm so tired of fighting with you, Ben." She heads toward a bathroom off the side of her bedroom. "I just finished packing. Haven't even started getting ready yet."

I resume my spot on her bed. "No worries. I've already made myself comfortable." I reach over and pick up the book sitting on her nightstand. "I'll just read until you're finished."

She peeks her head around the doorway of the bathroom and eyes the book in my hands. "Careful. That's a good one. It might change your mind about writing a romance novel."

I scrunch up my nose and shake my head. She laughs and disappears back into the bathroom again.

I open the first page of the book, expecting to skim over it. Before I know it, I'm on page ten.

Page seventeen.

Page twenty.

Thirty-seven.

Jesus, this is like crack.

"Fallon?"

"Yeah?" she says from the bathroom.

"Have you finished this book yet?"

"Nope."

"Well, I need you to finish it before you move to New York so you can tell me if she finds out he's really her brother."

She reappears in the doorway in a flash. "What?!" she yells. "He's her *brother*?"

I grin. "Gotcha."

She rolls her eyes and disappears into the bathroom again. I force myself to stop reading and toss the book aside. I look around Fallon's room and it already looks different from when I was in here an hour ago. She's removed all the pictures from her nightstand and I didn't even get a good look at them earlier. Her closet is almost empty, sans a few boxes on the floor.

I did notice when I walked in that she still had on the dress, though. I was hoping she wouldn't change her mind and pack it before I had a chance to intervene.

I see movement out of the corner of my eye, so I glance at the bathroom. She's standing in the doorway.

My eyes fall to the dress first. I have to give myself props for picking that one out. There's just enough showing at her neckline to keep me good and happy, but I'm not even positive I'll be able to look away from her face long enough to stare at her cleavage.

I can't tell what's different about her because it doesn't even look like she's wearing makeup, but she somehow looks even more beautiful than before. I'm glad I pushed my luck and asked her to wear her hair up, because she has it pulled up into some messy little knot on top of her head and I'm really digging it. I stand up and walk to where she's propped up in the doorway. I lift my hands to the doorframe above her head and I smile down at her. "Fucking beautiful," I whisper.

She smiles and then ducks her head. "I feel stupid."

"I barely know you, so I'm not about to argue with you over your level of intelligence, because you could very well be as dumb as a rock. But at least you're pretty."

She laughs and focuses on my eyes for a beat, but then her focus falls to my mouth and *God,* I want to kiss her. I want to kiss her so bad it hurts and now I can't smile anymore because I'm in too much pain.

"What's wrong?"

I grimace and grip the doorframe tighter. "I want to kiss you really, really bad and I'm doing everything in my power not to do that yet."

She pulls her neck back and her eyebrows draw together in confusion. "Do you always look like you're about to puke when you feel like kissing a girl?"

I shake my head. "Not until you."

She huffs and pushes past me. That did *not* come out how I meant it. "I didn't mean the thought of kissing you makes me sick. I meant I want to kiss you so bad it's making my stomach hurt. Kind of like blue balls, but in my stomach instead of my balls."

She starts laughing and brings both of her hands up to her forehead. "What am I gonna do with you, Ben the Writer?"

"You could kiss me and make me feel better."

She shakes her head and walks toward her bed. "No way." She sits down on her bed and picks up the book I was just reading. "I read a lot of romance, so I know when the timing is right. If we're going to kiss, it has to be book-worthy. After you kiss me, I want you to forget all about that Abitha chick you keep talking about."

I make my way to the other side of the bed and lie down next to where she's propped against the headboard. I roll onto my side and lift up on my elbow. "Abitha who?"

She grins at me. "Exactly. From now on when you meet a girl, you better be comparing them to me instead of her."

"Using you as a standard is completely unfair to the rest of the female population."

She rolls her eyes, assuming I'm kidding again. But in all honesty, the thought of comparing anyone to Fallon is ridiculous. There's no comparison. And it sucks that I've only spent a few hours with her and I already know that. I almost wish I'd never met her. Because I don't do real girlfriends and she's moving to New York and we're only eighteen and so . . . many . . . things.

I stare up at the ceiling and wonder how

this is going to work. How the hell am I supposed to just say goodbye to her tonight, knowing I'll never talk to her again? I lay my forearm across my eyes. I wish I wouldn't have walked into that restaurant today. People can't miss what they've never been introduced to.

"Are you still thinking about kissing me?"

I tilt my head back against the pillow and look up at her. "I moved beyond the kiss. Marry me."

She laughs and scoots down on the bed so that she's facing me. Her expression is soft with a trace of a smile. She reaches a hand out and presses her palm against my neck. My breath hitches. "You shaved," she says, running her thumb over my jaw.

I don't think a single part of me could possibly smile when she's touching me like this, because there's absolutely nothing good about the fact that I'm not going to feel this way again after tonight. It's fucking cruel.

"If I asked for your phone number would you give it to me?"

"No," she says, almost immediately.

I press my lips together and wait for her to explain why not, but she doesn't. She just continues to run her thumb back and forth over my jaw.

"Email address?"

She shakes her head.

"Do you have a pager, at least? A fax machine?"

She laughs, and it feels good to hear her laugh. The air was feeling way too heavy.

"I don't want a boyfriend, Ben."

"So you're breaking up with me?"

She rolls her eyes. "You know what I mean." She pulls her hand from my face and rests it on the bed between us. "We're only eighteen. I'm moving to New York. We barely know each other. And I promised my mother I wouldn't fall in love with anyone until I'm twenty-three."

Agree, agree, agree, and . . . *what*? "Why twenty-three?"

"My mother says the majority of people have their lives figured out by the age of twenty-three, so I want to make sure I know who I am and what I want out of life before I allow myself to fall in love. Because it's easy to fall in love, Ben. The hard part comes when you want out."

Makes sense. *If you're the Tin Man.* "You think you can actually control whether or not you fall in love with someone?"

"Falling in love may not be a conscious decision, but removing yourself from the situation before it happens is. So if I meet someone I think I might fall in love with . . . I'll just remove myself from their presence until I'm ready for it."

Wow. She's like a mini-Socrates with all this life advice. I feel like I should be taking notes. Or debating with her.

Honestly, though, I'm relieved she's saying these things because I was afraid she would kiss me drunk and convince me we were soul mates by the end of the night. Because Lord knows if she asked, I'd jump right in, knowing it's the absolute last thing I should do. Guys don't say no to a girl like her, no matter how unappealing relationships are to him. Guys see boobs coupled with a great sense of humor and think they've found the holy fucking grail.

But five years seems like an eternity. I'm pretty sure she won't even remember tonight after five years. "Will you do me a favor then and look me up when you're twenty-three?"

She laughs. "Benton James Kessler, you'll be too famous of a writer in five years to remember little old me."

"Or maybe you'll be too famous an actress to remember *me.*"

She doesn't respond to that. In fact, if anything, my comment made her sad.

We remain quietly in our positions, face

to face on her bed. Even with the scars and the obvious sadness in her eyes, she's still one of the most beautiful girls I've ever seen. Her lips look soft and inviting, and I'm trying to ignore the knots in my stomach, but every time I stare at her mouth, the intensity of trying to hold back actually causes me to grimace. I try not to imagine what it would feel like if I leaned forward and kissed her, but with her this close, I'm really wishing I'd have already somehow read every romance novel ever written, because what the hell makes a kiss *book*-worthy? I need to know so I can make it happen.

She's lying on her right side, and with the dress she's wearing, a lot of her skin is exposed. I can see where the scars begin, right above her wrist, all the way up her arm and neck, pouring across her cheek. I touch her face just like she was touching mine. I can feel her flinch beneath my palm, because I'm touching the part of her she didn't even want me *looking* at a few hours ago. I run my thumb over her jaw and then slide my hand down the length of her neck. She's tense everywhere beneath my touch. "Does this bother you?"

Her eyes flicker back and forth between mine. "I don't know," she whispers.

I wonder if I'm the only one who has ever touched her scars before. I've had accidents in the past where I've burned myself attempting to cook, so I know what it feels like when a burn heals. But her scars are a lot more prominent than a superficial burn. Her skin feels a lot softer to the touch than normal skin. More fragile. There's something about the way it feels beneath my fingertips that makes me want to keep touching her.

She allows it. For several quiet minutes, neither one of us speaks as I continue running my fingers over her arm and neck. Her eyes moisten, as if she's on the verge of tears. It makes me wonder if she doesn't like it. I can understand why this might make her uncomfortable, but for some twisted reason, I feel more comfortable with her right now than I have all day.

"I should hate this for you," I whisper, trailing my fingers over the scars on her forearm. "I should be angry for you, because going through this must have been excruciatingly painful. But for whatever reason, when I touch you . . . I like the way your skin feels."

I'm not sure how she'll take the words that just came out of my mouth. But it's true. I suddenly feel grateful for her scars . . .

because they're a reminder of how it could have been much worse. She could have died in that fire, and she wouldn't be next to me right now.

I run my hand down her shoulder, down the length of her arm, and back up again. When my eyes meet hers, there's evidence of a tear that just trailed down her cheek.

"One of the things I always try to remind myself is that everyone has scars," she says. "A lot of them even worse than mine. The only difference is that mine are visible and most people's aren't."

I don't tell her she's right. I don't tell her that as beautiful as she looks on the outside, I only wish I could look like that on the inside.

Fallon

"Shit. *Fallon!* Shit, shit, shit, dammit, shit, shit."

I hear Ben cursing like a sailor, but I don't understand why. I feel his hands meet my shoulders. "Fallon the Transient, wake the hell up!"

I open my eyes and he's sitting up on the bed, running one hand through his hair. He looks pissed.

I sit up on the bed and rub the sleep out of my eyes.

The sleep.

We fell asleep?

I look over at my alarm clock and it reads 8:15. I reach over and pick it up to bring it closer to my face. That can't be right.

But it is. It's 8:15.

"Shit," I say.

"We missed dinner," Ben says.

"I know."

"We slept for two hours."

"Yeah. I know."

"We wasted *two fucking hours,* Fallon."

He looks genuinely distraught. Cute, but distraught.

"I'm sorry."

He shoots me a look of confusion. "What? No. Don't say that. It's not your fault."

"I only slept three hours last night," I say to him. "I've been really tired all day."

"Yeah," he says with a frustrated sigh. "I didn't sleep much last night, either." He pushes himself off the bed. "What time is your flight?"

"Eleven-thirty."

"Tonight?"

"Yes."

"Like as in three hours from now?"

I nod.

He groans and rubs his hands down his face. "Shit," he says again. "That means you need to leave." His hands drop to his hips and he looks down at the floor. "That means *I* should leave."

I don't want him to leave.

But I need him to. I don't like this panicked feeling that's building in my chest. I don't like the words I want to say to him. I want to tell him I changed my mind, that he can have my phone number. But if I give him my phone number, I'll talk to him. All the time. And I'll be sidetracked by him and every little text he sends, and every phone call, and then we'll Skype all the time and before I know it I won't be *Fallon the Transient* anymore. I'll be *Fallon the Girlfriend.*

The thought of that should fill me with a lot more distaste than it does.

"I should go," he says. "You probably have a lot to do in the next few minutes so you can get to the airport."

I don't really. I'm already packed, but I don't say anything.

"Do you want me to leave?" I can tell he's hoping I say no, but there's so much of me that needs him to go before I use him as an excuse not to move to New York.

"I'll walk you out." My voice is small and apologetic. He doesn't react to my words right away, but he eventually presses his lips into a thin line and nods.

"Yeah," he says, flustered. "Yeah. Walk me out."

I slip on the shoes I had laid out to wear to dinner tonight. Neither of us says anything as we reluctantly head to the door. He opens it and walks out first, so I follow behind him. I watch him as he makes his way down the hall in front of me. His hand has a tight grip on the back of his neck, and I hate that he's upset. I hate that *I'm* upset.

I hate that we fell asleep and completely wasted our entire last two hours together.

We're almost to the living room when he stops and spins around. Once again, he looks like he's about to be sick. I stand still and wait for whatever it is he's about to say.

"It may not be book-worthy, but it'll have to do." He takes two quick steps toward me until his hands are in my hair and his mouth is on mine. I gasp in surprise and grab his shoulders, but I immediately fall into step with him and slide my hands to his neck.

He backs me against the wall and his hands and chest and lips are pressed hungrily against mine. He's gripping my face like he's afraid to let go and I'm fighting for breath because it's been so long since I've kissed anyone, I think I may have forgotten how to do it right. He pulls away long enough for me to inhale and then he's back and . . . hands and . . . legs and . . . tongue.

Oh, my God, his tongue.

It's been over two years since someone else's tongue has been inside my mouth, so I would assume I'd be a little more hesitant than I am. But the second he slides it against my lips, I immediately part them and welcome the warmth of a much deeper kiss. Soft. Mesmerizing. His mouth, coupled with the way his hand is sliding down my arm, is all too much. So much. Good much. So good. I just whimpered.

As soon as the sound leaves my mouth, he's pressing me harder against the wall. His left hand is caressing my cheek and his right hand is gripping me by the waist, pulling me against him.

I'm finished packing. He doesn't have to leave right this minute.

Does he?

He really doesn't. Sex releases endorphins and endorphins keep people awake, so having sex with Ben might actually benefit me before my flight. I haven't had sex in all my eighteen years put together, so imagine how many endorphins I have built up in here. We could have sex before my flight and I wouldn't need sleep for days. Imagine how productive I would be when I get to New York.

Oh, my God, I'm pulling him back to my room. If he comes back to my room with me, I won't be able to tell him no. Am I really willing to have sex with someone I'll never see again?

I'm crazy. I can't have sex with him. I don't even own a condom.

Now I'm pushing him back down the hall, away from my bedroom.

Jesus, he must think I'm crazy.

He shoves me against the wall again and acts like the last ten seconds of indecisiveness never even happened.

I'm dizzy. I'm so dizzy, it feels so good, my mother is *crazy.* Stupid, insane, absurd, and she's *wrong.* Why would a girl care to find herself when she'll never be able to make herself feel as good as a guy can? Okay, now I'm just being stupid. But Ben is making me feel really good things right now.

He groans and then I freaking lose it. My hands are in his hair and his mouth is all over my neck.

Grab my boob, Ben.

He totally reads my mind and grabs my boob.

Grab the other one.

God, he's so telepathic.

His lips move from my neck back to my mouth, but his hands are still on my breasts. I'm pretty sure mine are cupping his ass, pulling him even harder against me, but I'm too embarrassed at my behavior right now to acknowledge that.

"I would say get a room, but I thought that's what the two of you have been doing in there for the past two hours."

Amber.

What a bitch. I'm beating her up as soon as Ben leaves.

I can't believe I just had those thoughts. She's my best friend.

Endorphins are bad. They're evil and bad and make me think ridiculous thoughts.

Ben pulls his mouth from mine at the sound of her voice. His forehead presses against the side of my head and his hands leave their naturally assumed positions to meet the wall behind me.

I exhale a really, really, *really* pent-up breath.

"For real though," Amber says. "Glenn and I can see everything going on in this hallway. I thought I'd intervene before you got pregnant."

I nod, but I'm unable to speak yet. I think my voice got lost somewhere down Ben's throat.

He pulls away and looks down at me, and if Amber wasn't still standing there, I'd be kissing that mouth again.

"Fallon was just walking me out." His voice is raspy, and it makes me smile, knowing he's just as physically affected by me as I am by him.

"Uh-huh," Amber replies. As soon as she disappears from my peripheral vision, Ben grins and his mouth is back on mine. I smile against his lips and grab at his shirt, pulling him closer.

"*God,* you guys," Amber groans. "Seriously. It's five feet back to your bedroom and ten feet to the front door. Make a choice."

He pulls away again, but this time he pulls all the way away. Like three feet away, until his back meets the wall behind him. His chest is heaving as he runs his hands down his face. He glances back at my bedroom door, and then cuts his eyes to mine. He wants me to make the choice, but I don't want to. I kind of liked it when he took control and made the decision to kiss me. I don't want the next decision to be on me.

We stare at each other for what seems like an entire minute. Him wanting me to invite him back to my bedroom. Me wanting him to just *push* me back in there. Both of us knowing good and well that we should head toward the front door.

He straightens up and shoves his hands in his pockets and clears his throat. "Do you need a ride to the airport?"

"Amber's driving me," I say, somewhat disappointed that I do, in fact, already have a ride.

He nods and rocks back and forth on his feet. "Well, the airport is absolutely not in the direction of my house, but . . . I'll pretend it is if you want me to drive you."

Dammit, he's adorable. His words make me feel all warm and fuzzy, and . . . *I'm not a damn teddy bear. I need to suck it up.*

I don't accept his offer right away. Amber and I won't see each other again until she visits New York in March, so I don't know if she'd be mad if I told her I'd rather a guy I've only known half a day drive me to the airport.

"I don't mind," Amber says from the living room. Ben and I both look down the hallway. Glenn and Amber are sitting on the couch, staring at us. "Not only can we see you making out from right here, but we can also hear your conversation."

I know her well enough to know she's doing me a favor. She winks at me and when I look back at Ben, there's a little more hope in his expression. I casually fold my arms across my chest and tilt my head. "You don't happen to live near the airport, do you?"

His mouth pulls into a grin. "Actually, I do. How incredibly convenient."

Ben spends the next few minutes helping me with last-minute scrambling. I change out of the dress I had planned to wear and settle on yoga pants and a T-shirt so I'll be comfortable on the flight. He loads my suitcases in his car as I tell Amber goodbye.

"Remember, I'm all yours during spring break," she says. She hugs me, but neither of us are the type to cry over a silly goodbye. She knows as well as I do that this move is good for me. She's been one of my biggest cheerleaders since the accident, hoping I find the confidence I lost two years ago. And living inside this apartment isn't where that's going to happen. "Call me in the morning so I know you made it okay."

We finish our goodbyes and then I follow Ben to his car. He walks around to open the door for me, but before I climb inside I take one last look at my apartment door. It's a bittersweet feeling. I've only visited New York a handful of times and I'm not even sure if it's something I'll like. But this apartment is too comfortable, and comfort can sometimes be a crutch when it comes to figuring out your life. Goals are achieved through discomfort and hard work. They aren't achieved when you hide out in a place where you're nice and cozy.

I feel Ben's arms wrap around me from behind. He rests his chin on my shoulder. "You having second thoughts?"

I shake my head. I'm nervous, but I'm definitely not having second thoughts. *Yet.*

"Good," he says. "Because I didn't want to have to throw you in the trunk and drive you all the way to New York."

I laugh, relieved he's not like my father, selfishly trying to talk me out of taking this step. He keeps his arms wrapped around me as I turn around, but now I'm leaning against the car and he's staring down at me. I don't have much time to spare before I have to be checked in at the airport, but I don't want to rush getting there when I can soak this up for a few more minutes. I'll just run to my gate if I'm late.

"There's a quote that reminds me of you, from Dylan Thomas. My favorite poet."

"What is it?"

A slow smile warms its way across his mouth. He dips his head and whispers the quote against my lips. " 'I have longed to move away but am afraid; Some life, yet unspent, might explode.' "

Wow. He's good. And he makes it even better by pressing his warm mouth to mine, holding my face in the palms of his hands. I reach up and thread my hands through his hair, allowing him to have complete control over the speed and intensity of this kiss. He keeps it soft and concise, and I imagine he kisses the same way he writes. Gentle strokes of the keys, each word thought through and completed with purpose.

He kisses me like he wants this kiss to be

remembered. For which one of us, I don't know, but I allow him to take as much as he can from this kiss and I give him as much as I have. And it's perfect. Nice. *Really* Nice.

It's as if he really is my boyfriend and this is something we should be doing all the time. Which brings me back to the fact that being too comfortable can be a crutch. With kisses like these, I could see myself easily falling into Ben's life and forgetting how to live my own. Which is exactly why I need to follow through with this goodbye.

When the kiss finally breaks, he brushes the tip of his nose against mine. "Tell me something," he says. "On a scale of one to ten, how book-worthy was our first kiss?"

He has perfect comedic timing. I smile and nip at his bottom lip. "At least a seven."

He pulls back in shock. "Seriously? That's all I get? A seven?"

I shrug. "I've read some great first kisses."

He drops his head in mock regret. "I knew I should have waited. I could have made it a ten if I had a plan." He steps back, releasing me. "I should have taken you to the airport and then as soon as you got to security, I could have dramatically called out your name and run toward you in slow motion." He mimics the scene in slow motion, moving in place as he reaches an arm out toward me. "Faaallllooooon," he says in a long, drawn-out voice. "Dooon't Leeeave Meeeee!" I'm laughing hard when he stops acting out the scene and wraps his arms around my waist again.

"If you would have done it at the airport, it would have been at least an eight. Maybe a nine, depending on believability."

"A nine? That's it?" he says. "If that's a nine, what the hell could make it a ten?"

I think about that. What *does* make kissing scenes in books so great? I've read enough of them, I should know.

"Angst," I say. "Definitely need some angst to make it a ten."

He looks confused. "Why would angst make it a ten? Give me some examples."

I lean my head against the car and stare up at the sky as I think. "I don't know, it depends on the situation. Maybe the couple isn't allowed to be together, so the forbidden factor creates the angst. Or maybe they've been best friends for years and the unspoken attraction builds enough angst to make the kiss a ten. Sometimes infidelity creates good angst, depending on the characters and their situation."

"That's messed up," he says. "So you're saying if I were seeing another girl and I kissed you in the hallway like I did, it would have gone from a seven to a ten?"

"If you were seeing another girl, you would have never been inside my apartment to begin with." I suddenly stiffen at the thought. "Wait. You don't have a real girlfriend, do you?"

He shrugs. "If I did, would our next kiss be a ten?"

Oh, my God. Please don't say I just became the other woman.

He sees the fear on my face and he laughs. "Relax. You're the only girlfriend I have, and you're about to break up with me and move across the country." He leans in and kisses me on the side of my head. "Go easy on me, Fallon. My heart is fragile."

I press my head against his chest and even though I know he's kidding, part of me can't help but feel genuinely sad about saying goodbye to him. I read reviews a lot for the audiobooks I narrate, so I've seen the comments about how readers would do anything to make book boyfriends real. Here I am, convinced I'm standing in the arms of one, and I'm about to walk away from him.

"When is your first audition?"

He sure does have a lot of faith in me. "I haven't looked into it yet. Honestly, I'm kind of terrified to audition. I'm scared people will take one look at me and laugh."

"What's wrong with that?"

"With being laughed at?" I ask. "For one, it's humiliating. And it's a confidence killer."

He looks at me pointedly. "I *hope* they laugh at you, Fallon. If people are laughing at you, it means you're putting yourself out there to be laughed at. Not enough people have the courage to even take that step."

I'm glad it's dark, because I can feel my cheeks flush. He's always saying things that seem so simple, yet profound at the same time.

"You kind of remind me of my mother," I tell him.

"That's exactly what I was going for," he says sarcastically. He pulls me against his chest again and kisses me on top of the head. I need to get to the airport, but I try to stall it as long as possible because the looming goodbye is haunting me.

"You think we'll ever see each other again?"

His arms tighten around me. "I hope so. I would be lying if I said I'm not already plotting to hunt you down when you're twenty-three. But five years is a long time, Fallon. Who knows what could happen between now and then. Hell, I didn't even have hair on my nuts five years ago."

I laugh again, just like I've done with almost everything else he's said today. I don't know that I've ever genuinely laughed this much with one person.

"You really should write a book, Ben. A romantic comedy. You're kind of funny."

"The only way I'd be willing to write a romance novel is if you're one of the main characters. And *me,* of course." He pulls back and smiles down at me. "I'll make you a deal. If you promise to audition for Broadway, I'll write a book about the relationship we couldn't have thanks to distance and immaturity."

I wish he were serious, because I love that idea. If it weren't for the one glaring flaw. "We'll never see each other again, though. How would we know if the other stuck to the plan?"

"We hold each other accountable," he says.

"Again . . . we'll never *see* each other after tonight. And I can't give you my phone number."

I know better than to give him a way to contact me. There's too much I need to do on my own and if he had my phone number, my entire focus would be on what time each day he's supposed to call me.

Ben releases me and takes a step back,

folding his arms across his chest. He begins to pace back and forth as he chews on his bottom lip. "What if . . ." He stops and faces me. "What if we meet up again next year on the same day? And the year after that? We'll do it for five years. Same date, same time, same place. We'll pick up where we left off tonight, but only for the day. I'll make sure you're following through with your auditions and I can write a book about the days we're together."

I let his words sink in for a moment. I try to match the serious look on his face, but the prospect of seeing him once a year fills me with anticipation and I'm doing my best not to act too giddy. "Meeting up once a year on the same date sounds like a really good basis for a romance novel. If you fictionalized our story, I'd add it to the top of my TBR."

Now he's smiling. So am I, because the thought of being able to look forward to today's date is something I never thought would happen. November 9th has been an anniversary I've dreaded since the night of the fire, and this is the first time the thought of that date leaves me with a positive feeling.

"I'm serious about this, Fallon. I'll start writing the damn book tonight if it means

I'll get to see you next November."

"I'm serious, too," I say. "We'll meet every November 9th. Absolutely no contact in between, though."

"That's fair. November 9th or nothing. And we'll stop after five years?" he asks. "When we're both twenty-three?"

I nod, but I don't ask him what I'm sure we're both thinking. Which is what happens after the fifth year? I guess that's worth saving for another day . . . when we see if both of us actually stick to this ridiculous plan.

"I have one concern," he says, squeezing his bottom lip between his fingers. "Are we supposed to be . . . you know . . . monogamous? If so, I think we're both getting a raw deal, here."

I laugh at his absurdity. "Ben, there's no way I would ask you to do that for five years. I think the fact that we'll continue living our own lives is what makes this idea so great. We'll both get to experience life like we're supposed to at this age, but we also get to be with each other once a year. It's the best of both worlds."

"But what if one of us falls in love with someone else?" he asks. "Won't that ruin the book if we don't end up together in the end?"

"Whether or not the couple ends up

together at the end of a book doesn't determine whether that book has a happy ending or not. As long as the two people end up happy, it doesn't really matter if they end up happy together."

"What if we fall in love with each other? Before the five years is up?"

I hate that my first thought is how there's no way he'd ever fall in love with me. I don't know what I grow more tired of. The scars on my face or the self-deprecating thoughts in relation to the scars on my face. I dismiss the thoughts and force a smile.

"Ben, of course you're going to fall in love with me. Hence the reason for the five-year rule. We need firm guidelines so our hearts won't take over until you've finished your book."

I can see the contemplation in his eyes as he nods. We're both quiet for a moment as we ponder the deal we've just made. But then he leans against the car next to me and says, "I'll need to study up on my romance novels. You'll need to give me some suggestions."

"I can absolutely do that. Maybe next year you can take that kiss from a seven to a ten."

He laughs, resting an elbow on top of the car as he faces me. "So just to be safe, if kissing scenes are something you like most about books, what's your least favorite thing? I need to know so I don't screw up our story."

"Cliff-hangers," I say immediately. "And insta-love."

He makes a face. "Insta-love?"

I nod. "When two characters meet and supposedly have this great connection right off the bat."

He raises an eyebrow. "Fallon, I think we might already be in trouble if that's one of your least favorite things."

I think about his statement for a moment. He might be right. It's been a pretty unbelievable day with him. If he put today in writing, I'd probably roll my eyes and say it was too cheesy and unrealistic. "Just don't propose to me before my flight and I think we'll be fine."

He laughs. "Pretty sure I asked you to marry me when we were on your bed earlier. But I'll try not to get you pregnant before your flight." We're both smiling when he reaches for my door and motions for me to climb inside the car. Once we're on the road, I open my purse and pull out a pen and paper.

"What are you doing?"

"Giving you homework," I say. "I'll write down five of my favorite romance novels to get you started."

It makes me laugh thinking about Ben fictionalizing our story, but I also hope he actually does it. It's not every day a girl can say she has a genuine work of fiction loosely based on her relationship with the author. "You better make me funnier when you develop my character. And I want bigger boobs. And less flab."

"Your body is perfect. So is your humor," he says.

I don't know why I bite the inside of my cheek like I'm embarrassed to smile. Since when did flattery become embarrassing? Maybe it always has been but I just haven't been flattered enough to know.

At the top of the list of books, I write down the name of the restaurant and today's date, in case he forgets. "There," I say, folding up the paper and sticking it in his glove box.

"Get another piece of paper," he orders. "I have homework for you, too." He thinks quietly for a moment and then says, "I have a few things. Number one . . ."

I write down the number one.

"Make sure people laugh at you. At least once a week."

I scoff. "You expect me to go on an audition every *week*?"

He nods. "Until you get a role you want, yes. Number two, you need to date. You said earlier that I was the first guy you've brought back to your apartment. That's not enough experience for a girl your age, especially if I'm basing a romance novel on us. We need a little more angst. Go on at least five dates by the time I see you again."

"Five?" He's insane. That's five more than I planned to go on.

"And I want you to kiss at least two of them."

I stare at him in disbelief. He nudges his head toward the paper in my hands. "Write it down, Fallon. That's assignment number three. Kiss two guys."

"Are you about to tell me assignment number four is to find a pimp?"

He laughs. "Nope. Just three assignments. Get laughed at once a week, go on five dates, kiss at least two of them. Piece of cake."

"For you, maybe." I write down his stupid assignments and then fold up the paper and put it in my purse.

"What about social media? Are we allowed to Facebook stalk each other?" he asks.

Shit. I hadn't thought about that, even though I haven't really utilized social media much in the past two years. I reach over and grab Ben's phone. "We'll block each other," I tell him. "That way we can't cheat."

He groans, as if I just foiled his plans. I go through both of our phones and search our profiles, blocking one another on every social media platform I can think of. When I'm finished with that, I hand him back his phone and use mine to call my mother.

I had a really early breakfast with her before she left for work today. The breakfast also doubled as our goodbye. She'll be in Santa Barbara for two days, which is why Amber was going to drive me to the airport.

"Hey," I say when she answers the call.

"Hey, sweetie," she says. "Are you at the airport yet?"

"Almost. I'll text you when I land in New York, but you'll be asleep."

She laughs. "Fallon, mothers don't sleep when their children are hurtling through the sky at five hundred miles an hour. I'm leaving my phone on, so you better text me as soon as you land."

"I will, I promise."

Ben glances at me out of the corner of his eye, probably wondering who I'm talking to.

"Fallon, I'm really happy you're doing this," she says. "But I'm going to warn you, I might miss you a lot and I might sound sad when you call, but don't get homesick. I'll be fine. I promise. I'm sad that I won't get to see you as often, but I'm even happier that you're taking this step. And I promise that's all I'm going to say about it. I love you and I'm proud of you and I'll talk to you tomorrow."

"Love you, too, Mom."

When I hang up the phone, I catch Ben staring at me again.

"I can't believe you haven't introduced me to your mother yet," he says. "We've been dating for ten hours now. If it doesn't happen soon, I'll start to take it personal."

I'm laughing as I shove my phone inside my purse. He reaches over and takes my hand in his and holds it the entire way to the airport.

We're fairly quiet the rest of the drive. Aside from asking my flight information, the only other thing he says is "We're here."

Rather than pull into a parking garage like I was hoping he would, he pulls into the drop-off lane. I feel pathetic that I'm disappointed he didn't offer to walk me inside, because he drove me all the way to the airport. I can't be greedy.

He unloads my two suitcases from his trunk and I grab my purse and my carry-on from inside the car. He closes his trunk and then walks over to me. "Have a safe flight," he says as he kisses me on the cheek and gives me a quick hug. I nod and he makes his way back to his car. "November 9th!" he yells. "Don't forget!"

I smile and wave, but internally I'm confused and disappointed by the lack of emotion in his goodbye.

Maybe it's better this way, though. I was kind of dreading having to watch him drive away, but that *not* book-worthy goodbye somehow made it a little easier. Maybe because I'm kind of pissed about it.

I inhale a deep breath and push it out of my head as I watch his car move away. I grab my suitcases and head inside with not much time to spare before my flight. The airport is still buzzing despite it being so late at night, so I maneuver my way through the crowd and to a kiosk. I print my boarding pass, check my luggage, and make my way to security.

I try not to think about what I'm doing. How I'm about to move from a place I've lived my entire life to a city where I know absolutely no one. The thought of it makes me want to call a cab and go straight back to my apartment, but I can't.

I have to do this.

I have to force myself to make a life before

the one I'm not living swallows me whole.

I pull my driver's license out of my purse and prepare to hand it to the security agent as I wait in line. There are five people in front of me.

Five people is enough time to talk myself out of moving to New York, so I close my eyes and think about everything in New York that I'm excited about. Hot dog stands. Broadway. Times Square. Hell's Kitchen. The Statue of Liberty. The Museum of Modern Art. Central Park.

"Faaaallooon!"

My eyes flick open.

I turn around and Ben is standing at the revolving door. He begins running toward me.

In slow motion.

I cover my mouth with my hand and try not to laugh as he slowly stretches out an arm like he's reaching out for me. He's yelling, "Doooon't goooo yeeeet!" as he moves slowly through the crowd of people.

People from all directions stop to see what the commotion is all about. I want to dig myself a hole and hide but I'm laughing too hard to care about how embarrassing this is. What in the world is he doing?

When he finally reaches me after what seems like forever, a huge grin spreads across his face. "You didn't really think I was just going to drop you off and leave like that, did you?"

I shrug, because that's exactly what I thought just happened.

"You should know your own boyfriend better than that." He takes my face in his hands. "I had to create angst so I could try to make this kiss a ten." He presses his mouth to mine and kisses me with so much emotion, I forget all the things. Everything. I forget where I am. Who I am. There's a guy and I'm a girl and we're kissing and *the feels* and the knots in my stomach and the chills on my skin and the hand in my hair and my arms that feel too heavy and now he's grinning against my lips.

My eyelids flutter open and *I didn't even know kisses could really make eyelids flutter open.* But they do and mine did.

"On a scale of one to ten?" he asks.

The room feels like it's spinning, so I suck in a huge rush of air and try not to sway. "A nine. Definitely a solid nine."

He shrugs. "I'll take it. But next year, it'll be an eleven. Promise." He presses a kiss to my forehead and releases me. He begins to walk backward and I'm aware of everyone in our vicinity staring at us, but I can't help but not give a shit. Right before he reaches the revolving door, he cups his hands around his mouth and yells, "I hope the entire state of New York laughs at you!"

I don't think I've ever smiled so big. I lift a hand and wave goodbye as he disappears.

It really was a ten.

■ ■ ■ ■

Second November 9th

■ ■ ■ ■

Her tears and my soul, they live parallel
lives.
Run, ache, burn.
Repeat.
Her tears and my soul, they live parallel
lives.

— Benton James Kessler

Ben

When you swing upon a memory
So dark and far away
You get caught upon a mystery
That guides you through the day.
Although you're standing weak
And don't know your way around
I will always be there
For you when you're down.

I wrote that piece of shit poem when I was in the third grade. It was the first thing I ever showed anyone.

Actually, I don't even think I showed it to anyone. My mother found it in my room, which is how I came to respect the beauty of privacy. She showed everyone in my entire family and it made me never want to share my work again.

I realize now that my mother wasn't trying to embarrass me. She was just proud of me. But I still never show anyone the things

I write. It's almost like saying every thought out loud. Some things just aren't for public consumption.

And I don't know how to explain that to Fallon. She assumes, based on our agreement last year, that I'm writing a novel that she'll one day read. And as much as she claims it's fiction, every sentence I've written in the past year is more truthful than anything I'd ever admit out loud. I'm hoping after today I can start rewriting it in order to give her something to read, but the last year of writing down my fucked-up life has been kind of therapeutic.

And even though I've been busy with school and what I now call my "writing therapy," I still found time to complete the homework she gave me. *And then some.* I've read twenty-six romance novels, only five of which Fallon recommended. What she failed to tell me is that two of the novels she suggested were firsts in a series, so of course I had to finish the series.

So far in my "research" I've concluded that Fallon is absolutely right. Kisses in books and kisses in real life aren't exactly the same. And every single time I read one of these novels, I cringe when I think about the few times I kissed Fallon last year. They absolutely were not book-worthy, and even though I've been doing a lot of reading this past year, I'm still not sure what makes a kiss book-worthy. But I know she deserved better than what I gave her.

I'd be lying if I said I haven't kissed anyone since I kissed Fallon last November. I've been out with girls a few times since then, and when Fallon jokingly said she wanted me to compare every girl to her, she got her wish. Because that's exactly what happened with both the girls I kissed. One of them wasn't nearly as funny as Fallon. The other was way too self-absorbed. And neither of them had good taste in music, but that doesn't count since I have no idea what taste in music Fallon has.

It's definitely something I had planned to find out today. I have a list of things I need to know in order to work on the *real* novel I promised her. However, it looks like that list will go unanswered and the entire last year of studying romance novels and writing about our first November 9th together was for naught.

Because she didn't show up.

I look at the clock again to make sure it matches the time on my cell phone. *It does.*

I pull the slip of homework out to make sure I got the time right. *I did.*

I look around me once more to make sure

this is the same restaurant where we met last year. *It is.*

I know this, because the restaurant changed ownership recently and has a different name. But it's still the same building at the same address with the same food.

So . . . *where the hell are you, Fallon?*

She's almost two hours late. The waitress has refilled my drink four times. And five glasses of water in two hours is a lot for my bladder, but I'm giving myself half an hour before I go to the restroom, because I'm worried if I'm not sitting here when she walks in, she'll think I didn't show and she'll leave.

"Excuse me."

My pulse immediately quickens at her words and my head jerks up. But . . . *she's not Fallon.*

I immediately deflate.

"Is your name Ben?" the girl asks. She's wearing a name tag. *Tallie.* Tallie is wearing a *Pinkberry* name tag. How does Tallie know my name?

"Yeah. I'm Ben."

She exhales and points at her name tag. "I work down the street. Some girl is on the phone there and says it's an emergency."

Fallon!

I impress myself with how fast I'm out of

the booth and out the door. I run down the street until I get to Pinkberry and I swing the door open. The guy behind the counter looks at me strange and takes a step back. I'm out of breath and panting, but I point to the phone behind him. "Someone's on hold for me?" He grabs the phone, presses a button, and hands me the receiver.

"Hello? Fallon? Are you okay?"

I don't immediately hear her voice, but I can tell it's her from her sigh alone.

"Ben! Oh, thank God you were still there. I'm *so* sorry. My flight was delayed and I tried calling the restaurant, but their number was disconnected and then my flight was boarding. I finally figured out the number by the time I landed, and I've tried calling several times but I just keep getting a busy signal, so I didn't know what else to do. I'm in a cab now and I'm really, really sorry I'm so late but I had no way of getting in touch with you."

I didn't know my lungs could hold this much air. I exhale, relieved and disappointed for her but completely stoked that she actually did it. She remembered and she came and we're actually doing this. Never mind the fact that she's now aware I was still waiting at the restaurant two whole hours later.

"Ben?"

"I'm here," I say. "It's fine, I'm just glad you made it. But it's probably faster if you just meet me at my house; the traffic is a nightmare here."

She asks for the address and I give it to her.

"Okay," she says. She sounds nervous. "I'll see you in a little while."

"Yeah, I'll be there."

"Oh, wait! Ben? Um . . . I kind of told the girl who answered the phone that you would give her twenty bucks if she took you the message. Sorry about that. She just acted like she wasn't going to do it, so I had to bribe her."

I laugh. "No problem. See you soon."

She tells me goodbye and I hand the phone to Tallie, who is now standing behind the register. She holds out her hand for the twenty dollars. I pull out my wallet and hand her the twenty.

"I would have paid ten times that for her phone call."

I pace back and forth in the driveway.

What am I doing?

There is so much wrong with this. I barely even *know* the girl. I spent a few hours with her and here I am committing to writing a book about her? About *us*? What if we don't even click this time? I could have been having a manic episode last year and was just in an exceptionally receptive and good mood. She might not even be funny. She could be a bitch. She could be stressed out over her flight delay and she might not even *want* to be here.

I mean, who *does* that? What sane person would fly across the country to see someone for one day who they barely know?

Probably not many people. But I would have been on a flight without hesitation today if we were supposed to meet up in New York.

I'm rubbing my hands down my face when the cab rounds the corner. I'm trying to mentally psych myself into believing that this is perfectly normal. It's not crazy. It's not commitment. We're friends. Friends would fly across the country to spend time together.

Wait. *Are we friends?* We don't even communicate, so that probably wouldn't even qualify as acquaintances.

The cab is pulling into the driveway now.

For fuck's sake, lose the nerves, Kessler.

The car stops.

The back door opens.

I should greet her at the door. It's awkward

with me being so far away.

I'm walking toward the cab when she begins to step out.

Please be the same Fallon I met last year.

I grip the door handle and pull it the rest of the way open. I try to play it cool, to not come off nervous. Or worse, *excited.* I've studied enough romance novels to know girls like it when the guys are somewhat aloof. I read somewhere those kinds of guys are called alpha males.

Be a jackass, Kessler. Just a little bit. You can do it.

She steps out of the car, and when she does, it's like in the movies where everything is in slow motion. Not at all similar to my version of slow motion. This is much more graceful. The wind picks up and strands of hair blow across her face. She lifts her hand to pull the hair away, and that's when I notice what a difference one year can make.

She's different. Her hair is shorter. She has bangs. She's wearing a short-sleeved shirt, which is something she admitted to never doing before last year.

She's covered in confidence, from head to toe.

It's the sexiest thing I've ever seen.

"Hey," she says, as I reach behind her to close her door. She seems to be happy to see me and that alone makes me smile back at her.

So much for playing aloof.

I literally lasted zero seconds when it came to the alpha-male alter ego I've been practicing.

I release a yearlong pent-up breath and I step forward and pull her into the most genuine embrace I've ever given anyone. I wrap my hand around the back of her head and pull her to me, breathing in the crisp winter scent of her. She immediately wraps her arms around me and buries her face against my shoulder. I feel a sigh escape her and we stand in the same position until the cab has backed out of the driveway and disappears around the corner.

And even then, we don't let go.

She's squeezing the back of my shirt in her fisted hands and I'm trying not to be obvious about the fact that I might be a little bit obsessed with her new hairstyle. It's softer. Straighter. Lighter. Refreshing, and *fuck, it hurts.*

Again.

Why is she the only one who makes me wince like this? She sighs against my neck and I almost push her away, because *dammit, this is too much.* I'm not sure what bothers me more. The fact that we seem to have picked up right where we left off last year or the fact that last year wasn't a fluke. If I'm being honest, I kind of think it's the latter. Because this past year was hell having to go every minute of the day with her on my mind and not knowing if I'd ever see her again. And now that I know she's committed to this idiotic plan of mine to meet up once a year, I foresee another long year of agony ahead of me.

I'm already dreading the second she leaves, and she just now showed up.

She lifts her head from my shoulder and looks up at me. I brush her bangs back with my hand to see more of her face. Despite how frantic she sounded on the phone earlier, she seems completely peaceful right now.

"Hello, Fallon the Transient."

Her smile grows even wider. "Hello, Ben the Writer. Why do you look like you're in pain?"

I try to smile, but I'm sure the look on my face right now isn't an attractive one. "Because keeping my mouth off of you is really painful."

She laughs. "As much as I want your mouth on me, I must warn you that a hello kiss is probably only going to be a six."

I promised her an eleven. It'll have to wait.

“Come on. Let’s go inside so I can find out what color panties you have on.” She’s laughing that familiar laugh as I grab her hand and walk her toward the house. I can already tell I have nothing to worry about. She’s the same Fallon I remember from last year. Maybe even a little better.

So . . . maybe that means I have *everything* to worry about.

FALLON

I wasn't expecting this when he said to meet him at his house. I was more or less expecting an apartment, but this is a fairly modern two-story house. A *house*-house. He closes the front door behind me and heads for the stairs. I trail behind him.

"You didn't bring luggage?" he asks.

I don't want to think about how little time I'll actually be here. "I'm heading back tonight."

He stops mid-step and faces me. "Tonight? You aren't even staying the night in California?"

I shake my head. "I can't. I have to be back in New York by eight in the morning. My flight is at ten thirty tonight."

"The flight is more than five hours," he says, concerned. "With the time difference, you won't even get home until after six in the morning."

"I'll sleep on the plane."

His eyebrows draw apart and his mouth tightens. "I don't like that for you," he says. "You should have called. We could have changed the date or something."

"I don't know your phone number. Besides, that would have ruined the entire premise of your book. It's November 9th or nothing, remember?"

I think he may be pouting, but I do recall him being the one to make that rule.

"I'm sorry I was late. We still have six hours left before I have to head to the airport."

"Five and a half," he clarifies. He begins walking up the stairs again. I follow him all the way to his room, but now I feel like he's upset with me. I know there were probably ways around flying in and out on the same day, but to be honest, I wasn't even sure he would show up. I thought he probably had crazy, spontaneous days with fake girlfriends all the time and he wouldn't even remember me. I figured I wouldn't be too embarrassed with myself for believing he would show up if I was able to get right back on the plane a few hours later and pretend it never happened.

But not only did he show up, he was still waiting two hours later.

Two hours.

It's extremely flattering. I would have probably given up after the first hour, thinking he stood me up.

Ben opens a door and motions for me to walk in first. He smiles at me as I walk into his room, but his smile feels forced.

He has no right to be upset with me. We agreed to meet today and yes, I was late, but I showed up. I spin around and put my hands on my hips, ready to defend myself if he says another word about how little time we have. He closes the door and leans against it, but rather than bring it up again, he begins to kick off his shoes. The disappointment is gone from his face and he actually looks . . . I don't know . . . *happy.*

After his shoes are off, he steps quickly toward me and shoves me. I let out a shriek when I fall backward, but before I can panic, my back meets a cloud. Or a bed. Whatever it is, it's the most comfortable thing I've ever lain on.

He steps forward with a smirk on his face and a gleam in his eye. "Let's get comfortable," he says. "We have a lot of talking to do." He stands between my knees and lifts one of my legs to remove my shoe. They're just flats, so he slides it off easily. Rather than drop my foot, he runs his hand slowly down my leg as he lowers it to the bed.

I forgot how hot it is in California. He really needs to turn on a fan.

He lifts my other leg and removes that shoe in the same fashion, moving his hand down my leg at a torturous pace, all the while grinning at me.

Is the elevation different here than in New York? God, it's so hard to breathe in this room.

Once I'm barefoot, he steps around me and takes a seat at the head of the bed.

"Come here," he says.

I flip onto my stomach and he's lying on a pillow with his head propped up on his hand. He pats the pillow next to him. "I don't bite."

"Damn shame," I say as I crawl my way to where he is. I lie down on the pillow and face him. "Ninety percent of our time together since we met has been spent on a bed."

"Nothing wrong with that. I love your hair."

His words send me into a tizzy, but I smile like I hear it every day. "Why, thank you."

We quietly take each other in for a moment. I was starting to forget what he looked like, but now that I'm in front of him it's like I never even left. He looks less like a teenager now than he did last year. And it makes me wonder if, when I see him again next year, he'll look just like a man. Not that there's any difference between a man and a nineteen-year-old, because they're the same thing.

"We don't have much time," he says. "I have a ton of questions. I have a book to write and I know absolutely nothing about you."

I open my mouth to argue, because it seems like he knows everything about me. But then I clamp it shut, because I guess he doesn't really know much about me. We only spent one day together.

"Did you write anything this year?"

He nods. "I did. Did you kiss anyone this year?"

I nod. "I did. Did you?"

He shrugs.

"*Did* you, Ben?"

He nods. "A few."

I try not to let that affect me, but exactly how many constitutes a few?

"And did you compare them all to me?"

He shakes his head. "I told you last year, that's completely unfair to the rest of the female population. You're incomparable."

I'm so glad I came today. I don't care if I don't sleep for a week, it would be worth it just to have that compliment.

"How about your guys? Did you go on all

five dates?"

"Guy," I correct him. "There was just one. I tried."

He raises an eyebrow, so I immediately go into defense mode. "Ben, you can't expect me to put myself out there in a brand-new state when I've never really been *out* there. It takes time. I was so proud when I kissed the one guy. He thought I was stoked because of the kiss, but I was only happy because I crossed something off my homework."

He laughs. "Well, one will do, I guess. But that means your homework for this year just got a lot harder."

"Yeah, well. So will yours, then. And speaking of, I want proof of this book you're writing. I want to read something you wrote about us."

"No," he says immediately.

I lift up on the bed. "What? No? You can't tell me you wrote this year and not prove it to me. Give me something."

"I don't like people to read what I write."

I laugh. "Seriously? That's like an opera singer refusing to make sound when she performs."

"It's nothing like that. I'll let you read it when I'm finished."

"You're going to make me wait *four years*?"

His lip curls up in a grin when he nods.

I fall back down onto the pillow with a defeated flop. "Sigh."

"Did you just *say* sigh? Out loud? Instead of actually *sighing*?"

"Eye roll."

He laughs and scoots closer to me. Now I'm looking up and he's looking down and that would be fine and dandy if he wasn't looking at me like he's planning out exactly how his lips are going to mesh with mine.

I suck in a breath as his hand slides over my jaw. "I missed you, Fallon," he whispers. "A lot. And screw it if I'm not supposed to admit that, but I tried the whole alpha-male thing for two seconds and I just can't do it. So you don't get alpha-Ben today. I'm sorry."

Wow. Is he . . .

He is.

"Ben," I say, narrowing my eyes. "Are you . . . *booksting* me?"

He cocks an eyebrow. "Booksting?"

"Yeah. When a hot guy talks books with a girl. It's like sexting, but out loud and with books instead of sex. Nor does it have to do with texts. Okay, so it's nothing like sexting, but it made sense in my head."

He falls onto his back in laughter. I scoot toward him and place my hand on his chest as I lean over him. "Don't stop," I tease in a seductive voice. "Give me more, Ben. Did you read eBooks or . . ." I run my finger slowly down his chest. "*Hard*backs?"

He pulls his hands behind his head and a smug look washes over his face. "Oh, they were hardbacks, all right. And I'm not sure if you're ready for this, but . . . I have my very own TBR pile. You should see it, Fallon. It's *huge.*"

I let out a moan, but I'm not so sure it's pretend.

"I also know what makes a kiss book-worthy now," he says. "So be prepared." He lifts up onto his elbow again and loses the smile. "Seriously though. This female attraction to the alpha-male throws me off a little bit, because I'm not anything like the guys you read about."

Yeah. You're better.

"I could never drive a motorcycle, or fight another man just for fun. And as much as I've fantasized about having sex with you this year, I don't think I could ever say, '*I own you,*' with a straight face. And I've always wanted a tattoo, but probably just a small one, because no way in hell I could endure the pain. Overall, the books were interesting but they also made me feel highly inadequate."

He can't be serious. "Ben, not all the guys in the books I read are like that."

He tilts his head. "But you obviously like the bad boys if you like reading about them."

"Actually, that's not true," I tell him. "I enjoy reading books like that because it's not at all the life I lead. It's completely different than any situation I'll ever be in, thank God. But I get entertainment out of it. Because as much as I like to read about a guy telling a girl she's so, so wet for him . . . if anyone ever said that to me during sex, I wouldn't be turned on by it. I would be terrified I accidentally peed on myself."

Ben laughs.

"And if you and I were having sex and you told me you *owned* me, I would literally crawl out from under you, put on my clothes, walk out of your house, and go puke in your front yard. So just because I like reading about those kinds of guys, doesn't mean I need my *real*-life guys to act like that."

He grins. "Can I keep you?"

Too bad he's only kidding. "I'm all yours for the next five hours."

He pushes me flat on my back. "Tell me

about this *boy* you kissed." His use of the word *boy* somehow seems like an insult to the guy. I like it. Jealous Ben is cute. "I need to know all the details about your kiss so I can add a subplot to the book."

"A *sub*plot?" I ask. "Does that mean you have an *actual* plot already?"

His expression doesn't waver. "So how did you meet him?"

"Rehearsals."

"Did you go on a date with him?"

"Two."

"Why only two? What happened?"

I want to say "sigh" again out loud. I really don't want to talk about him. "Nothing came of it. Do we really have to talk about it?"

"Yep. It was part of the agreement."

I groan. "Fine. His name is Cody. He's twenty-one. We were auditioning for the same play and we had a nice conversation. He asked for my number and I gave it to him."

"You gave him your phone number?" Ben asks, dejected. "Why won't you give *me* your phone number?"

"Because I actually like you. Anyway, we went out that weekend and kissed a few times. He was nice. Funny . . ."

Ben makes a face. "Funnier than me?"

"Your humor is incomparable, Ben. Stop interrupting me. So I agreed to go out with him a second time. We went back to his place to watch a movie. We started making out and . . . I just . . . I couldn't do it."

"Couldn't do it? Like *it* it? Or just make out with him?"

I don't know what's more strange. Talking to Ben about making out with another guy or the fact that I'm so comfortable talking to Ben about making out with another guy.

Well, up to this point, anyway. Now I just want to shut up.

"I couldn't do either. It was . . ." I close my eyes, not wanting to tell him the real reason why I couldn't do it. But it's Ben. He's easy to talk to.

"It was different. He made me feel . . . I don't know. *Flawed.*"

I can see the roll in Ben's throat when he swallows. "Explain," he says, his voice clipped. I like that he seems a little upset, like he doesn't actually *want* to hear about me making out with someone else. I especially like how he seems a little protective of me.

I think Ben has more alpha in him than he gives himself credit for.

I blow out a heavy breath, preparing for the honesty I shouldn't really want to share, but for some reason *want* to share.

"Last year when you touched me, you made me feel . . . pretty. Like I didn't have any scars. Or . . . not like that, I said that wrong. You made me feel like the scars were part of what *made* me pretty. And I've never once felt like that, nor did I think I'd *ever* feel like that. So when I was with Cody, I noticed everything. How he only touched the right side of my face. How he only kissed the right side of my neck. How, when we were making out, he insisted the lights be off."

Ben makes a face like he's in pain again, but this time he's very convincing. "Go on," he says, forcing the words out of his mouth.

"He tried to take off my bra at one point and I just couldn't do it. I didn't want him to see it. He was really nice about it and didn't ask me to keep going. And if I'm being honest, that bothered me a little. I kind of wanted him to console me and act like he still wanted me, but he seemed a little relieved that I stopped it."

Ben rolls onto his back and rubs his hands up and down his face. After a moment, he resumes his position, looking down on me. "Please don't ever speak to that fucking douchebag again."

A surprising wave of heat rolls over me

with those words. His thumb brushes my jaw and his expression is full of sincerity. "What didn't you want him to see?"

The confusion on my face prompts him to be more detailed. "You said, *'I didn't want him to see it.'* But if your shirt was already off and he already saw your scars, what is it you're referring to?"

I swallow. I want to pull a pillow over my face and hide. I can't believe he caught that.

In fact, I think I *will* pull a pillow over my face.

"Stop," he says, when I try to grab for the pillow. He tucks it back under my head and leans in closer. "It's *me,* Fallon. Don't be embarrassed. Tell me what you were referring to."

I inhale a deep breath, hoping more air in my lungs will somehow give me more courage to answer him. And then I release the breath as slow as possible so I can drag out having to answer him.

I cover my eyes with my arm and say it as fast as I can. "My left breast."

I wait for him to ask more questions, or make me move my arm, but he doesn't. I can't believe I just told him that. I've never told anyone that, not even Amber. During the fire, not only was most of the left half of my body burned, but as if that wasn't punishment enough, I was injured when they tried to pull me out the top-story window. Luckily I don't remember anything between falling asleep that night and waking up in the hospital, but the scars are a daily reminder. And my left breast bore the brunt of most of it. And I'm not stupid. I know to guys, breasts are supposed to be beautiful and symmetrical, and mine aren't.

I feel Ben's hand meet my wrist and he pulls my arm from my face. He gently palms my cheek. "Why would it bother you for anyone to see it? Because it's scarred?"

I nod, but then I shake my head. "This is so embarrassing, Ben."

"Not to me," he says. "And it sure as hell shouldn't be for you. I've seen you without a shirt already, remember? As I recall, it was pretty magnificent."

"You've seen me without a shirt, but you should see me without a bra. You would understand."

Ben immediately lifts up onto his elbow. "Okay."

I stare at him in disbelief. "That wasn't an invitation."

"But I want to see it."

I shake my head. I even laugh, because there's no way in hell I'm just going to plop my boob out of my shirt so he can gawk at its hideousness.

"I want to do the book justice, and your injuries are something I have to talk about. So you should let me see it. We'll consider it research."

It feels like his words just backhanded my heart. "What?" My voice is so unsteady, it sounds like I'm crying. But I'm not. *Yet.* "What do you mean you'll have to talk about it in the book? You aren't really writing about my scars, are you?"

Confusion encompasses his face. "It's part of your story. Of course I'm writing about it."

I lift up on my elbows and narrow my eyes in his direction. "I wanted you to fictionalize me and make me *pretty,* Ben. You can't make the main character a freak show. No one wants to identify with that. Main characters should be beautiful and . . ."

Ben immediately rolls on top of me and covers my mouth with his hand. He inhales a deep breath in preparation for what seems like a fight. He releases it quickly, his jaw twitching with irritation.

"You listen to me," he says, keeping his hand secured over my mouth so that I can't interrupt him. "It pisses me off that you allow something so trivial to define such a huge part of you. I can't make you pretty in this book, because that would be an insult. You're fucking *beautiful.* And you're funny. And the only times I'm not completely enamored by you are the moments you're feeling sorry for yourself. Because I don't know if you've realized this yet, but you're *alive,* Fallon. And every time you look in the mirror, you don't have the right to hate what you see. Because you survived when a lot of people don't get that lucky. So from now on when you think about your scars, you aren't allowed to resent them. You're going to embrace them, because you're lucky to be on this earth to see them. And any guy you allow to touch your scars better thank you for that privilege."

My chest hurts.

I can't breathe.

He removes his hand from my mouth and when he does, I gasp for breath. My eyes rim with tears and I can't stop myself from shaking as I try to suppress them. Ben lowers himself completely on top of me, cradling my head in his hands. He presses his lips to the side of my head and then whispers, "You deserved that, Fallon."

And I nod, because he's right.

He's right.

Of course he's right. I'm alive and I'm healthy and yes, the fire left its thumbprint on my skin, but it didn't take the most important parts of me. It wasn't able to reach anything beneath the surface. So why am I treating myself like it did?

I have to stop doing this to myself.

"Shh," he whispers, thumbing the tears on my cheeks. My emotions are all over the place. I'm so pissed that he felt he has the right to even talk to me that way, but the fact that he just talked to me that way made my heart wish it had lips so it could kiss him. And I'm pissed off at myself for being so self-centered these last few years. Sure, the fire sucked. Yes, I wish it never happened. But it did and I can't change it so I need to get over it.

I want to laugh, because everything he just said feels like a weight has been removed from my chest and I'm breathing for the first time in three years.

Everything feels different. Newer. Like the air is buzzing, reminding me that I'm lucky to be here, breathing it in.

So I do just that. I take in a deep breath and I throw my arms around him, burying my head in the crevice of his neck and shoulder.

"Thank you," I whisper. "You asshole."

I feel him laughing, so I lie back down on my pillow and allow him to wipe more tears away. He's looking down at me like I'm a beautiful mess, and I'm not going to allow myself to question that. Because I am. I'm a beautiful fucking mess and he's lucky to be on top of me right now.

I slide my hands to his chest and feel his heart pounding through his shirt. It's pounding as hard as mine is.

We lock eyes and he doesn't ask permission when he dips his head and brushes my mouth with his. "Fallon, I'm worked up so damn tight. I'm going to kiss you now and I'm not sorry."

And then his lips claim mine. My head is swimming, my body feels like it's floating and I can't move my arms. But I don't have to, because he raises my hands above my head and interlocks our fingers, pushing them into the mattress. His tongue slides against mine and there's so much feeling in it, it's as if he's kissing me the same way he looks at me. From the inside out.

He slowly plants kisses down my neck, keeping my hands secured to the bed, not allowing me to touch him back while he explores my skin. *God, I've missed him.* I've missed the way I feel when I'm with him. I wish I could have this every day. Once a year isn't near enough.

The pressure on my right hand disappears

as he runs his fingers down the length of my arm, all the way to my waist. His mouth has returned to mine and he's kissing me again as his hand slowly begins to crawl inside my shirt. Just feeling his fingertips on my skin reminds me of why I think about him every night when my head meets my pillow.

"I'm taking off your shirt," he says.

I don't even hesitate.

I don't even hesitate?

He pulls the shirt over my head and tosses it behind him. His eyes fall to my breasts, covered with a black lace bra that I was convinced he wouldn't see tonight. He smiles a devilish smile, running his fingertips over the lace. He cups my right breast in his hand, dragging his thumb over the fabric covering my nipple. The second he does that, I flinch, because I've read enough books to know that the next move is going to be touching me *beneath* the fabric. My entire body tenses because I don't think I want him to remove my bra. I don't want him to see all of me. No one has ever seen all of me.

"Baby," he says, sliding his lips across my chest. "Relax, okay?"

I could try, but now I'm tense because he called me baby and not because he's about to go where no one has gone before.

I've always found that term of endearment to be a little grating, but it so works when he says it.

I thread my fingers through the back of his hair and guide him toward my left breast, wondering how this went from zero to ten in a matter of seconds. *Oh, God, he's pulling down my bra strap.* His mouth is right there, trailing over the curve of my breast and his fingers are pulling the material lower . . . lower . . . lower . . . *gone.*

I feel the air against my exposed breast, but my eyes are closed too tight to see the look on his face. But I can feel his lips as he kisses his way across my chest without hesitation, sliding his tongue against my skin, sucking and kissing and squeezing and . . . *enjoying.*

"Fallon."

He wants me to look at him, but I'm much more comfortable with my eyes closed.

"Open your eyes, Fallon."

I can do this.

I open my eyes and I'm staring up at the ceiling.

I can do this.

I slowly bring my gaze down until I'm looking him in the eyes. "You're beautiful. Every inch of you is so beautiful." He presses his lips between my breasts and then drags them slowly across my skin, running his tongue over my scars. I wait for him to make an excuse . . . to back away from me.

But he doesn't. He grins up at me instead. "Are you okay? Can I keep going?"

My first inclination is to shake my head, because I shouldn't want him to. Any time I've imagined this happening with a guy in the past, I picture myself with a perfect body and no scars. But here I am, staring down at Ben as he explores every part of me I've wished were different. And he's actually enjoying it.

And . . . so am I.

I nod, and maybe moan again because *holy shit he looks hot.* The fact that I'm the reason for that heated look in his eyes makes me feel even more desirable than when I imagine being perfect. He kisses his way back up my neck until he's hovering over me. He slides a hand to the nape of my neck and dips his head.

"I'm sorry. I don't know how to slow myself down when I'm with you."

But not only does he slow himself down. He stops completely, because the door to his bedroom swings open.

Ben lies on top of me in a flash, covering me, but he isn't fast enough for me to miss the girl standing in the doorway, wide-eyed.

Oh, God. The door. A girl.

"Ben?" she says.

I think I might panic.

"Can we have a minute, Jordyn?" Ben says, without looking back at her.

The door quickly slams shut and a muffled apology comes from the other side of it. "Sorry! Oh, wow, *so* sorry!"

Her reaction isn't that of a pissed-off girlfriend, so that fills me with relief. It does little to relieve my embarrassment, though.

"I'm so sorry," Ben says. "I had no idea she was home." He gives me a quick peck on the mouth and then lifts up. "Don't worry. This is way more embarrassing for her than it is for us."

I pull my bra back up over my breasts and I sit up on the bed. "Speak for yourself."

Ben retrieves my shirt from the foot of the bed and returns to me, helping me pull it over my head. He's grinning.

"It's not funny," I whisper.

He laughs quietly. "If you knew Jordyn, you'd know that this is actually hilarious."

I feel out of the loop and it isn't until this moment that I realize how very little I actually know about Ben. "Is she your sister?"

"She will be in a few days," he says, answering me as he slips on his shoes.

"She's marrying my brother Kyle this weekend. They're having the wedding out back."

He has a brother?

I'm reminded of how little I actually know about his family.

"The wedding is here? Do they live here?"

He nods. "My brothers and I inherited the house after my mom died. We all live here since there's plenty of space. My older brother travels a lot, so he's gone more than he's here, though. Kyle and Jordyn share the master bedroom downstairs."

I don't know why I assumed Ben was an only child. And I had no idea his mother passed away. I feel like this guy whose mouth was just devouring my breasts is a complete stranger. He must see the confusion and embarrassment still on my face, so he leans over me and smiles reassuringly. "We'll play twenty questions later and you'll know almost everything about me. As boring as my life is. But for now, I want you to meet my future sister." He pulls on my hands until I'm standing. I put my shoes back on and follow him out of the bedroom. We get to the top of the stairs and he stops and gives me the sweetest, softest kiss before continuing his descent to find Jordyn.

Blame it on the fact that I'm a sucker for

romance novels, but I've been convinced that the grander the gesture, the greater the love. Some of my favorite scenes from the books I read are those pivotal points in the arc of the story when the guy declares his love for the girl in a huge way. But the way this one little kiss from Ben just left me feeling, I think I've been overlooking the best parts of romance novels. Maybe the grand gestures don't matter nearly as much as all the inconsequential things between the two main characters.

It makes me want to go back and reread everything I've ever read, now that I'm experiencing these things with someone in real life.

"I'm so sorry," someone is saying as Ben pulls me into the kitchen. "I had no idea you were home and I was looking for scissors but you *are* home and she's *definitely* not a pair of scissors."

She's cute. Shorter than me, California-blond hair and a face that can't hide a single emotion. Because right now, just looking at her, I can tell she's about to crack.

"Jordyn, this is Fallon," Ben says, gesturing toward me.

I wave and Jordyn immediately crosses the room and hugs me. "Nice to meet you, Fallon. Don't be embarrassed, it's perfectly normal for Ben to have girls in his room."

I cut my eyes to Ben and he lifts his hands in defense like he has no idea why she just said that. I lift my palms up in a "help me" gesture, because she's clinging tight and I don't know what I'm supposed to do. Ben clears his throat and Jordyn finally releases me.

"Oh God, that totally came out wrong," she says, shaking out her hands. "It's not *normal* for him to have girls in his room. Not at all what I meant," she says. "I just mean it's nothing to be ashamed of, we're all adults. I wasn't implying that you're one of many. In fact, he rarely ever brings girls here so that's why I didn't think twice before walking into his room, because it's so rare I never thought he'd actually be *in* there. With you. With a girl." She's pacing now, and every time I catch a glimpse of her face, she looks on the verge of tears. I've never seen anyone more in need of a hug than she is right now.

I walk over to her and she stops pacing. I place both of my hands on her shoulders. I take a deep, exaggerated breath, straightening my posture. She copies the movement, dragging air into her lungs. I calmly exhale, and she follows suit. I smile. "It's okay, Jordyn. Ben and I are absolutely fine. But you look like you could use a drink. Or ten."

She nods feverishly and then slaps her hand over her mouth as soon as the tears come.

Oh, Jesus. What now? I look to Ben for help, but he's looking at me like this is completely normal behavior for her. He does make his way toward her though, turning her around to face him.

"Hey," Ben says soothingly, pulling her into a hug. "What's wrong?"

She shakes her head, pointing toward another room. "The placeholders came and half of them are spelled wrong and the tables and chairs were supposed to be here this morning, but they moved delivery to tomorrow and tomorrow doesn't work because tomorrow is when I'm supposed to have my last fitting and now I have to be here for the delivery and my mom's flight was canceled so she can't help me finish the flower arrangements tonight and . . ."

Ben cuts her off. "Calm down," he says. He motions toward the refrigerator, so I walk to the kitchen and find a half-full bottle of wine. I pour Jordyn a glass while Ben calms her down. When I hand it to her, she's sitting on a bar stool, wiping at her tears.

"Thank you," she says as she takes the

wine. "I'm normally not this crazy or high-strung but it's the worst week of my life. And I know it'll be worth it in the end but . . ." She eyes me hard. "Never get married. Ever. Unless you go to Vegas."

I make it look like I'm soaking in her advice, but her stress level is enough to make anyone not look forward to a wedding.

"Wait," she says, pointing at me. "Your name is Fallon? As in Fallon O'Neil?"

Oh, no. It's not often I get recognized from the show, but when it does happen, it's usually by girls who are about Jordyn's age. Girls who probably watched the show religiously.

"You aren't the actress who used to star on that detective show, are you?"

Ben's arm goes around my shoulder like he's proud of that fact. "She sure is."

"No way!" she says. "I used to watch that show all the time! Well, until they replaced you with that one chick who couldn't act worth a flip."

That comment makes me feel good. I couldn't bring myself to watch the show after I was replaced, but I won't lie and say I wasn't a little relieved that it went off the air two seasons later due to a drop in ratings.

"Why did you quit the show?" she says. And then, "Oh. Wait, I remember. You were injured, right? Is that where you got the scars from?"

I can feel Ben's arm immediately tense. "Jordyn," he says.

I appreciate that he's attempting to intercept the conversation for my sake, but it's hard to be offended by Jordyn when it's obvious she's just curious and not at all judging.

"It's fine," I say, as soon as she looks like she's about to apologize. "It was an unfortunate accident, and it sucked that I had to quit the show. But I'm grateful I survived. It could have been a lot worse."

I feel Ben press a kiss against the side of my head, and I assume it's because he appreciates that the encouraging words he said to me upstairs might have actually sunk in.

The front door slams and everyone's attention shifts from the conversation about my career to the sound of a man's voice.

"Where's my little bitch?" he calls out.

Oh, lord. I hope this isn't the groom.

"Ian's home," Ben says. He grabs my hand and pulls me toward the living room. "Come meet my big brother."

I follow Ben into the living room to see a man kneeling down by the front door, petting a little white dog. "There's my little bitch," he says sweetly to the dog. As sweet as that sentence can sound, anyway.

"Look what the cat flew in," Ben says, getting the guy's attention.

It isn't until Ian stands up that I notice he's in a pilot's uniform. Ben immediately motions toward me. I'm not gonna lie, meeting new people is awkward enough. But meeting Ben's family is a whole new level of awkward.

"Ian, this is Fallon. Fallon, Ian."

Ian immediately steps forward and grabs my hand, shaking it. He and Ben look so much alike, I can't help but stare. He's got Ben's strong jaw and they have the same mouth, but Ian is slightly taller and has blond hair.

"And Fallon is your . . ." He leaves the sentence hanging, waiting for Ben to finish it. But Ben stares at me and waits for *me* to finish it.

What the hell? Talk about being put on the spot.

"I'm Ben's . . . *plotline*?"

Ben laughs loudly, but Ian cocks a curious eyebrow. He looks even more like Ben when he does this. "You finally writing an actual book?" Ian asks him.

Ben rolls his eyes and grabs my hand to

pull me back toward the stairs. "She's not my plotline, she's my girlfriend and today is our one-year anniversary."

Jordyn is in the living room now, standing next to Ian. They're both looking at Ben like he's been keeping the world's biggest secret.

"You've been dating for a whole *year*?" Jordyn asks, directing her question at me. Before I can tell her he's only kidding, she throws her hands up in defeat. "Ben, you told me you weren't bringing a plus one! I didn't order enough chairs and *oh, my God,* it's probably too late!" She storms out of the room to go make an unnecessary phone call.

I slap Ben on the arm. "That was so mean! She's already stressed as it is."

He laughs and then rolls his eyes dramatically with a groan. "Fine." He follows after Jordyn and as soon as it's just me and Ian in the room, the front door opens. *Again.* Jesus Christ, how many people can fit in this house?

When the next guy walks through the front door, he sees Ian first. They hug and he slaps Ian on the back. "You said you didn't come in until tomorrow."

Ian shrugs. "Miles took today's runs for me so I could get here sooner. Weather is supposed to be bad tomorrow and I didn't want to get delayed."

The brother I don't know yet says, "Dude, if you would have missed the rehearsal dinner, Jordyn would have my . . ." His voice trails off when he notices me standing in the middle of the living room. I expect him to say something, but he just carefully eyes me up and down with suspicion, as if they don't have visitors very often. Ian steps in and motions toward me.

"Have you met Ben's girlfriend?"

The guy's expression doesn't change, other than an almost unnoticeable arch of his brow. He quickly straightens up and walks toward me. "Kyle Kessler," he says, extending a hand. "And you are?"

"Fallon," I say in a slightly intimidated voice. "Fallon O'Neil."

Unlike Ian and Ben, Kyle doesn't give off the welcoming vibe. It's not that he gives off an unfriendly vibe . . . he's just nothing like his brothers. He's more serious. More intimidating. For a second, I see him glance at the left side of my face and it makes me wonder what he thinks of Ben for bringing someone like me home. But then I remember Ben's words to me upstairs, and how lucky Ben is to have brought someone like me home. Rather than follow through with my initial urge to let my hair fall in my face, I stand taller — more confident. Kyle releases my hand when Ben walks back into the living room.

"All is well with Jordyn," he says. Ben stops short when he sees Kyle. His eyes widen a little, as if he's shocked to see Kyle, and I notice a shift in his demeanor. He tries to cover it up with a smile. "You said you wouldn't be home until tonight."

Kyle drops his keys onto a nearby table and then points at Ben. "We need to talk."

I can't place the tone in Kyle's voice. He doesn't sound outright angry, but he also doesn't seem to be pleased with Ben.

Ben shoots me a reassuring smile before following Kyle out of the room. "Be right back," he says.

I'm left alone with Ian again. I shove my hands in the pockets of my jeans, unsure of what to do with myself while I wait for Ben.

Ian bends down and scoops up the little white dog at his feet. He nods his head toward the stairs. "I haven't showered in three days. That's where I'll be if either of them asks."

"Yeah," I say. "It was nice meeting you, Ian."

He smiles. "You too, Fallon."

And now I'm alone. These last few minutes have been all kinds of strange. Ben's family is . . . interesting.

I look around the living room, trying to get a clue as to who Ben is. There are pictures on the mantel of him and his brothers. I pick one up to get a closer look. It's hard to tell now, but in the earlier pictures it's clear that Ben is the baby and Ian is the oldest. I just have no idea how many years separate the brothers. Maybe two or three?

I don't see any pictures of their mother anywhere. It makes me wonder how long ago she died and where their father is. Ben hasn't mentioned anything about him yet.

I hear a loud thud come from the hallway. Worried it might be Jordyn, I walk in that direction. I immediately pause when I see Ben pressed up against the wall with Kyle's arm against his throat.

"Are you an idiot?" Kyle says through clenched teeth. Ben is looking at Kyle like he wants to kill him, but he isn't making an effort to fight back. Just as I'm about to rush down the hallway to pull Kyle off of him, Ben catches sight of me out of the corner of his eye. Kyle then turns to see what caught Ben's attention and as soon as he sees me, he takes a step back, releasing Ben.

I'm so confused by what just happened. Kyle is standing between Ben and me, looking back and forth between us. Just when it looks as if he's about to turn and walk away, he spins around and decks Ben right in the eye, slamming him into the wall behind him.

"What the hell!" I yell at Kyle. I rush to Ben and he holds up a hand, keeping me at a distance.

"It's okay," he says. "Go upstairs. I'll be up in a minute." He's covering his eye with his hand, and Kyle is still standing there, looking like he wants to hit him again. But he immediately backs down when Jordyn comes rushing around the corner to take in the scene. She looks back and forth from Kyle to Ben in shock, like this is completely out of character for both of them.

Which makes this entire scene even more confusing. I don't have brothers, so as far as I know, brothers punch each other all the time. But going by Jordyn's reaction, that's not the case in this household. She'll probably break down in tears again any second.

"Did you just *hit* him?" she says to Kyle.

For a split second, Kyle looks ashamed, as if he wants to apologize. But then he blows out a quick breath and turns his attention to Ben. "You deserved that," he says, backing out of the hallway. "You fucking *deserved* that."

Ben

We're in my bathroom and I'm leaning against the counter as she dabs the wet washcloth against my eye, wiping away the blood.

I can't believe Kyle hit me in front of her. I'm so pissed and I'm trying to relax, but it's hard. Especially when she's pressed against me in the bathroom like this, touching my face with her fingertips.

"Do you want to talk about it?" She reaches down for a Band-Aid and begins tearing it open.

"No."

She presses the Band-Aid to my face and smooths it out. "Should I be worried?" She tosses the paper in the trash can and puts the washcloth in the sink.

I face the mirror and finger the swelling around my eye. "No, Fallon. You should never be worried when it comes to me. Or Kyle, for that matter."

I still can't believe he hit me. In all my life, he's never hit me. He's come very close a time or two. Either he's really stressed about his wedding or I've really pissed him off this time.

"Can we get out of here?" I ask.

She shrugs. "I guess. Where do you want to go?"

"Wherever you are."

Just seeing her smile releases so much of my tension. "I have an idea," she says.

"Are you cold?"

It's the third time I've asked her and she keeps saying no, but she's shivering. I pull her against me and wrap the blanket more securely around us.

She wanted to come to the beach, despite the fact that it's almost dark and November. We got takeout from Chipotle, of course, and she set up a makeshift picnic with blankets we took from my house. We finished eating about half an hour ago and we've just been making small talk, getting to know more about each other. But with the heaviness of what happened back at the house, all of the questions so far have been safe. But neither of us has asked the other a question in at least two minutes, so we may be all out of small talk. Or maybe the silence is a question in itself.

I'm holding her hand under the blanket and we're both just staring at the waves as they crash against the rocks. After a while, she lays her head on my shoulder.

"I haven't been to the beach since I was sixteen," she says.

"Are you scared of the ocean?"

She lifts her head off my shoulder and pulls her knees up, wrapping her arms around them. "I used to come all the time. Whenever I had a day off, this is where I'd be. But then the fire happened and it took a long time to recover. I was in and out of the hospital and physical therapy. The sun isn't good for skin when it's trying to heal, so I just . . . never came back. Even after it was okay to be in direct sunlight again, I no longer had the confidence to show up to a place where everyone revealed the most amount of skin they could get away with."

Once again, I'm at a loss for what to say to her. I hate knowing the fire took away so much of her confidence, but I think I'm still clueless when it comes to how much it actually took away from her life.

"It feels good to be back," she whispers.

I squeeze her hand, because I'm sure that's all she really wants.

We sit in silence again, and my mind keeps

going back to what happened with Kyle in the hallway. I don't know how much she heard, but she's still here, so it couldn't have been much. However, to say she saw a different side to Kyle than I would have wanted her to see is an understatement. She probably thinks he's an asshole, and based on the few minutes she witnessed of him, I wouldn't blame her.

"When I was in fourth grade, there was this older kid who used to pick on me," I tell her. "Every day on the bus he would either hit me or say mean things to me. It went on for months, and there were a couple of times I would actually get off the bus with a bloody nose."

"Jesus," she says.

"Kyle is a couple years older than me. He was in middle school, but we rode the same bus because we went to a fairly small school. One day, after the kid hit me right in front of Kyle, I expected him to take up for me. To beat the kid's ass, because I'm his little brother. That's what big brothers are supposed to do. Protect their little brothers from bullies." I stretch my legs out in front of me and sigh. "But Kyle just sat there, staring at me. He never intervened. And when we got home, I was so angry with him. I told him it was his job as my brother to teach the bullies a lesson. He laughed and said, 'And how will that teach *you* anything?'

"I didn't know what to say, because what the hell was I supposed to be learning by getting my ass kicked every day? Kyle said, 'What is stopping one bully going to teach you? Nothing. If I intervened, what would you gain from that besides learning to rely on someone else rather than yourself? There will always be bullies, Ben. You need to learn how to deal with them yourself. You need to learn how to not let them get to you. And me beating up some kid for you isn't going to teach you a damn thing.' "

Fallon faces me. "Did you listen to him?"

I shake my head. "No, I went to my room and cried because I thought he was just being mean. And the kid continued to pick on me for weeks after that. But then one day, it just clicked. I don't know what it was, but I slowly started defending myself. I stopped letting him get to me as much as he did. Stopped acting so scared around him. And after a while, when he realized his insults didn't bother me, he finally backed off."

She's quiet, but I can tell she's wondering why I'm telling her this story.

"He's a good brother," I say to her. "He's a good person. I hate that you saw the side of him you did today, because that's not him. He had a right to be upset with me and no, I don't want to talk about it. But my brothers are really good people and I just wanted you to know that."

She's looking at me appreciatively. I wrap my arm around her and pull her to my chest as I lay down on the blanket beneath us. I'm looking up at the stars now, surprised at how long it's been since I've actually seen them.

"I was excited about the idea of having a sibling," she says. "I know I acted like I wasn't happy when my dad told me last year, but I've always wanted a sister or brother. Unfortunately, the girl my dad was engaged to wasn't pregnant after all. She thought he had money thanks to his semi-celebrity status. When she found out he was actually broke, she left him."

Wow. I don't feel so bad about my family drama she witnessed today. "That's awful," I say to her. "Was he upset?" Not that I care if he was upset. The man deserves any negative karma that's returned to him with the way he treated her that day.

She shrugs. "I don't know. My mom told me all that. I haven't even spoken to him since last year."

That makes me sad for her. As much of a douchebag as he is, he's still her father, so I know that has to hurt. "What kind of person fakes pregnancy to trap a man? That's messed up. Although it does sound like a great plotline for a book."

She laughs against my chest. "It's tripe and way overused as a subplot." She rests her chin on her arms and smiles at me. The moonlight is hitting her face, shining down on her like she's on a stage.

Which reminds me . . .

"Are you ever going to tell me about this rehearsal you mentioned earlier? What's it for?"

She loses the smile. "Community theater," she says. "Tomorrow is opening day and we have dress rehearsals in the morning, which is why I need to be back so early. I don't have a lead role and it doesn't pay anything, but I enjoy it because a lot of the actors look to me for advice. I don't know why, maybe because I've had a lot of experience in the past, but it feels good. It's nice that I'm not cooped up in my apartment all the time."

I like hearing that. "What about work?"

"My schedule is flexible. I'm still recording audiobooks and I get enough work to pay the bills, so that's good. Although I did have to move apartments because my rent was a little steep, but . . . overall things are going well. I'm happy there."

"Good," I say to her, running my fingers through her hair. "I'm happy you're happy there."

And I am. But I'm not going to lie, a part of me was selfishly hoping I'd see her today and she'd tell me New York didn't work out. That she lives in L.A. again and she thinks her five-year rule is stupid and that she wants to see me tomorrow.

"Do you even have a job?" she asks. "I can't believe I don't know that about you. I let you fondle my breasts and I don't even know what you do for a living."

I laugh. "I go to UCLA. Full-time student with a double major, so it doesn't leave much time for work. But I don't have many bills. I have enough money left over from my mom's inheritance to support myself through college, so it works for now."

"What are your two majors?" she asked me.

"Creative writing and Communications. The majority of writers don't have much luck finding a career to sustain themselves, so I want to have a backup plan."

She smiles. "You don't need a backup plan because in a few years, you'll have a bestselling novel to pay your bills."

I hope she doesn't actually think that.

"What's it called?" she asks.

"What's *what* called?"

"Our book. What's the title going to be?"

"*November Nine.*"

I watch her reaction, but her expression reveals nothing of what she thinks of the title. After a few seconds, she lays her head on my chest so I can't see her face anymore.

"I didn't tell you this last year," she says, her voice much quieter than before. "But November 9th is the anniversary of the fire. And being able to look forward to seeing you on this date makes me not dread the anniversary as much as I used to. So thank you for that."

I suck in a quiet breath, but before I can even give her a response, she scoots closer and presses her lips firmly to mine.

Fallon

"Are you sure about this?"

He nods, but everything else about his demeanor says he's not.

Half an hour ago, we were making out on the beach. Five minutes into our kiss, he sat straight up and announced he wanted a tattoo. *"Tonight,"* he said. *"Right now."*

So here we are. He's sitting in the chair, waiting on the tattoo artist, and I'm leaning against the wall, waiting for him to chicken out.

He won't tell me what the tattoo means. He's getting the word *poetic* across his left wrist, written inside a music staff. I don't know why he won't tell me the meaning behind it, but at least it's not my name. I mean, I like the guy. A lot. But permanently inking a girl's name into your skin is a pretty alpha-male thing to do this early on in a relationship. Especially on the wrist. And why did I just refer to this as a relationship?

Oh, God. What if that's why he's getting a tattoo? What if he's trying to come off as more of a tough guy? I should probably warn him that he's doing it wrong.

I clear my throat to get his attention. "Um. I hate to say this Ben, but a wrist tattoo of the word *poetic* isn't very alpha-male. It's quite the opposite, actually. You sure you don't want to go with a skull? Some barbed wire? Something bloody, maybe?"

His lip curls up into a crooked grin. "Don't worry, Fallon. I'm not doing this to impress girls."

I don't know why I love that answer as much as I do. The tattoo artist walks back into the room and points at Ben's wrist where he drew the outline of the tattoo a few minutes earlier. "If you like the placement, we'll get started."

The tattoo is sketched in ink from one side of his wrist to the other. He nods and tells the guy he's ready. Ben motions to me. "Can she sit in my lap and distract me?"

The guy shrugs, pulling Ben's arm in front of him, but he says nothing. As soon as the thought begins to cross my mind that this guy is probably wondering what Ben is doing with someone who looks like I do, Ben interrupts my bout of insecurity. "Come here," he says, patting his leg. "Distract me."

I do what he says, but the only way I can sit on his lap is if I straddle him. At least I'm in jeans, but I still feel awkward that I'm sitting like this in the middle of a tattoo parlor. Ben's hand comes to rest on my waist and he squeezes. I can hear the buzz of the needle and the slight difference in the sound once it presses into his skin. He doesn't even make a face other than giving me a tiny smile. I do what I can to distract him, so I continue the small talk we shared on the beach.

"What's your favorite color?"

"Malachite green."

I make a face. "That's a very specific green, but okay."

"It's what color your eyes are. Also happens to be my favorite mineral."

"You have a favorite *mineral*?"

"Do now."

I look down to avoid him seeing my embarrassed smile straight on. I feel his hand squeeze my waist again. I'm guessing the needle is distracting him more than I am, so I throw out another question.

"What's your favorite food?"

"Pad Thai," he says. "Yours?"

"Sushi. They're almost the same thing."

"Not even close," he says.

"They're both Asian food. What's your

favorite movie?"

"These questions are boring. Try harder."

I drop my head back and look up at the ceiling while I think. "Okay, who was your first girlfriend?" I ask, bringing my eyes back to him.

"Brynn Fellows. I was thirteen."

"I thought you said her name was Abitha."

He grins. "You have a good memory."

I raise a serious brow. "It's not that I have a good memory, Ben. I'm just insanely jealous and unstable when it comes to your past loves."

He laughs. "Abitha was the first girl I kissed. Not my first girlfriend. I was fifteen, dated her for a year."

"Why'd you break up?"

"We were sixteen." He says that like it's a valid reason. He can see the question in my expression so he says, "That's what you do when you're dating at sixteen. You break up. What about you? Who was your first boyfriend?"

"Real or fake?"

"Either," he says.

"You." I watch his eyes closely to see if there's pity in them, but it looks more like pride. "How many people have you slept with?"

He tightens his mouth. "Not answering that."

"More than ten?"

"Nope."

"Less than one?"

"Nope."

"More than five?"

"I don't kiss and tell."

I laugh. "Yes you do. In five years, you'll be telling the whole world about us in your book."

"Four years," he clarifies.

"When's your birthday?" I ask him.

"When's *yours*?"

"I asked you first."

"But what if you're older than me? Isn't that a turnoff for girls? Dating guys younger than them?"

"Isn't it a turnoff for guys to date girls with scars on over half their face?"

His hand squeezes my waist and he eyes me hard. "Fallon." He says my name like it's an entire lecture in itself.

"I was trying to be funny," I say.

He doesn't smile. "I don't think self-deprecation is very funny."

"That's only because you aren't the self who's doing the deprecating."

The corner of his mouth twitches as he tries to hold back his smile. "July Fourth," he says. "The whole country celebrates my birthday every year. It's quite epic."

"July 25th, which means you are officially older than me. I can safely pursue you now and not be considered a cougar."

He runs his hand up my waist a couple of inches, and then his thumb moves side to side, slowly. "You can't pursue the willing, Fallon."

Oh, dang. He deserves a kiss for that comment, but there's a guy with a tattoo gun two feet away and I'm not the type of girl who would make out with a guy in public. Apparently I draw the line at straddling them.

"There's something I need to know about you," he says with a poignant stare. "And when I ask you this question, I want you to think very long and hard about the answer, because it might make or break this connection we have."

I swallow hard. "Okay. What do you need to know?"

He winces, just a little, and I'm not sure if it's from the tattoo gun or because he's nervous to ask the question. "Okay," he says. "If you could only listen to one band for the rest of your life, which band would you choose, and why?"

I instantly relax. This is easy. I thought he

was about to dig a whole lot deeper than my favorite band.

"X Ambassadors."

"Never heard of them," he says.

"I've seen them twice," the guy with the tattoo gun says. Ben and I both look at him, but he's focused on his work.

I look back at Ben and arch my eyebrow. "Why would my favorite band make or break us?"

"A lot can be said about a person through their taste in music. Pretty sure I read that in one of the books you gave me. If you would have picked a band I hated, it would have been a major turnoff."

"Well, you might still hate them once you listen to them, so we aren't in the clear yet."

"In that case, I'll never listen to them," he says confidently.

"Not if I have anything to do with it."

"What's your favorite lyric by them?" he asks.

"It changes depending on my mood."

"Well then, what's your favorite lyric right now?"

I close my eyes briefly and hum one of the songs in my head until I get to the lyric that fits this moment. I open my eyes and smile. "You're so gorgeous, 'cause you make me feel gorgeous."

A faint smile works its way across his mouth. "I like that," he says, brushing his thumb across the skin of my waist. We stare at each other for a while. I can see the rise of his chest becoming more prominent, and knowing he's getting worked up despite having a needle piercing his skin makes me feel a little triumphant.

I think about maybe just leaning forward and giving him a small peck on the mouth, but before I can, the tattoo artist says, "Done!"

I slide off his lap and we look at the finished product before it's bandaged up. It turned out great, but I still don't know what prompted it or why he needed it tonight, but I'm glad I got to be here with him while he had it done.

He stands up and pulls his wallet out of his pocket to tip the guy. When he takes my hand in his to walk me to his car, every step I take grows heavier and heavier, because I know with each step, we're closer to another goodbye.

On our drive to the airport, I'm on edge the entire way. I keep asking myself if this new urge to not want to get on that plane to go back to New York is a result of my feelings for Ben or for New York.

I know I told him at the beach that I'm

happy in New York, but I'm still almost as unhappy there as I was here. I just don't want him to know that. I'm hoping my involvement in the community theater will help me make a few more friends. After all, it's only been one year. But it's been a tough year. And as much as I tried to stick with the homework he gave me, going on audition after audition is exhausting when all I get are rejections. It makes me wonder if my father is right. I might be dreaming too big. And despite Ben having given me a lot of my confidence back, it doesn't make an industry built on looks any less shallow.

And Broadway is so far out of my reach it's laughable. The amount of people who show up for auditions makes me feel like a small ant in a massive colony. The only chance I probably have of standing out is if the role requires someone who actually has facial scars. And so far, I haven't gotten that lucky.

"Do you need another dramatic airport scene?" he asks as we approach the terminal.

I laugh and tell him absolutely not, so he parks in the parking garage this time. Before we walk inside the airport, he pulls me to him. I can see sadness in his eyes and I know without a doubt he can see in my expression how much I don't want to say goodbye. He trails the backs of his fingers down my cheek and I shiver.

"I'll come to New York next year. Where do you want to meet?"

"In Brooklyn," I tell him. "That's where I live. I want to show you around my neighborhood and there's this really great tapas restaurant you have to try." I type the address to one of my favorite restaurants into his phone. I also type in the date and time, not that it's easily forgotten. I hand it back to him.

He slides the phone in his back pocket and pulls me in for another hug. We hold the hug for at least two solid minutes, neither of us wanting to let go. His hand is cradled around the back of my head and I try to memorize how his hand feels there. I try to memorize how he smells just like the beach where we spent over three hours together tonight. I try to memorize how my mouth rests right at the height of his neck, as though his shoulders were made for me to rest my head on them.

I lean into him and kiss his neck. A soft peck and nothing more. He lifts my head off his shoulder, tilting my face up to his, scrolling over my features. "I thought I was tougher than a word," he says. "But I just discovered that having to say goodbye to you is one of the hardest things I've ever had to do."

I want to say, *"Then beg me to stay,"* but his mouth is on mine, and he's kissing me, hard. He's saying goodbye with the way his lips move over mine, the way his hands caress my cheeks, the way his mouth moves to my forehead and presses one single, gentle kiss right in the center of it before he releases me. He practically pushes away from me, as if putting distance between us will make this any easier. He walks backward until he's at the edge of the curb, and all my words are lodged in my throat, so I press my lips tightly together and try not to let them loose. We stare at each other for several seconds, the pain in this goodbye evident in the air between us. And then he turns and jogs back toward the parking garage.

And I try not to cry, because that would be silly.

Right?

I've never liked window seats, so when I hear the woman in the aisle seat say something to the affect of hating aisle seats, I offer her mine.

I'm not scared of flying unless I'm looking out the window. And if I'm in a window seat, I feel I'm taking it for granted if I *don't* look out the window. And then I spend the entire flight staring at the world below us and it makes me panic more than if I just don't put myself in that position.

I set my purse beneath the seat in front of me and try to get comfortable. I'm relieved Ben is coming to New York next year because the flight from L.A. to New York is one of my least favorite things.

I close my eyes and hope I can get a few hours of sleep. I won't have time to sleep before rehearsals tomorrow, and I would just sleep in, but tomorrow is opening day and I have to be there for the last rehearsal.

"Hey."

I hear Ben's voice and smile, because that means I'm definitely going to sleep just fine if I'm already confusing reality with dreams.

"Fallon."

My eyes flick open. I look up to see Ben standing next to me. *What in the ever loving hell?*

I look at his hand and he's holding a plane ticket.

I sit up straight. "What are you doing?"

Someone is trying to squeeze past him, so he moves to where he's standing as close to me as he can get. When the man passes, Ben kneels down. "I forgot to give you homework for this year." He hands me a folded sheet of paper. "I had to buy a plane ticket in order to get it to you before you took off, so that means you have to follow through with it or I'm out a lot of money for naught. And who actually says naught? Anyway. That's all. Totally not an alpha-move, but whatever."

I look at the paper in my hands and then back up at him. *Did he seriously buy a plane ticket just to give me homework?*

"You're insane."

He grins, but then has to stand again to let someone else pass. A flight attendant tells him he needs to clear the aisle and take his seat. He winks at me. "I better go before I get stuck on the plane." He leans down and gives me a small peck on the lips.

I try to hide the flicker of sadness I know is evident in my eyes. I force a smile just before he turns and makes his way toward the exit. A flight attendant intercepts him and asks why he's not in his seat. He mutters something about a family emergency, so she allows him to pass, but right before he's out of my line of sight, he turns around and winks.

And then he's gone.

Did that really just happen?

I look down at the paper in my hands and

I'm nervous to even open it, wondering what homework assignment could possibly be worth the purchase of a plane ticket.

Fallon,

I lied. Kind of. I don't have a lot of homework for you because I think you're doing a good job at adulting. I mostly wanted to give you this letter because I wanted to thank you for showing up today. I forgot to thank you earlier. It sucks that you have to go a day without sleep, but it means a lot that you sacrificed that sleep to follow through with our arrangement. I'll make it up to you next year, I promise. As for this year, there's only one thing I want you to do.

Go visit your father.

I know, I know. He's an asshole. But he's the only father you have, and when you told me you haven't spoken to him since last year, I couldn't help but feel at fault for that. I feel guilty for the fight you guys got into because my butting in didn't help matters. I should have stayed out of it, but had I stayed out of it, I wouldn't have had the privilege of finding out what kind of panties you had on. So I guess I'm saying I don't really regret butting in, but I do feel bad that maybe your relationship with your father wouldn't be so strained had I just minded my own business. So for that, I think maybe you should give him another chance.

When I realized I forgot to ask you to do this one small thing, it was worth the $400 plane ticket I just had to buy. So don't let me down, okay? Call him tomorrow. For me.

Next year, I want all the hours of November 9th I can get with you. Let's meet an hour earlier and I'll stay until midnight.

In the meantime, I hope you still get laughed at.

Ben

I read the note through again before folding it. I'm happy he's no longer on the plane, because the smile on my face is embarrassing.

I can't believe he just did that. And I can't believe I'm going to suck it up and call my father tomorrow simply because Ben asked me to.

But even more than that, I'm in shock he spent that much money on a plane ticket just to give me this letter. That seems like more of a grand gesture than an inconsequential moment. And I love it just as much, if not more than the inconsequential things he does.

Maybe I don't know the first thing about falling in love, because I've been telling myself I'm not falling for him yet. That it's too soon.

But it's not. What's happening inside my heart right now is way too consequential to deny. I think I've been misjudging the whole concept of insta-love. Now if I can just figure out how we can finish these next few years with a happy ending.

■ ■ ■ ■

Third November 9th

■ ■ ■ ■

She “loved me” in quotations
She kissed me in bold
I TRIED TO KEEP HER in all caps
She left with an ellipsis . . .
— Benton James Kessler

Fallon

I brought a notebook to the restaurant with me.

It's a little embarrassing, but so much has happened this year, I started taking notes back in January. I'm also a neat freak, so Ben is lucky in that regard. He won't have to do much research on me, because it's all here. All four guys I went out with, all the auditions I went on, the fact that I'm speaking to my father again, the four callbacks I received, the one (very small) role I actually landed in an off-Broadway play. And how as excited as I was about it, I miss the community theater more than I expected to. Maybe because I enjoyed everyone wanting my advice. Now that I've got a small role in a slightly larger production, it feels different. Everyone is trying to climb their way to the top and they'll crawl over anyone to get there. There are a lot of competitive people in this world, and I've discovered I'm not really one of them. But today I'm not going to dwell on what is or isn't going right in my life, because today is all about Ben and me.

I have our entire day mapped out. After we eat breakfast, we're doing typical touristy things. I've lived in New York for two years now and I've still never been to the Empire State Building. After lunch, though, is the part I'm the most excited about. I was walking past an art studio a couple of weeks ago and noticed a flyer for an event called "The life and death of Dylan Thomas. But mostly the death." He's brought up Dylan Thomas's name a couple of times, so I know he likes his work. And the fact that the event takes place in that studio today of all days isn't nearly as fascinating as what else I learned from the flyer.

Dylan Thomas died in New York City in 1953.

On November 9th.

What are the odds? I had to Google that information just to make sure it was right. It is. And I have no idea if Ben even knows that about Dylan Thomas. I'm kind of hoping he doesn't so I can see the look on his face when I tell him.

"Are you Fallon?"

I look up at the waitress. She's the same

waitress who has refilled my Diet Pepsi twice. But this time she has an apologetic look about her . . . and a phone in her hands.

My heart sinks.

Please just let him be late. Please don't let him be calling me because he isn't coming today.

I nod. "Yeah."

She pushes the phone at me. "He says it's an emergency. You can bring the phone back to the counter when you're done."

I take it out of her hands and pull it to my chest with both hands. But then I quickly pull it away, because I'm afraid he'll be able to hear my heart pounding on his end of the line. I look down at it and inhale a slow breath.

I can't believe I'm reacting this way. I had no idea how much I've been anticipating today until the threat that it might be taken away from me. I slowly lift the phone to my ear. I close my eyes and mutter, "Hello?"

I immediately recognize the sigh that comes from the other end of the line. It's crazy how I don't even have to hear his voice to recognize him. That's how embedded he is in my mind. Even the sound of his breath is familiar.

"Hey," he says.

It's not the kind of desperate greeting I wanted to hear. I need him to sound panicked — late. Like he's just walking off the airplane and he's terrified I'll leave before he has a chance to get here. Instead, it's a lazy hey. Like he's sitting on a bed somewhere, relaxed. Not at all in a panic to get to me.

"Where are you?" I utter the dreaded question, knowing he's about to give me an answer that's almost three thousand miles from New York.

"Los Angeles," he says. I close my eyes and wait for more words to come, but they don't. He fails to follow it up with any type of explanation, which only means he feels guilty.

He's met someone.

"Oh," I say. "Okay." I try not to be transparent, but my sadness is audible.

"I'm really sorry," he says. I hear the truth in his words, but it does little to comfort me.

"Is everything okay?"

He doesn't answer my question immediately. The silence grows thick between us until he sucks in a rush of air.

"Fallon," he says, his voice faltering on my name. "I don't even know how to say this gently, but . . . my brother? Kyle? He uh . . . he was in a wreck two days ago."

I cover my mouth with my hand as his words rush through me. "Oh, no. Ben, is he okay?"

More silence, and then a weak, "No."

The word is spoken so quietly, it's as if he's in a state of disbelief.

"He um . . . he didn't make it, Fallon."

I'm unable to respond to that sentence. I don't know what to say. I have absolutely no useful words. I don't know Ben well enough to know how to console him over a phone, and I didn't know Kyle well enough to express my sadness over his death. Several seconds pass before Ben speaks again.

"I would have called before now, but . . . you know. I didn't know how to reach you."

I shake my head as if he can see me. "Stop. It's okay. I'm so sorry, Ben."

"Yeah," he says, saddened. "Me too."

I want to ask him if there's anything I can do, but I know he's probably tired of hearing that. More silence engulfs the line and I'm angry at myself for not knowing how to respond to this. It's just so unexpected, and I've never experienced anything like what he must be going through right now, so I don't even try to fake empathy.

"This is killing me," he says, his voice in a

rushed whisper. "I'll see you next year, though. I promise."

I squeeze my eyes shut. I can hear the underlying hurt in his side of our conversation and it makes me ache for him.

"Same time next year?" he asks. "Same place?"

"Of course." I try to get the words out before I burst into tears. Before I tell him I can't wait another year.

"Okay," he says. "I have to go. I'm really sorry."

"I'll be fine, Ben. Please don't feel bad . . . I understand."

Silence hangs between us, until he finally sighs. "Goodbye, Fallon."

The line disconnects before I speak again. I look down at the phone and tears are blurring my vision.

I'm heartbroken. Crushed.

And I'm such an asshole, because as much as I want to convince myself I'm crying over the loss of Ben's brother, I'm not. I'm crying for completely selfish reasons, and recognizing that I'm such a pathetic human makes me cry even harder.

BEN

I'm clenching the cell phone in my hand in an attempt to avoid punching through my bedroom door. I was hoping the waitress would tell me she wasn't there. I was hoping she didn't show up so I wouldn't have to disappoint her. I'd rather she have met someone else, fallen in love and forgotten about me than to be responsible for the disappointment I just heard in her voice.

I roll from my shoulder to my back and let my head fall against the door. I look up at the ceiling and fight back the tears that have been trying to take over since I found out about Kyle's wreck.

I haven't cried yet. Not even once.

What good would it have done Jordyn if I was a broken mess when I delivered the news that her husband died a week shy of their one-year anniversary? Three months before the birth of their first child? And what good would it have done Ian if I had been a blubbering mess on the phone when I had to tell him his little brother was dead? I knew he'd have to make arrangements to come straight home after I got off the phone with him, so I needed him to know that I was fine. I had things under control here and he didn't need to rush.

The closest I've come to crying was just now, on the phone with Fallon. For some reason, it was harder telling her the news than anyone. And I think it was because I knew Kyle's death wasn't the real factor in our conversation. It was the unspoken fact that we've both been anticipating this day since we had to tear ourselves apart last year.

And as much as I wanted to reassure her that I'd be there next year, all I wanted to do was fall to my knees and beg her to come here. Today. I've never needed to wrap my arms around someone more than I do right now, and I'd give anything to have her here with me. To just be able to press my face in her hair and feel her arms around my waist, her hands on my back. There isn't a single thing in this world that could comfort me like she could, but I didn't tell her that. I couldn't. Maybe I should have, but asking her to come to me at the last minute is more of a request than I could ever make.

The doorbell rings, and I stand at attention, pulling myself from the regret I feel over the phone call I just had to make. I toss my cell phone onto the bed and head downstairs.

Ian is opening the front door when I reach the bottom step. Tate steps inside and her arms go around his neck. I'm not surprised to see her and Miles here. Miles and Ian have been best friends since before I was born, so I'm glad Ian has them. It does make me wallow in a little bit of a deeper pool of self-pity, knowing his best friends are here with him and the only person I want is three thousand miles away.

Tate releases Ian and hugs me. Miles walks through the front door and hugs Ian, but says nothing. Tate turns around and reaches for one of the bags in Miles's hand, but he pulls it from her.

"Don't," he says, his eyes falling to her stomach. "I'll take all our stuff to the room. You go to the kitchen and make yourself something to eat, you still haven't had breakfast."

Ian closes the door behind him and looks at Tate. "Is he still not letting you lift anything?"

She rolls her eyes. "I never thought I'd get tired of being treated like a princess, but

I'm *so* over it. I can't wait until this baby comes and his attention is focused on her and not me."

Miles smiles at her. "Not gonna happen. I'll have more than enough attention for both of you." Miles nods a greeting at me as he passes, heading toward the guest bedroom.

Tate looks at me. "Is there anything I can do? Please put me to work. I need to feel useful for a change."

I motion for her to follow me into the kitchen. She pauses when she sees the countertops. "Holy shit."

"Yeah," I say, looking at all the food. People have been dropping casseroles off for two days. Kyle worked for a software company that employed about two hundred people and the building is only seven miles from our house. I'm pretty sure more than half of them have brought food by over the last couple days. "We've already filled up the refrigerator, plus the one in the garage. But I feel bad just throwing stuff out."

Tate pushes the sleeves up on her blouse and scoots past me. "I have no qualms with throwing away a perfectly good casserole." She opens one of the containers, sniffs it and makes a face. She quickly shuts it. "That's definitely not a keeper," she says, tossing the entire dish in the trash. I'm standing in the kitchen watching her, realizing for the first time that she looks to be about as far along as Jordyn. Maybe a little further.

"When are you due?"

"Nine weeks," she says. "Two weeks ahead of Jordyn." She glances up at me, pulling the lid off another container. "How is she?"

I take a seat at the bar, releasing a deep breath as I do. "Not good. I can't get her to eat anything. She won't even leave her room."

"Is she asleep?"

"I hope. Her mother flew in last night, but Jordyn doesn't want to interact with her, either. I was hoping she'd be able to help."

Tate nods, but I notice her wipe at a tear when she turns around. "I can't imagine what she's going through," she says in a whisper.

I can't, either. And I don't want to try. There's too much that needs to be done before Kyle's funeral for me to get caught up in what the hell is going to happen to Jordyn and their baby.

I walk to Ian's room and knock on his door. When I enter, he's pulling a different shirt over his head. His eyes are red and he swipes at them quickly before bending to put on his shoes. I pretend I don't notice he's been crying.

"You ready?" I ask him. He nods and follows me out the door.

He's been taking this really hard, as he should. But it's just one more reason why I can't let this break me. Not yet. Because right now I'm the only one holding us all together.

A few days ago, I assumed I'd be spending today with Fallon in New York. I never imagined I'd be spending it at a funeral home, picking out a casket for the one person in this world who knew me better than anyone.

"What do you plan to do with the house?" my uncle asks. He pulls a beer from the refrigerator. As soon as he closes the door, he opens it again and takes out a casserole dish. He lifts the corner of it and sniffs it, then shrugs and grabs a fork from a nearby drawer.

"What do you mean?" I ask, just as he shoves a spoonful of chilled noodles in his mouth.

He waves the fork around the room. "The house," he says with a mouthful. He swallows and stabs at the casserole again. "I'm sure Jordyn will move back to Nevada with her mother. Are you just gonna stay here by yourself?"

I hadn't thought about it, but he's right. It's a big house, and I doubt I'll want to stay here by myself. But the thought of selling it fills me with dread. I've lived in this house since I was fourteen. And I know my mother is gone, but she would never want us to sell this house. She even said so herself.

"I don't know. I haven't really thought about it."

He pops the lid on his beer. "Well if you plan to sell it, make sure you let me list it. I can get you a great price."

My aunt speaks up from behind me. "Seriously, Anthony? Don't you think it's a little too soon?" She looks at me. "I'm sorry, Ben. Your uncle is an asshole."

Now that she brought it up, I guess it is in poor taste to be discussing this with me just ten minutes after they show up.

I've lost count of who all is at my house right now. It's almost seven in the evening and at least five cousins have stopped by. Two sets of aunts and uncles have brought us casserole dishes and Ian and Miles are on the porch out back. Tate is still running around the house cleaning, despite Miles's desperate pleas for her to rest. And

Jordyn . . . well. She still hasn't left her bedroom.

"Ben, come here!" Ian yells from outside. I gladly escape the conversation with my uncle and open the screen door. Ian and Miles are both sitting on the porch steps, staring out over the backyard.

"What?"

Ian turns around. "Did you contact his old job and let them know? I didn't even think about it."

I nod. "Yeah, I called them yesterday."

"What about that friend of his with the red hair?"

"The one who was in the wedding?"

"Yeah."

"He knows. Everyone knows, Ian. It's called Facebook."

He nods and then turns back around again. He's hardly ever here because of his schedule, so I guess showing up and not knowing what he can do to help makes him feel useless. He's not, though. The simple fact that he's allowing me to stay preoccupied with all the busy work is actually helping a little bit. Especially after not being able to see Fallon today like I was supposed to.

I close the back door and bump into Tate.

"Sorry," she says, sidestepping around me.

"I think I've convinced Jordyn to finally eat something." She rushes to the refrigerator and shoots my uncle a dirty look as she watches him dig through each of the casserole dishes.

"Stop snacking and let's go," my aunt says to him. "We have that dinner with Claudia and Bill."

They hug me goodbye and say they'll see me at the funeral. When my aunt isn't looking, Uncle Anthony slips me his Realtor card. When I shut the front door behind them, I lean against it and exhale.

I think having to interact with all the visitors is the worst part of this whole family-member-death thing. I don't remember visitors being this frequent when my mother died several years ago, but then again, Kyle was alive to play the part I'm playing right now. I sulked in my bedroom like Jordyn is doing right now, hiding away from all the people. The thought of Kyle taking care of things back then when he was so young fills me with guilt. He had to have been hurting over her death just as much as I was, but I needed him to hold things together since I did nothing but fall apart.

I slide my hands down my face, wanting it all to be over with. I want the day to end so we can get tomorrow over with and then the funeral will come and go. I just want things to settle down. But then again, I'm scared of how I'll feel when the dust finally does have a chance to settle.

I kick off the door and head toward the kitchen when the doorbell rings. *Again.* I groan, just as Tate passes me with a plate of food. "I would get it, but . . ." She looks down at the plate and drink in her hands.

"If you can just get her to eat something, I'll entertain the ten million visitors."

Tate nods a sympathetic agreement, heading back toward Jordyn's room.

I swing open the door.

I blink twice to ensure I'm really seeing her.

Fallon glances up at me and I don't say anything right away. I'm scared if I speak, the aberration will disappear.

"I would have called first," she says, looking nervous. "I didn't know your number. But I just . . ." She blows out a quick breath. "I just wanted to make sure you were okay."

I open my mouth to speak, but she holds up a hand to stop me. "I just lied to you, I'm sorry. I'm not here to see if you're okay. I know you're not okay. I just couldn't function after you hung up. The thought of not seeing you today and having to wait another year completely gutted me and . . ."

I step forward and shut her up with my mouth.

She sighs against my lips and wraps her arms around me, clasping her hands together behind my back. I kiss her hard, unable to believe that she's actually standing here. That she went straight to the airport after hanging up with me today and spent money on a ticket to fly all the way to Los Angeles just to see me.

I continue to kiss her as I pull her into the house with me. My arm is around her waist, securing her against me, afraid that if I let her go she'll vanish into thin air.

"I need . . ."

She tries to speak, but my mouth pressed to hers is preventing her from it. She opens the front door and tries to pull away from me. I release her just enough so that she can say what she's trying to say. "I have to tell the driver he can go. I wasn't sure you'd want me here."

I step around her and swing the door open wider. I wave the driver off and then close the door and grab her hand.

I pull her up the stairs, toward my room.

Away from everyone in the world I don't want to see or speak to right now.

She's the only one I wanted with me today, and here she is. Just for me. Because she missed me.

If she's not careful, I might just fall in love with her.

Tonight.

Fallon

He closes his bedroom door behind us and pulls me in for a long hug.

I've second-guessed my decision to show up today since the minute I bought my ticket. I almost turned around a hundred different times. I didn't think he'd want to see me with everything going on in his life right now. I thought maybe he would be angry that he told me he'd see me next year, but I showed up unannounced anyway.

I never anticipated seeing the relief wash over his face when he opened the door. I never anticipated him kissing me like he missed me just as much as I've missed him. I never thought he'd just stand here and hug me for as long as he's been hugging me. He hasn't spoken a single word to me yet, but his actions have said a million thank yous.

I close my eyes and keep my head pressed against his chest. He has one hand wrapped around the back of my head and the other hand secured around my back. I could stand here all night. If this is all we did — if he never even speaks a single word — it's worth the trip.

I wonder if he feels the same way? If thoughts of me consume him all day long like thoughts of him consume me? If everything he does and everywhere he goes, he wishes he were sharing it with me?

He kisses the top of my head and then plants his hands on my cheeks, tilting my face up to his. "I can't believe you're here," he says. I can see a smile at war with the devastation in his expression. I don't speak, because I still don't know what to say. I just run my hand down the side of his face and brush my thumb over his lips.

I shouldn't be surprised that he's even more appealing this year than last. He's all man now. Gone are the pieces of boy I could still catch a glimpse of the last time I saw him.

"How are you holding up?" I'm still stroking his face and he's still stroking mine, but he doesn't answer me. Instead, he connects his lips with mine and walks me backward, away from the door. He gently lowers me onto the bed, adjusting me so that I'm lying on his pillow. He breaks our kiss and slides over me. He doesn't lie adjacent to me. Instead, he presses his head against my chest and listens to my heartbeat as he secures his arms tightly around me. I bring my hand up and begin to stroke his hair in long, slow movements.

We lie quietly for so long, I begin to wonder if he's fallen asleep. But after a few minutes, his grip around me grows desperate. He tilts his face until it's completely buried in my shirt, and his shoulders begin to shake as he starts to cry.

It feels like my heart explodes into millions of tiny tears, and I want to wrap myself around him while he mourns. But his cry is so quiet, I can tell he doesn't want me to acknowledge it. He just needs me to let him cry, so that's exactly what I do.

Five minutes pass before he pulls himself together, but half an hour passes before he finally pulls away from me. He lifts off my chest and lies down next to me on his pillow. I roll over to face him. His eyes are still red, but he's no longer crying. He reaches to my face and brushes away a strand of hair, looking at me appreciatively.

"How did it happen?" I ask.

The sadness immediately reenters his eyes but he doesn't hesitate with his answer.

"He was on his way home from work when his car ran off the road," he says. "A slip of attention. Three seconds and he hit a damn tree. He and Jordyn were supposed to leave on vacation that night and I'm pretty sure he was texting her when it happened, based on what the police told me. I'm hoping she hasn't figured that out yet, though. I hope she never does." I quietly begin tracing my fingers over his hand. "She's pregnant," he adds.

My fingers pause their movement and I gasp.

"I know," he says. "It's shit luck. They're supposed to be celebrating their anniversary this weekend."

I hadn't thought of that, but as soon as he brings it up, I think about Jordyn last year and the frenzy she was in as she prepared for her impending wedding with Kyle. And now, just one year later, she's having to prepare for his impending funeral. "That's so sad. How far along is she?"

"She's due in February."

I try to put myself in her shoes. I'm almost positive she's twenty-four now. I can't imagine being that young and losing a husband months before the birth of my first child. It's incomprehensible.

"When do you go back to New York?" he asks.

"First thing tomorrow morning. I can stay at my mother's tonight, though, if I need to. I have to be up really early."

He brings his mouth to mine. "You aren't sleeping anywhere but in this bed."

A loud knock prevents his lips from reaching me and his attention moves to the door. It swings open and Ian walks in, looks at me and then does a double take.

He points at me, but is looking at Ben. "There's a chick in your bed."

We both sit up. When we do, Ian cocks his head, narrowing his eyes in my direction. "Wait. I've met you before. Fallon, right?"

I won't lie; it feels good that his brother remembers me. Not that my face is one a person easily forgets. But he didn't have to remember my name and he did, so that can only mean that girls aren't in Ben's bed very often.

"It was nice of you to come," Ian says. "You hungry? Came up to let Ben know that dinner's on the table."

Ben groans as he scoots off the bed. "Let me guess. Casserole?"

Ian shakes his head. "Tate was craving pizza, so we ordered delivery."

"Thank God." Ben pulls me up. "Let's go eat."

Ben

"Let me get this straight," Miles says, looking at me and Fallon from across the table. "You blocked each other on social media. You don't know each other's phone numbers, so no contact whatsoever. But you've met up every year since you were eighteen?"

"Crazy, huh?" Fallon says, lowering her glass to the table.

"It's a little bit like *Sleepless in Seattle,*" Tate says.

I immediately shake my head. "It's nothing like that. They only agreed to meet up once."

"True. It's like *One Day,* then. That movie with Anne Hathaway?"

Again, I dismiss her comparison. "That just focuses on one particular day every year, but the two people still interact throughout the year like normal. Fallon and I have no contact." I don't know why I'm being so defensive. I think writers just naturally become defensive when their ideas are compared to other ideas, even if it's done innocently. But mine and Fallon's story is one-of-a-kind, and I feel somewhat protective of it. *Very* protective of it, actually.

"When will you stop? Or do you plan on doing this for the rest of your lives?"

Fallon glances at me and smiles. "We stop when we're twenty-three."

"Why twenty-three?" Ian asks.

Fallon answers the next few questions being fired at us, so I use the opportunity to excuse myself from the conversation to refill my drink. I lean against the counter and watch all of them interact from the kitchen.

I'm happy she's here. I feel like having her here somewhat eases the grief everyone is feeling. She wasn't tied to Kyle in any way, so no one feels forced to walk on eggshells around her. She's like the breath of fresh air we all needed this week. I know I already thanked her for coming today, but one day I'll tell her exactly how much it means to me that she showed up.

She glances at me from her chair, and when she sees the small smile on my face, she excuses herself from the table and walks into the kitchen.

My entire body relaxes when her arms

slide around my waist. She plants a kiss on my arm and then stifles a yawn.

"You tired?"

She looks up at me and nods. "Yeah. Still on New York time, and it's after midnight there. You mind if I use your shower before we go to bed?"

I lift my finger to her mouth. "You have something in your teeth." She bares her teeth and I wipe what looks like a piece of pepper from her tooth. "All gone," I say, giving her a quick peck on the lips. "And yes, you can use my shower. Let me know if you need assistance." I wink at her, just as Ian leans against the counter beside us, narrowing his eyes at me.

"Did you just pick something out of her teeth?"

I don't say anything because I don't know what he plans to do with my answer.

"I'm being serious," he says, looking at Fallon now. "Did he just pick something out of your teeth?"

She nods hesitantly.

Ian smirks. "Wow. My brother is in love with you."

I can feel Fallon freeze against me.

"That's not awkward at all," I say sarcastically.

Ian shakes his head with a sly grin. "It's

not awkward, Ben. It's cute. You're in love."

"Stop," I say to him.

Ian releases a lighthearted laugh, and for once, I don't mind being picked on by him. It's the most air that's been let in this house in two days.

"People don't do gross things like that unless they're in love," Tate says from the table. "It's a proven fact. It's on the Internet or something."

I grab Fallon's hand and pull her out of the kitchen, away from the teasing. "Good night, guys. Fallon has other pressing hygiene issues I need to assist her with."

I hear them laughing as we exit the kitchen and walk upstairs together.

To my bedroom.

Where we'll spend the night.

Together.

In my bed.

It's tricky knowing I won't see her for another year, so I have no idea how far she's willing to take it. I think that would all depend on how far she's taken it with guys in the past.

Of course I don't want to think about her with anyone else, but that's the whole point of meeting her every year. I want to make sure she's experiencing life like every girl her age should, and that means experiencing different people. But every night I close my eyes, I selfishly pray that she's sleeping in her bed alone.

I want to ask her about it, but I'm not sure how to bring it up.

I open my bedroom door and follow her inside. It's different walking into my room with her this time. It almost feels like there are expectations that have to be met before we exit this room in the morning. Conversations that need to be had. Bodies that need touching. Minds that need sleep. And not enough time to cram it all in before she'll leave me again for another year.

I close and lock the door behind me. She's facing the bed as she reaches up and pulls her hair into a knot, securing it with a rubber band she's had around her wrist all day. I take a moment to admire the perfection of the curve between her neck and shoulder. I step forward and slip my arms around her waist so that I can press my lips against that very spot. I shower her in soft kisses from her shoulder to her ear and back down again. I kiss away the chills I'm responsible for. She makes a quiet sound, somewhere between a sigh and a moan.

"I'll let you shower," I tell her without releasing her. "Towels are under the sink."

She squeezes my hands that are wrapped

around her waist and then breaks away from me. Rather than head toward the bathroom, she walks toward my closet. "Can I sleep in one of your shirts?" she asks.

I glance at the closet and then at her. My manuscript is in my closet, sitting on the shelf. What I've written of it, anyway. At this point, the last thing I want her to do is read a single word of it. I grip the back of the shirt I'm wearing and pull it over my head.

"Here," I say, handing it to her. "Wear this one."

She grabs the shirt from my hands, but as soon as she looks up, she stops mid-step. She swallows, staring straight at my stomach. "Ben?"

"Yeah?"

She points at my stomach. "You have abs?"

I laugh and look down at my abdomen. She said it like it was a question, so I give her the obvious answer. "Um . . . yeah? I guess."

She covers her mouth with my shirt, hiding her grin. "Wow," she says, her words muffled by my shirt. "I like them."

And then she rushes toward the bathroom and closes the door.

Fallon

I made sure to lock the door before getting into the shower. Not that I wouldn't want to take a shower with him, but I'm just not at that point yet. To me, showering with someone registers higher on my scale for potential humiliation than most things, including sex. At least with sex I'll be hiding under the covers in the dark.

Sex.

I think about that word. I even roll it around on my tongue as I rinse the conditioner out of my hair. "Sex," I say quietly. It's such a weird word.

The older I get, the more apprehensive I become at the thought of losing my virginity. On the one hand, I'm ready to experience what all the fuss is about. It has to be great or it wouldn't be such a huge factor in the lives of all mankind. But that also scares me, because if I end up *not* liking sex, I'll be a little bit disappointed in mankind as a whole. Because it seems to be the root of a lot of evil, so if it's mediocre and I don't instantly want more of it, I'll feel a little misled by the entire world.

Perhaps I'm being a bit melodramatic, but whatever. I'm too nervous to get out of the shower, even though I rinsed the conditioner out of my hair several minutes ago. I have no idea what Ben's expectations are for tonight. If he wants to sleep, I would totally understand. He's been through hell and back this week. But if he wants to do something *besides* sleep, I will absolutely, without a doubt, be a willing participant.

After I dry off, I pull his shirt over my head. I look in the mirror and admire the way it hangs off my shoulders. I've never worn another guy's t-shirt before, and I've always wondered if it felt as good as I imagined it would feel.

It does.

I pull the towel off my head and run my fingers through my hair a few times. I take Ben's toothpaste and squeeze some onto my finger and then rub it in my mouth for a minute. When I'm done, I take a deep, calming breath, and then I turn out the lights and open the door.

His lamp is on and he's lying on the bed, facing the center of it, with his hands tucked beneath his head. He's kicked his covers onto the floor and is wearing nothing but his socks and a pair of boxers. I stand here and admire him for a moment, since his eyes are closed. He might actually be sleeping, but it doesn't disappoint me at all. Tonight's for him and him only, because I know he's hurting. I just want to help him while I'm here, so if he needs sleep, I'll do what I can to ensure he gets the best night of sleep he's ever had.

I walk to the lamp and switch it off and then pick his covers up off the floor. I gently sit on the bed and cover us both as I lie down next to him with my back to his chest. I try not to wake him as I adjust my pillow.

"Shit."

I roll over at the sound of his voice. It's dark in the room, so I can't tell if he was talking in his sleep or if he's awake. "What is it?" I whisper.

I feel an arm go around my waist, and he pulls me closer. "I left the light on so I could see you walk out of the bathroom wearing my shirt, but you take really long showers. I think I fell asleep."

I smile. "I'm still wearing it. You want me to turn the lamp on?"

"Fuck yes, please."

I laugh and roll over toward the lamp. I

switch it on and then face him again. His eyes are unmoving, yet somehow all over me.

"Stand up," he says, lifting up onto his elbow. I stand up and his eyes never meet mine. They're roaming over my thighs, my hips, my breasts. I don't mind that he isn't looking at my face. I don't mind at all.

The hem of his shirt falls several inches above my knees. It's just long enough to where he can't tell that I'm not wearing underwear right now. It's also just short enough to where he's probably *praying* I'm not wearing underwear right now.

His eyes drop to my legs again and he begins to speak slowly, as if he's reciting poetry. "The only sea I saw, Was the seesaw sea, With you riding on it. Lie down, lie easy. Let me shipwreck in your thighs." His eyes drag up my body until they meet mine. "Dylan Thomas," he says.

I release a slow breath. "Wow," I say. "Poetry porn. Who knew?"

Ben smiles at me lazily. He lifts a finger and points at me. "I'd like to have my shirt back now."

"Now?"

He nods. "Right now. Before you turn off the lamp. Take it off, it's mine."

I laugh nervously and begin to reach for

the lamp. Before I'm able to turn the light off, he jumps up and walks across the mattress, hopping to the floor directly in front of me. His eyes are playful, yet somehow stern at the same time. He grabs the hem of my shirt and pulls it up without hesitation, yanking it off my head. He throws it somewhere behind him and I'm immobile in front of him, completely exposed. His eyes read every curve of my body before he lets out a shaky breath.

"Holy shit," he mutters.

I can't recall a single time, even before the fire, when I've felt this beautiful. He's soaking me up like it's a privilege rather than a favor. And when he leans forward and takes my face in his hands, I part my lips and wait for his kiss because I've never wanted it like I want it right now.

His lips are moist, and he kisses me with entitlement. His tongue is rough and unapologetic, and I love it. I love feeling needed this way. I realize, as his fingers are slowly trailing down my spine, that angst doesn't have to be a factor for a kiss to be a ten, after all. Because angst is nowhere in this kiss, and it's already a nine.

He pulls me flush against him, my naked chest pressed against his. *Okay, it's a ten now.*

He turns us around and lowers me to the

bed, but doesn't lie on top of me. He adjusts us to where we're side by side and my head is on a pillow, but his mouth is still on mine. Quiet, desire-filled sounds begin to leave my mouth, each one of them a direct result of what this kiss is building inside me.

I don't even care that the lamp is still on. If it means he'll be looking at me again like he looked at me before this kiss, I'll let him turn *all* the lights on. I'd even let him install fluorescents.

"Fallon," he says quickly after tearing his mouth from mine. I open my eyes and find him looking down at me. "We've read the same books. You know the rules. If you want me to stop or slow down, just . . ."

I shake my head. "It's perfect, Ben. So perfect. I'll tell you if there's something I don't want to do, or if I get nervous. I promise."

He nods, but it still seems as though there's something else he wants to say. Or ask. And then I remember that we've never really had this discussion.

"I've never done this, but that doesn't mean I'm not ready," I tell him.

I feel his body stiffen, just slightly. "You're a virgin." He says it as more of a realization than a question.

"Yeah, but only for a few more minutes."

My comment forces him to smile, but then worry consumes his expression. His eyes grow immediately sober and his smile falls into a grim line. He shakes his head softly. "I don't want to be your first, Fallon. I want to be your last."

I take in a quiet rush of air as his words sink in. He's not even kissing me, and those words just made this moment a twelve. I touch his cheek with the tips of my fingers and smile up at him. "I want you to be my first *and* last."

Ben's eyes darken and then he slides his body over mine, caging me in with his arms. I can feel him hard against me and I try not to whimper. "You can't say things like that unless you mean them, Fallon."

I meant it with everything I am. For the first time, I realize that I don't care about the five years. I don't care that I'm not twenty-three. All I care about is Ben and how I feel when I'm with him, and how I want so much more of this. "I want you to be my *only,*" I say, my voice quieter, but with more resolve.

He winces as if he's in pain, but I know by now that's a good thing. A very good thing.

He brushes his thumb over my lips. "I *want* to be your only, Fallon. I want it more than anything. But it's not happening tonight unless you promise me that I'll be able to hear your voice tomorrow and every day that follows."

I nod, surprised we're having this conversation. I wasn't anticipating this at all when I got on that flight this morning. But I know it's right. I'm never going to meet anyone who makes me feel the way he does. People don't get this lucky more than once in the same lifetime. "I promise."

"I'm serious," he says. "I want your phone number before you leave in the morning."

I nod again. "You can have it. I *want* you to have it. And my email address. I'll even go buy an all-in-one printer with a fax machine so I can give you that number, too."

"Baby," he says, his lips forming a smile. "You have already made this the best sex I've ever had, and I'm not even inside you yet."

I bite my lip as I run my fingers up his arms, sliding them up his neck until I'm cupping his face. "What are you waiting for?"

He pulls in a raspy breath. "To wake up, I think." He lowers his mouth and kisses my neck. "I'm dreaming, right?"

I shake my head, just as he moves his hips

against me. A moan escapes my mouth and the gentle kiss against my neck grows wilder.

"*Definitely* dreaming," he mutters. His mouth meets the base of my throat and he touches the tip of his tongue to my skin, dragging it up my throat until he's kissing me again. It's by far the sexiest thing I've ever felt.

Seconds turn into minutes. Fingers turn into hands. Teasing turns into torture. Torture turns into unimaginable pleasure.

His boxers have met their fate on the floor. In an insurmountable display of willpower, he's pressed against me, but still not inside me.

"Fallon," he whispers, moving his lips slowly across mine. "Thank you for this beautiful gift."

As soon as his words brush over my mouth, he covers me in a deep kiss. My whole body tenses from the burst of pain that ripples through me as he pushes inside of me, but the perfection of the way we fit together makes the pain a mere inconvenience.

It's beautiful.

He's beautiful.

And somehow, with the way he's looking down at me, I even believe *I'm* beautiful.

He presses his mouth against my ear and

whispers, "No combination of written words could ever do this moment justice."

I smile between moans. "How are you going to write about it, then?"

He kisses me, softly, right on the corner of my mouth. "I guess I'll just have to fade to black . . ."

I'm not sure if sex is supposed to make you feel like you've just lost a part of yourself to the person inside you, but that's exactly what it felt like. It felt as if the second we joined together, a tiny piece of our souls got confused and a piece of his fell into me and a piece of mine fell into him. It was by far the single most intense moment I've ever shared with another person.

I feel a warmth creeping up my face like I want to cry, but I keep the tears at bay. I just know that there's no way I can tell him goodbye after this. It'll tear me apart, way worse than last year. I can't go another day without him being a part of my everyday life. Not after this.

His arm is wrapped around me, and even though it's been several minutes and he's already been to the bathroom and crawled back into bed, he's still breathing like he was just inside me a matter of seconds ago. I like this part of sex, I think. The aftermath.

The quiet. Still feeling connected after the physical connection is no longer there.

His lips meet my shoulder — the scarred one — and he places the gentlest kiss against my skin. So soft and thought out, it feels like so much more than just a kiss. It feels like a promise, and I'd give anything to be able to read his mind right now.

"Fallon," he whispers, pulling me closer to his side. "You know all those romance novels you made me read for research?"

"I only made you read five. The others were of your own accord."

He runs his nose along my jawline until his lips are at my ear. "Well," he continues, "I was thinking about some of the things those guys say when they're with a girl. The ones we said we'd never say? Like when a guy tells a girl he owns her? I know we've laughed about it before, but . . . *holy shit.*" He pulls back and holds me captive with an intense stare. "I've never wanted to say anything like I wanted to say those things to you while I was inside you. It took everything I had not to."

I never thought a sentence could make me whimper, but it absolutely does. "If you did . . . I wouldn't have asked you to stop."

He drags his lips across my cheek until he reaches my mouth. "I'm not saying those things to you until you really *are* mine." He wraps his arms around me, cradling me against him, begging me without words for whatever it is he's not saying. I can feel it. The desperation.

"Fallon," he says, his words strained against his throat. "I don't want to say goodbye to you when we wake up."

His words carve a hole right in the center of my heart. "You'll have my phone number this time. You can call me."

"Every single day?" he asks, hopeful.

"I'll be mad if you don't."

"Twice a day?"

I laugh.

"Can I *see* you every day?"

I shake my head, because that one isn't really possible. "That'll be kind of expensive," I say to him.

"Not if I live in the same city as you."

My smile immediately disappears. Not because that sounds unappealing. But because that's not an innocent remark. People can't just threaten to move across the country for someone if they don't actually mean it.

I swallow the lump in my throat. "What are you saying, Ben?"

He rolls onto his side again and props his head up on his hand. "I'm thinking about selling the house, if Ian is okay with it. According to Jordyn's mother, she's moving back home. Kyle is gone. Ian is never even here. The only person I want to be near lives in New York. I wonder what she would think if I moved there."

I can't believe we're having this conversation. As much as I know we need to talk about this without the rush of sex clouding our minds, I can't think of anything I want more than to see him every day. To have him be a part of my life.

Except for one small detail.

"What about the book?" I ask him. "We're supposed to meet up three more times. Don't you want to finish it?"

He contemplates my question for a short moment before slowly shaking his head. "No," he says simply. "Not if it means we can't be together." His expression doesn't falter.

He's serious. He actually wants to move to New York. And I want him there more than I've ever wanted anything.

"You're gonna need a jacket."

His smile transforms his entire face. He reaches a hand up to my cheek and traces my jaw, brushing his thumb over my lips. "And they lived happily ever after."

■ ■ ■ ■

Yesterday evening when he opened the door and I saw him for the first time in a year, I could see the pain in every single aspect of him. It was like the death of his brother aged him five years.

But right now, he looks somewhat like he did the first time I saw him. Unkempt and scruffy. Adorable. Beautiful. It's the most at peace I've seen him since I arrived.

I kiss him lightly on the cheek and roll off the bed without waking him. I put on my clothes and slip out of his bedroom, heading downstairs to see if there's any cleaning I can do before I wake him up to say goodbye.

It's almost four in the morning. The last thing I expect is to see someone in the kitchen, but Jordyn is seated at the bar.

She looks up at me as soon as I walk in. Her eyes are red and puffy, but she's not crying. She's got an entire box of pizza in front of her and she's taking a huge bite out of a slice of pepperoni.

I feel bad for walking in on her. Based on my conversation with Ben, she's wanted nothing but solitude the last couple of days. I debate walking back to Ben's room to give her privacy. She must see my hesitation, because she scoots the box toward me.

"You hungry?" she asks.

I kind of am. I take a seat next to her and grab a slice of pizza. We sit together in silence until she finishes a second slice. She stands and takes the box of pizza to the refrigerator. She hands me a soda when she returns to the bar. "So you're the girl Ben's writing the book about?"

I pause the can at my lips, shocked she knows about it. No one else at the dinner table seemed to know anything about his book. I nod again and then take a drink.

She forces a smile and looks down at her hands, laced together on the bar in front of her. "He's a great writer," she says. "I think the book is going to be huge for him. It's a clever idea."

I clear my throat, hoping she doesn't hear the shock in my voice. "Have you read any of it?"

"Bits and pieces," she says, smiling again. "He's really picky about which parts I'm allowed to read, but I was an English major, so sometimes he asks my opinion."

I take another drink, just to keep myself from speaking just yet. I want to ask her about it, but I don't want her to know that I haven't read a single word of it yet.

"Kyle was so happy for him when he signed with his agent." Her eyes begin to mist when she mentions Kyle's name.

I look away from her.

An agent?

Why didn't he tell me he signed with an agent?

"How is he?" she asks.

"Ben?"

She nods. "I haven't really interacted with anyone yet. I know it's selfish of me, because I'm not the only one hurting. But I just . . ."

I put my hand on top of hers and squeeze. "He's okay. And he understands, Jordyn. Everyone does."

She wipes a tear away with a nearby napkin. Seeing her try to hold it in creates pressure in my chest. I hurt for her, especially knowing what she's about to face alone.

"I just feel bad. I've been so caught up in everything I've lost the past two days, I haven't even thought about how much it affects Ian and Ben. I mean, they both live here. And now they're stuck with a girl who's about to have a baby. The last thing I want is for them to feel obligated to help me, but . . . I really don't want to go back to Nevada. I can't move back in with my mother when this is my home. I just . . ."

She presses her hands against her face. "I don't know what to do. I don't want to burden anyone, but I'm scared I can't do this on my own."

I put my arms around her and she begins to cry into my shirt. I had no idea she didn't want to move back in with her mother. I wonder if Ben is even aware of that.

"Jordyn."

We both look up when Ben calls her name. He's standing in the doorway to the kitchen with a distraught look on his face. When she looks up at him, she starts crying even harder. He walks over to her and puts his arms around her, so I stand up and walk around the bar, giving them space.

"You aren't going anywhere, okay?" he says. "You're my sister. You're Ian's sister. And our nephew will be raised in the home that you and Kyle planned for him to be raised in." He pulls back and brushes the hair out of her face. "Promise me you'll let us help you."

She nods, wiping more tears away. She can barely get out the words *thank you* between sobs.

I can't watch her cry anymore. I'm on the verge of tears myself just knowing how scared she is. I rush up the stairs and back into Ben's bedroom, where I can gather my thoughts. So many things are running through my head, most of them fears. I'm afraid he's making a decision out of haste. I'm afraid if I tell him how much I wish he would move to New York, he would actually do it, and it's obvious his sister-in-law needs him here. Not to mention the possibilities he'd lose by giving up on the book. I feel the more genuine the story is, the better chance he'll have of selling the book. Yes, I would love to start a real relationship right now, but that's not what we agreed on in the beginning. If we just up and end our arrangement in the middle without continuing to meet up on November 9th, he'll be giving up on what his agent obviously thought would make a great book.

I can't believe he has an agent.

That's huge, and I don't know why he didn't tell me. As much as I want to believe he's okay with not finishing the book, I fear that he's making this decision based on the high emotions from the last few days. The last thing I want is for him to make a choice as big as moving across the country and then regretting it after he does it. Of course I'd give anything to have him with me every day, but even more than that I want him to be happy with whatever decision he makes. I know three years is a long time for us to wait, but those three years could make a huge difference in his success as an author. The fact that our story is true might make it appealing to readers, and even though I haven't read any of it yet, I'm convinced he needs to finish it.

I don't want to be the reason he doesn't finish what he started out to do. Years from now, he'll look back on tonight and he'll wonder if he made the wrong choice. If maybe our lives would have still turned out the same and we would still end up together, but by waiting three years, he also would have met his goal of writing the book he promised to write.

He's made such a huge difference in my life. More than he'll ever know. If it weren't for him, I don't think I would have ever regained my confidence. I know I wouldn't have had the courage to audition anywhere. Just having him in my life one day a year has had such a positive effect on me, I'd hate myself if I did the exact opposite for him.

And none of that includes what just transpired over the last ten minutes. There's no way he can move to New York when his family needs him now more than ever. Jordyn is going to need him here way more than I need him in New York. He and Ian are both going to need to be here for her and I refuse to be the one to convince him to leave her at a time like this.

I grab my phone and call for a cab before I change my mind.

Ben

I close the door to Jordyn's bedroom when I hear Fallon's footsteps coming down the stairs. I walk around the corner to meet her and she gasps, clutching a hand to her heart.

"You scared me," she says, taking the last step. "How is she?"

I glance down the hallway toward Jordyn's bedroom. "Better," I say. "I think the pizza helped."

Fallon smiles appreciatively. "It wasn't the pizza that made her feel better, Ben." She takes two more steps, toward the front door this time. I finally notice the purse around her shoulder and the shoes on her feet. She looks prepared to leave.

She shuffles, putting her weight on one foot. She shrugs, as if I asked her a question, and then she looks back up at me. "Earlier . . ."

"Fallon," I interject. "Please don't change your mind."

She winces, looking up and to the right as if she's trying to hold back tears. *She's not changing her mind. She can't.* I rush toward her and grab both of her hands. "*Please.* We can do this. Maybe I can't move right away, but I will. Things just need to settle around here first."

She squeezes my hands and releases a sigh. "Jordyn said you got an agent." Her voice sounds somewhat offended, and she has a right to be. I should have told her that before she heard it from somewhere else, but my mind has been a little preoccupied today.

I nod. "Yeah, a couple months ago. I submitted the book idea to a few and this one really likes it." I realize where this is going, so I shake my head. "It doesn't matter, Fallon. I can write something else."

A stream of light strolls across the walls, and she glances over her shoulder. Her cab is here.

"Please," I beg. "Just give me your phone number, at least. I'll call you tomorrow and we'll figure it out then, okay?" I'm trying to keep my voice soothing and hopeful, but it's hard hiding the panic that's building up in my chest.

She regards me with a look that resembles pity. "It's been an emotional couple of days,

Ben. It's not fair of me to let you make this kind of decision right now." She presses her lips to my cheek and then turns for the front door. I follow her out, determined not to let her change her mind like this.

When she reaches the cab, she faces me with a steadfast look. "I would never forgive myself if I didn't encourage you to follow your dreams like you encouraged me to follow mine. Please don't ask me to be the reason you give them up. It isn't fair."

I can feel the desperate appeal in her words, and it forces all of my words back down my throat. She wraps her arms around me, pressing her face against my neck. I hold her tight, hoping if she feels how much I need her to stay with me that she'll change her mind. But she doesn't. She releases me and opens the door to the cab.

I've never wanted to use physical force on a girl before, but I want to push her to the ground and hold her there until the cab drives away.

"I'll come here next year," she says. "I want to meet your nephew. We'll meet at the restaurant again, okay? Same time, same place?"

What?

Did we even experience the same past eight hours?

Did she fall down the stairs and hit her head?

No, I'm not agreeing to this. She's crazy if she thinks I'm just going to give her a high five and tell her I'll see her in a year. I shake my head adamantly and close the door to the cab, refusing to let her climb inside.

"*No,* Fallon. You can't just agree to love me, and then take it back because you think it's not what's best for me. That's not how this works."

She's startled by my words. I think she expected me to let her go without a fight, but she's not the kind of girl you choose your battles for. She's the kind of girl you fight to the death for.

She leans against the cab and crosses her arms over her chest. Her eyes are focused on the ground, but mine are focused on her.

"Ben," she says, her voice barely above a whisper. "You don't need to be in New York. You need to be here. I'll just be a distraction, and you'll never finish your book. It's only three more years. If we're meant to be together, three years is nothing."

I laugh, but my laugh is short and humorless. "Meant to be together? Are you listening to yourself? This isn't one of your fairy tales, Fallon. This is *real life,* and in the real world you have to bust your ass for the happy ever after!" I grip the nape of my neck and take a step away from her, trying to collect my frustration and bottle it back up, but it's pouring out of me every time I think about how she can so easily climb into this cab, knowing she won't see me for an entire year. "When you find love, you take it. You grab it with both hands and you do everything in your power not to let it go. You can't just walk away from it and expect it to linger until you're ready for it."

I don't know where this is coming from. I've never been angry at her before, but I'm so fucking pissed because this hurts. It hurts to know we just shared what we did upstairs in my room and then after giving it a little thought, she decides it didn't mean shit to her. That *I* don't mean shit to her.

Her eyes are wide and she's watching me struggle through every single emotion a guy can possibly have. This week has been full of them. From Kyle's death, to having to call Fallon yesterday morning, to seeing her at my front door, to breaking down on her in my bed, to making love to her in the same spot. If I were to put the week's emotions on a graph chart, it would look like tidal waves.

I see her glance at the cab as if she's contemplating her decision. I step forward and put my hands on her shoulders, forcing her attention back on me. "Don't walk away from this."

Her shoulders drop with her sigh. She gives her head a soft shake. "Ben, I'm not walking away from this. I'm not doing anything we didn't agree to the first day we met. I'm the one sticking to the rules, here. We agreed on five years. And yes, we had a little hiccup upstairs where we almost caved and —"

I cut her off. "A hiccup?" I point to the house. "Did you just refer to us agreeing to start a relationship as a . . . *hiccup*?"

Her expression is immediately apologetic, but I don't want to hear an apology. I'm obviously in the wrong here, because when I made love to her I knew what was happening between us was something most people don't even know exists. And if she even remotely felt the same, there's no way in hell she would be saying these things right now.

My stomach clenches and I want to double over in pain. But instead I hold steady and I offer her one last chance to prove to me that the entire past day wasn't completely one-sided.

I grip her face until my fingers are wrapped around the nape of her neck. I brush my thumbs across her cheeks and encourage her to look up at me. I touch her softly — as gentle as my fingers are capable of touching her. She swallows, and I can see that my change in demeanor is making her nervous.

"Fallon," I say, keeping my voice calm and sincere. "I don't care about the book. I don't even want to finish it. All I care about is you. Being with you every day. Seeing you every day. I'm not finished falling in love with you yet. But if you don't want to finish falling in love with me, then you need to tell me right now. Do you want me to be a part of your life on more than just November 9th? If you say no, I'll turn around and walk right back inside that house and things can go back to how they were before you showed up here yesterday. I'll continue working on the book and we'll meet up next year. But if you say yes . . . if you tell me you want to spend every single day on the calendar this year falling in love with me, then I'm going to kiss you. And I promise it'll be an eleven. And I'll spend every day after today proving to you that you made the right choice."

My hands remain firm on her face. Her eyes remain firm on mine.

And then a tear slowly begins to take

shape and rolls down her cheek. She shakes her head, "Ben, you can't —"

"Yes or no, Fallon. That's all I want to hear."

Please say yes. Please tell me you aren't finished falling in love with me yet.

"You need to be here for your family this year. You know that as well as I do, Ben. The last thing we need is a relationship over a cell phone. And that's exactly what will happen, because we'll spend every spare second wanting to talk to each other instead of focusing on our goals. We'll alter everything just to be together, and it shouldn't be that way. Not yet. We need to finish what we started."

I let all of that go in one ear and out the other, because it isn't the answer I want. I lower myself until I'm at eye level with her. "Yes. Or no."

She inhales a shaky breath. And then, in a weak effort at sounding sincere, she says, "No. No, Ben. Go back inside and finish your book."

Another tear falls, but this time it falls from *my* eye.

I take a step back and I let go of her. When she climbs into the backseat of the cab, she rolls down her window, but I won't look at her face. I stare at the ground beneath my feet, waiting to see if it will split in two and swallow me whole.

"The one thing I want more than anything is for the whole world to laugh at you, Ben." I can hear the tears in her voice. "And they can't do that if I don't do for you what you did for me the day we met. You let me go. You *encouraged* me to go. And I want the same for you. I want you to follow your passion instead of your heart."

The cab begins to back away, and for a split second I think maybe she'll realize how fucked up her priorities are, because *she's* my passion. The book was just an excuse.

I debate running after her — giving her a book-worthy performance. I could chase down the cab and when it comes to a stop, I could pull open her door and whisk her into my arms and tell her I'm in love with her. That I finished falling in love with her almost immediately after I started, because it was a straight plummet from the top to the bottom. A whoosh. An instant. Insta-love.

But she hates insta-love. Apparently she hates semi-instant love and slow love and love at a snail's pace and love in general and . . . "Fuck!"

I curse at the empty street, because for once, I get exactly what I deserve.

■ ■ ■ ■

Fourth November 9th

■ ■ ■ ■

In her darkness, she is silent.
In my darkness, she screams.
— Benton James Kessler

Fallon

Even counting the night I was called up from being the understudy, I wasn't this nervous. I'm over an hour early, but our booth was already taken when I arrived here this morning, so I chose the one next to it.

I tap my fingers on the table, my eyes flicking to the door anytime someone enters or exits.

I have no idea how I'm going to start this conversation. How do I tell him that as soon as I pulled away last year, I knew I'd made the biggest mistake of my life? How do I tell him I made that last-minute decision for his benefit? That I thought if I told him I didn't want to fall in love with him, that I would be helping him in some way? And most important, how do I bring up the fact that I moved back to Los Angeles just for him? Well, not exactly *just* for him. I did make a huge career change a few months ago.

Back when I was in community theater, I

was asked to help out with lines a lot because people had confidence in my talent. I guess you could say I taught acting in a sense. The joy I got from that stuck with me and over time, I realized that I enjoyed assisting the actors with their parts more than I enjoyed *being* the actor.

It took a few months to finally accept that maybe my goal wasn't to be an actress anymore. People change. They grow. Passions evolve, and mine evolved into wanting to help others develop their own talents.

I looked into schools all over the country, but with my mother, Amber, and yes, Ben, being in Los Angeles, it was a no-brainer for which city I ended up choosing.

As much as I question my decision for not agreeing to be with him last year, I know it was for the best in the long run. I've never been more at peace with my career choice as I am right now, and I'm not sure it would have happened had Ben been in the picture. So even though mistakes were made, I don't have any regrets. I think things are working out exactly as they should.

But as Ben and I can both probably attest, a lot can change in a year, so I'm terrified he may have changed his mind. He may not even want to be with me like he did last year. He may still be so pissed at me, he doesn't even show up.

But that's not really why I'm nervous.

I'm nervous because I know he *will.* He always shows up. But this year, I have no idea where we stand. We left on really bad terms last year and I take complete blame, but he has to understand that if the shoe were on the other foot, he would have done the same for me. If I had made such a huge declaration in the midst of so much suffering, he would have acknowledged that maybe I wasn't in the best place to make such a life-altering decision. And he certainly can't fault me for encouraging him to stay and help out his family. His brother had just died. His sister-in-law needed him. His nephew would need him. It was the right thing. He would have done the same for me. He just took it as hard as he did because he was already having such an emotional week.

I almost feel like showing up unannounced last year was a bad idea. I feel like my time there did more damage than it did good.

My thoughts are interrupted when a hand comes to rest on my shoulder. I look up, expecting to see Ben standing there. And I do . . . but it's not just Ben. It's Ben and . . . *a baby.*

His nephew.

I know this immediately because he has Ben's eyes. *Kyle's* eyes.

All of this is coming at me at once and I try to process each thing separately. First, the fact that Ben showed up. And he's smiling at me as I stand up to hug him, so that's enough to elicit a huge sigh of relief.

Second, his arm is wrapped around this baby boy who is perched up on his hip, leaning his head against Ben's chest. Seeing him with his nephew like this assures me that both of us made the right choice last year, whether he agreed to it at the time or not.

I was hoping to meet his nephew at some point today, but I thought I'd have a chance to talk to Ben first, one-on-one, about how we left things last year. But I can adapt. Especially for a baby as cute as this one.

He's grinning shyly at me and I can see so much of Jordyn in him. He's almost equal parts Jordyn and Kyle. I wonder how that is for her . . . to see so much of Kyle when she looks at her son.

When Ben releases me from the hug, he smiles down at the little boy. "Fallon, I'd like you to meet my nephew, Oliver." He picks up Oliver's tiny wrist and waves it at me. "Oliver, this is Fallon."

I lift my hand and Oliver immediately reaches his arms out to me. Shocked, I let him come to me, pulling him against me the same way Ben was holding him. It's been a long time since I've held a baby, but I'd much rather Ben's nephew want me to hold him than cry if I tried.

"He likes the pretty ladies," Ben says with a wink, releasing him once I have hold of him. "Let me grab a high chair."

Ben walks away, so I take a seat with Oliver, setting him on the table in front of me. "Aren't you a cutie," I say to him. And he is. He seems like a very happy baby and that makes me happy for Jordyn. But still, sadness seeps in when I think about Kyle never being able to meet his son. I push the thought out of my head when Ben returns with a high chair.

He pushes it against the edge of the booth and then secures Oliver in it. I didn't even notice the diaper bag Ben had over his shoulder until he removes it to take a seat. He fishes through the bag until he finds a container of snacks, and then he sets some Cheerios out on the table in front of Oliver, but not before wiping it down first. The whole time, he talks to Oliver in a respectful, peer type of way. He doesn't indulge in baby talk, and I'd be lying if I said it isn't adorable seeing him interact with an infant like they're on the same level.

Ben really has this baby thing down. It's impressive. And . . . kind of sexy.

"How old is he now?"

"Ten months," Ben says. "He was born New Year's Day. A few weeks early, but he was fine."

"So the whole world celebrates his birthday with fireworks, just like they do yours?"

Ben grins. "You know, I never even thought about that." Oliver plays with the Cheerios in front of him, completely content with not being the center of attention. Which is a relief, because maybe Ben and I will be able to have a serious conversation despite being in the company of his nephew.

Ben reaches his hand across the table and squeezes mine, and my chest heats up from the small gesture. "It's really good to see you, Fallon," he says, brushing his thumb over mine. "Really good."

The sincerity in his eyes makes me want to lunge across this table and kiss him right here. He doesn't hate me. He isn't mad at me. I feel like I just took my first breath of pure air in a year.

I flip my hand over to hold his, but as soon as I do, he pulls away to push Oliver's snacks closer to him. "I'm sorry I had to bring him. Jordyn had to work today and the sitter canceled last minute."

"It's fine," I tell him. And honestly, it is. I love watching him interact with Oliver. It adds another layer to him that I haven't witnessed before. "How is Jordyn?"

"Good," Ben says, nodding like he's trying to convince himself of this, too. "Really good. She's such a great mom. Kyle would be proud." He says the last sentence quieter than the rest. "What about you? How's New York?"

I don't know how to answer that. I don't feel now is the right time to bring it up, so I avoid the question. "This is always so weird," I say. "Seeing you for the first time in a year. I never know what to say or do." I'm lying. It's never been weird before, but thanks to last year, it feels very awkward today.

He reaches across the table and places his hand over my wrist, giving it a light squeeze. "I'm nervous, too," he says reassuringly. His eyes drop to our hands, and then he pulls his back and clears his throat. It's cute how he's trying to be respectful in front of Oliver. "Have you ordered yet?" He picks up the menu and stares at it silently for a moment, but I can tell he isn't reading it.

He's more nervous than he should be, but we did leave things off in an awkward place last year. I worry that it isn't nerves plaguing him, but maybe a little bit of bitterness. I know I hurt him last year, but surely he's had time to understand why I did what I did. And hopefully he knows that walking away from him when he was in so much pain was probably harder on me than it was on him. I've spent the entire last year with a heavy heart because it's constantly on my mind.

We both order something to eat and he makes sure to add a side of mashed potatoes for Oliver, which I find adorable. I try to alleviate our nerves with small talk. I tell him about how I decided my new goal in life is to open a talent studio. He smiled and said I was no longer, *"Fallon the Transient."* I asked him what my new name was and he looked at me thoughtfully and said, *"Fallon the Teacher."* And I loved the sound of that.

He said he graduated college this past May and it made me sad that I wasn't there for that, but I know there will be plenty of milestones in the future. I'll go to his graduation ceremony when he gets his advanced degree, because he says that's what he's working toward now. He got a job doing freelance for an online magazine and decided to further his career with a master's in technical writing.

During a lull in our conversation, Ben

spoons a bite of mashed potatoes into Oliver's mouth. The baby rubs his eyes and looks as though he's about to nod off right into his bowl.

"Can he say any words yet?"

Ben smiles down at Oliver, brushing a hand over his tiny head. "A couple. I'm pretty sure he says them by accident, though. He mostly talks gibberish." Ben laughs and then says, "He did say his first curse word, though. We keep his baby monitor on at night and last week, clear as day, he said the word *shit.* Little guy is starting early," he says, pinching Oliver playfully on his cheek. Oliver smiles up at him, and when he does, everything hits me at once.

Ben treats Oliver like a father would treat a son.

Oliver looks at Ben like he's his dad.

Ben referred to himself and Jordyn as a *"we."*

And they keep Oliver's baby monitor on at night . . . which means . . . *they share a bedroom*?

I suck in a breath the moment I feel my entire world turn on its axis. I grip the table when the clarity hits.

I feel like such an idiot.

Ben notices the change in my demeanor immediately, and when my eyes lock with his, he begins to slowly shake his head, realizing his slip up. "Fallon," he says quietly. But he adds no additional words to follow up my name. It's clear that I know, and he does nothing to dismiss my assumption. He's drowning in an apologetic look.

Instant jealousy.

Building, raging, *insane* jealousy. I'm forced to get up from my seat and rush to the bathroom, because I refuse to let him see how much this completely destroyed me in a matter of seconds. He calls after me, but I don't pause. I'm thankful he brought Oliver with him, because now he can't run after me.

I rush straight to the sink and I grip the edges of it, staring at myself in the mirror.

Calm down, Fallon. Don't cry. Save the heartbreak for when you get home.

I'm not prepared for this. I have no idea how to deal with this. It feels like my heart is literally breaking. Cracking right down the middle, bleeding out into my chest, filling my lungs with blood, making it impossible to breathe.

Holding the tears back proves even more difficult when the door to the bathroom opens and shuts. I look up to see Ben standing there, holding Oliver, looking at me with a deep layer of regret.

I close my eyes so I don't have to see his reflection in the mirror. I drop my head between my shoulders and I just start crying.

Ben

This isn't how I meant for her to find out. I was going to tell her, and soon, but I wanted to ease into it. Not that I expected her to be heartbroken over the fact that I'm dating Jordyn. In fact, I thought the chances of her being happy for me were greater than the chances of her being upset by it. I never expected this reaction from her. Why is she acting like she cares this much when she made it clear last year that she wasn't interested in anything more than the arrangement we made?

But it's obvious by the way she's reacting that she does care. That she did care. But for whatever reason, she refused to be with me when I needed her the most.

I try to hold it together, considering I'm holding Oliver, but every part of me wants to drop to my knees and scream.

I take a few hesitant steps forward until I'm right behind her. I gently grip her elbow with my hand, wanting to turn her around, but she brushes my hand away and walks to the other side of the restroom. She grabs a paper towel and wipes at her eyes, her back still to me.

"I didn't mean for it to happen." The words fall out of my mouth, as if they'll somehow comfort her. I want to take them back immediately. It doesn't matter that Fallon left such a big hole in my heart, I couldn't help it if someone else found their way in. It doesn't matter that Jordyn and I were both destroyed after the death of Kyle. It doesn't matter that things didn't progress between us until well after Oliver was born. It doesn't matter that I'll never feel the same connection with Jordyn that I had with Fallon, but Oliver makes up for anything our relationship lacks.

The only thing that matters to Fallon is the unexpected twist in our story. One neither of us saw coming. One neither of us even wanted. And one she's partly responsible for. I have to remember that. As much as she's hurting right now, she hurt me just as much — if not worse — when she chose New York over me.

I look down at Oliver and his head is resting against my chest — his eyes closed. It's well past time for his morning nap, so I readjust him so that he's lying in my arms. Every time I look at him, there's a swelling in my heart. One that's so different from any feeling Fallon or Jordyn could ever create. And I have to remind myself of that. It's not about either of them. It's about this little guy in my arms and what's best for him. He's the only thing that should matter, and I've been telling myself that for months. I thought that little reminder would be all it took to get me through this moment with Fallon, but now I'm not so sure.

Fallon takes a deep breath and releases it before turning around. When she locks eyes with mine, it's evident how much of her I just destroyed. My knee-jerk reaction is to make it better, to tell her how I really feel. How — since the moment I kissed Jordyn for the first time — I've been nothing but a confused mess.

Actually, I've been a confused mess since the second Fallon pulled away in that cab last year.

"Are you in love with her?" She immediately covers her mouth with her hand, shaking her head in regret for asking the question. "Please don't answer that." She walks toward me and drops her eyes to the floor. "I need to leave," she says as she passes me.

I back up until I'm pressed against the door, holding it shut. "Not like this. Please, don't leave yet. Give me a chance to explain."

I can't let her leave without her understanding the whole situation. But even more so, I'm hoping she'll explain what the hell happened last year and why she's acting like this news is actually affecting her like it is.

"Explain what?" she says quietly. "Do you want me to stand here and listen to you explain how you didn't mean to fall in love with your dead brother's wife? Do you expect me to argue with you when you tell me it isn't just about what *you* want anymore, but about what's better for your nephew? Do you expect me to apologize for lying to you last year when I said I didn't want to love you?"

Each word of the last sentence to leave her mouth is like weights bearing down on me, sinking me to the bottom of a lake. *She lied to me?*

"I get it, Ben. It's my fault. I'm the one who walked away last year when you tried to love me."

She tries to reach around me for the door handle, but I move to block her. I pull her to my side, wrapping my free hand around the back of her head and pressing her face to my shoulder. I press my lips against the side of her head, trying not to be affected by the way she feels in my arms. She grips my shirt and I feel her begin to cry again. I want to pull her closer, hold her tighter in my arms, but Oliver prevents me from doing that in more ways than one.

I want to say something that will comfort her, but at the same time I'm so pissed at her. At how carelessly she threw around my heart last year when I handed it to her. And how she's doing it again now that it's too late.

It's too late.

Oliver begins to squirm in my arms, so I'm forced to release her so that he doesn't wake up. She uses the opportunity to slip around me and out the bathroom door.

I follow her out of the bathroom and watch as she grabs her purse from our booth and heads straight for the door. I head to the booth and grab the diaper bag. Our food is still sitting on the table, but I think it's safe to say we won't be eating it. I drop cash on the table and head outside.

She's next to a car, fumbling around in her purse. By the time she retrieves her keys, I'm standing next to her. I yank the keys out of her hands and walk toward my car, which is parked right next to hers.

"Ben!" she yells. "Give me my keys!"

I unlock my car and crank it. I roll down the windows and then move to the backseat and strap Oliver in his car seat. When I'm positive he's still asleep, I walk back to her car.

"You can't leave hating me," I say, putting the keys back in her hand. "Not after everything we've been —"

"I don't *hate* you, Ben," she interjects. Her voice is offended and there are still tears streaming down her cheeks. "This was part of the deal, wasn't it?" She wipes at her eyes, almost angrily, and then she continues. "We live our lives. We date other people. We fall in love with our dead brother's wives. And in the end, we see what happens. Well, we've reached the end, Ben. A little early, but it's *definitely* the end."

I look past her, too ashamed to make eye contact with her. "We still have two more years, Fallon. We don't have to end it today."

She shakes her head. "I know I promised, but . . . I can't. There's no way in hell I'm putting myself through this again. You have no idea what this feels like," she says, holding her hand to her chest.

"Actually, Fallon. I know *exactly* what it feels like."

I peg her with my stare, wanting her to

see that I'm not taking all the blame for this. If she wouldn't have walked away last year and completely devastated me, I wouldn't have spent the majority of the year resenting her. I would have never put myself in a position with anyone — much less Jordyn — to risk what I could have had with Fallon. But I thought Fallon only felt a fraction of what I felt for her.

She has no idea how heartbroken she left me. She has no idea that Jordyn was there for me when she wasn't. I was there for Jordyn when Kyle wasn't. And after losing two people we both loved, only later to be united with Oliver . . . it wasn't something we planned. I'm not even sure I wanted it. But it happened, and now I'm the only father Oliver knows. And why does it all feel so wrong now? Why does it feel like I somehow fucked up my life even more?

Fallon pushes around me to try and open the door to her car. And that's when it feels like I've been punched in the gut.

I can't breathe.

I don't know why it took me this long to notice. I grab her hand and squeeze it before she opens the door. The quiet plea forces her to pause and look up at me.

I look at her car for a beat and then back at her. "Why did you drive here today?"

Confusion clouds her expression. She shakes her head, "That was our agreement. It's November 9th."

I squeeze her hand even harder. "Exactly. You usually come straight from the airport when we meet. Why are you in a car and not a cab?"

She stares up at me, defeat consuming her eyes. She expels a quick breath and looks at the ground. "I moved back," she says with a shrug. "Surprise."

Her words impale my chest, and I wince. "When?"

"Last month."

I lean against her car and bury my face in the palms of my hands, trying to keep it together. I came here today, hoping for clarity. Hoping that seeing Fallon would stop the war that's been raging inside of me since things started up with Jordyn.

And clarity is exactly what I'm getting. Since the second I walked into the restaurant and laid eyes on her, that feeling was back in my chest. The one I've never felt with any other girl. The feeling that makes me so terrified, I think my heart is about to burst right out of me.

I've never had that feeling with anyone but Fallon, but I still don't know if that's enough to make a difference. Because

Fallon was right when she said it isn't about what *I* want. It's about what's better for Oliver. But even that doesn't seem like sound logic when I'm standing right in front of the only girl who has ever made me feel this way.

Now that Oliver is sound asleep in the car next to us and no longer in my arms, I pull Fallon to me. I wrap my arms around her desperately, needing to feel her against me. I close my eyes and try to think of words that will fix this, but the only words that come are all the things I shouldn't say. "How did we let this happen?"

I know as soon as the words leave my mouth that I'm being unfair to Jordyn. But Jordyn is also being unfair to me, because she'll never love me like she loved Kyle. And she has to know that I'll never feel about her the way I feel for Fallon.

Fallon tries to pull away, but I hold her tight. "Wait. Please just answer one question."

She relents and stays wrapped in my arms.

"Did you move back to L.A. for me? For us?"

As soon as I ask the question, I can feel her deflate. I can feel my heart tumbling down the walls of my chest. Her lack of denial forces me to squeeze her tighter.

"Fallon," I whisper. "*God,* Fallon." I lift her chin and force her to look up at me. "Do you love me?"

Her eyes grow wide with fear, as if she has no clue what the answer to that question is. Or maybe the question scares her because she knows exactly how she feels about me, but she wishes she didn't feel that way. I ask her again. I plead with her this time. "*Please.* I can't make this decision until I know that I'm not alone in how I feel about you."

She looks me pointedly in the eyes with an adamant shake of her head. "I'm not about to compete with a woman who is raising a child on her own, Ben. I won't be the one who took you from her when she's already been through too much. So don't worry, you don't have to make any decisions. I just made it for you."

She tries to push past me, but I grab her face and try to plead with her. I can see the resolve in her eyes before I even speak. "Please," I whisper. "Not again. We can't make it through this if you walk away again."

She looks up at me, vexed. "You didn't give me a choice this time, Ben. You showed up in love with someone else. You share another woman's bed. Your hands touch someone who isn't me. Your lips make promises against skin that isn't mine. And no matter who is at fault for that, whether it's mine for walking away last year or yours for not knowing I did it for your own good, none of it changes things. It is what it is." She slips from my grasp and opens her car door, looking up at me through damp lashes. "They're lucky to have you. You're a really great father to him, Ben." She gets in her car, completely unaware that she's about to pull away with my heart. I stand here, frozen, unable to stop her. Unable to speak. Unable to plead. Because I know there's nothing I could say that would change things. Not today, anyway. Not until I make things right in all the other areas of my life.

She rolls down her window, wiping another tear from her cheek. "I won't be back next year. I'm sorry if this ruined your book, that's the last thing I wanted. But I just can't do this anymore."

She can't give up for good. I grip the door of her car and lean in to the open window. "*Fuck* the book, Fallon. It was never about the book. It was about you, it always was."

She stares at me, silent. And then she rolls up her window and pulls away, never once slowing down as I pound on the back of her car, chasing her until I can't anymore.

"Shit!" I yell, kicking at the gravel beneath

my feet. I kick it again, stirring up dust. "Goddammit!"

How am I supposed to go back to Jordyn now when I no longer have a heart to give her?

■ ■ ■ ■

Fifth November 9th

■ ■ ■ ■

My flaws are draped in her mercy
Revered by her false perception
And with her lips upon my skin
She will undress my deception.
— Benton James Kessler

Fallon

Previously, when I would think about events in my life, I would organize those events chronologically in my mind as *before the fire* and *after the fire.*

I don't do that anymore. Not because I've grown as a person. Quite the opposite, actually, because now I think about my life in terms of *before Benton James Kessler* and *after Benton James Kessler.*

Pathetic, I know. And even more so because it's been exactly a year since we went our separate ways and I still think about him just as much as I did before *after Benton James Kessler.* But it's not so easy to rid my thoughts of someone who had such an impact on my life.

I don't wish ill on him. I never have. Especially after seeing how torn he was with his decision when we parted ways last year. I'm sure if I cried and begged him to choose me, he would have. But I would never want to be with anyone because I had to beg. I don't even want to be with anyone if there's even a remote possibility that there's a third party at play. Love should be between two people, and if it isn't, I'd rather bow out than take part in the race.

I'm not one to believe things happen for a reason, so I refuse to believe it was our fate not to end up together. If I believed that, then I'd have to believe it was fate for Kyle to die at such a young age. I'd much rather believe shit just happens.

Injured in a fire? *Shit happens.*

Lost your career? *Shit happens.*

Lost the love of your life to a widow with an infant? *Shit happens.*

The last thing I want to believe is that my fate has already been mapped out for me and I get no say in where or who I end up with. But if that's the case and my life will turn out the same in the end, no matter what choices I make, then why does it matter if I leave my apartment tonight?

It doesn't. But Amber seems to think it's a big deal.

"You can't stay here and mope," she says, plopping down on the couch next to me.

"I'm not moping."

"Yes, you are."

"Am not."

"Then why won't you come out with us?"

"I don't want to be a third wheel."

"Then call Teddy."

"Theodore," I correct.

"You know I can't call him Theodore with a straight face. That name should be reserved for members of the royal family."

I wish she would get past his name. I've been out with him several times now and she still brings it up every time. She can see the irritation on my face, so she continues to defend herself.

"He wears pants with tiny, embroidered *whales* on them, Fallon. And the two times I've gone out with you guys, all he does is tell stories about being raised in Nantucket. But no one in Nantucket talks like a surfer, I can promise you that."

She's right. He talks about Nantucket like everyone should be jealous he's from there. But besides that small quirk and his pretentious choice in pants, he's one of the only guys I've been around that can take my mind off Ben for more than an hour.

"If you hate him as much as you seem to, why are you insisting I invite him out with us tonight?"

"I don't hate him," Amber says. "I just don't like him. And I'd rather you come tonight with him than sit here and mope about how it's November 9th and you aren't spending it with Ben."

"That's not why I'm moping," I lie.

"Maybe not, but at least we can both agree that you *are* moping." She picks up my phone. "I'm texting Teddy to tell him to meet us at the club."

"That's going to be awkward for you and Glenn, considering I won't even be there."

"Hogwash. Get dressed. Wear something cute."

She always wins. I'm here . . . at the club. Not at home, moping on my couch where I wish I could be.

And why did Theodore have to wear the pants with whales on them again? That just makes Amber the winner *and* right.

"Theodore," Amber says, fingering the rim of her almost-empty drink. "Do you have a nickname or does everyone just call you Theodore?"

"Just Theodore," he says. "My father is referred to as Teddy, so the nickname gets confusing if we both use it. Especially when we're back in Nantucket around family."

"Riveting," she says, dragging her eyes over to me. "Want to walk to the bar with me?"

I nod and scoot out of the booth. As we

make our way to the bar, Amber threads her fingers through mine and squeezes. "Please tell me you haven't had sex with him."

"We've only been out four times," I tell her. "I'm not that easy."

"You had sex with Ben on the third date," she says in retort.

I hate that she brought up Ben, but I guess when you're discussing your sex life, the only guy you've ever slept with is surely going to be part of the conversation.

"Maybe so, but that was different. We knew each other a lot longer than that."

"You knew each other for three days," she says. "You can't count entire years when you only interacted once a year."

We reach the bar. "Change of subject," I say. "What do you want to drink?"

"Depends," she says. "Are we drinking because we want to remember this night forever? Or because we want to forget the past?"

"Definitely forget."

Amber turns to the bartender and orders four shots. When he puts them in front of us, we hold up the first shot and clink our glasses together.

"To waking up on November 10th and having no memory of the 9th," she says.

"Cheers to that."

We down the shots and then immediately follow those up with the next two. I don't usually drink a lot, but I'll do whatever it takes to speed up the night just so I can get it over with.

Half an hour passes and the shots have definitely done their job. I'm feeling good and buzzed, and I don't even mind it that Theodore is being a little handsy tonight. Amber and Glenn left the booth a couple of minutes ago to hit the dance floor, and Theodore is telling me all about . . . *shit.* I have no idea what he's talking about. I don't think I've been listening to him at all.

Glenn slides back into the booth across from us and I try to stay focused on Theodore's face so he'll think I'm listening to him jabber about some fishing trip he takes with his cousin during summer solstice. When the hell is summer solstice, anyway?

"Can I help you?" Theodore says to Glenn, which is odd, considering he said it in an unpleasant tone. I turn to face Glenn.

Only . . . it's not Glenn.

Brown eyes are staring back at me and I suddenly want to push Theodore's hands off of me and crawl across the table.

Fuck you, fate. Fuck you to hell.

A slow smile spreads across Ben's face as he returns his attention to Theodore. "Sorry to interrupt," Ben says, "but I'm going from table to table, asking couples a few questions for a paper I'm working on for grad school. Do you mind if I ask you two a few?"

Theodore relaxes once he realizes Ben isn't here to mark his territory. Or so he thinks. "Yeah, sure," Theodore says. He reaches across the table to shake his hand. "I'm Theodore, this is Fallon," he says, introducing me to the only man who has ever been inside me.

"Nice to meet you, Fallon," Ben says, clasping my hand with both of his. He makes a quick brush of his thumbs over my wrist, and the contact of his skin on mine is scorching. When he releases my hand, I look down at my wrist, sure it left a mark.

"I'm Ben."

I raise what I'm hoping comes off as an uninterested, lazy eyebrow. *What in the world is he doing here?*

Ben's gaze slides from my eyes to my mouth, but then he focuses on Theodore. "So how long have you lived in Los Angeles, Theodore?"

So many things to process in my alcohol-riddled mind right now.

Ben is here.

Here.

And he's probing my date for information.

"Most of my life. Going on twenty years, I guess."

I glance at Theodore. "I thought you grew up in Nantucket."

He shifts in his seat and laughs, squeezing my hand that's resting on top of the table. "I was born there. Wasn't raised there. We moved here when I was four." He turns his attention back to Ben, and *dammit,* Amber wins again.

"So," Ben says, pointing a finger back and forth between Theodore and me. "You two dating?"

Theodore puts his arm around me and pulls me against him. "Working on it," he says, smiling down at me. But then he looks back at Ben. "These are oddly personal questions. What kind of paper are you writing?"

Ben pops his neck with his hand. "I'm studying the probability of soul mates."

Theodore chuckles. "Soul mates? That's graduate-level work? God help us."

Ben raises an eyebrow. "You don't believe in soul mates?"

Theodore wraps his arm around me and leans back in his seat. "Are you saying you do? Have you met your soul mate?" Theodore glances around the room half-jokingly. "Is she here with you tonight? What's her name? Cinderella?"

My eyes slowly make the journey to Ben's. I'm not sure I want to hear her name yet. He's eyeing me hard, trading glances with the fingers that are sliding up and down my arm.

"She's not here with me," Ben says. "In fact, I was actually stood up by her today. Waited for over four hours but she never showed."

His words are like icicles. Beautiful and sharp as a knife. I swallow the lump in my throat.

He actually showed up? Even after I told him last year I wasn't coming? His words are doing too many things to me right now, and it feels all wrong since I'm sidled up next to a guy I wish would stop touching me.

"What girl is worth waiting four hours for?" Theodore says with a laugh.

Ben leans back in his seat, but I'm eyeing his every movement. "Just this one," he says quietly, to no one in particular. Or maybe his words were only meant for me.

Speaking of Amber. Or maybe I *wasn't* speaking of Amber, I can't remember now that Ben is here and my brain isn't functioning properly. But Amber is back.

My eyes grow wide when I look up at her. She's looking between me and Ben like one of us is a mirage. I totally get it, because I feel the same way. Might just be the alcohol, though. I shake my head and widen my eyes to let her know not to acknowledge that she knows Ben. Hopefully she understands my silent instructions.

Glenn is walking up behind her and I try to do the same with him, but as soon as he reaches the booth, he smiles and yells, "Ben!" He slides in next to him and throws an arm around him like he's just found his best friend.

Yeah, Glenn's drunk.

"You know this guy?" Theodore says, pointing at Ben.

Glenn starts to point at me, and that's when he sees the look on my face. Good thing he's not too drunk to decipher it. "Ummm . . ." He stutters. "We . . . um. We met earlier. In the bathroom."

Theodore chokes on his drink. "You met in the *bathroom*?"

I take the opportunity to slide out of the booth, in desperate need of a break. This is way too much.

"Want me to come with you?" Amber

asks, grabbing my elbow.

I shake my head. I think we both know I'm hoping Ben follows me so he can explain what the hell he's doing here.

I walk quickly toward the bathroom, slightly embarrassed by how fast I just made a break for it. It's funny how a grown adult can just forget how to function properly in the presence of someone else. But I feel like my insides are so hot, they're beginning to scorch my bones. My cheeks are warm. My neck is warm. Everything is warm. I need to splash water on my face.

I walk into the bathroom and even though I don't need to pee, I do anyway. I'm wearing a skirt that Amber forced me to put on and it's so easy to use the bathroom when you're in a skirt, it's stupid not to take advantage of the opportunity. Besides, I'm pretty sure I'm getting a cab home right after I punch Ben in the face, so I might as well use the restroom while I'm here.

Why am I justifying the fact that I'm peeing?

Maybe because I really know all I'm doing is wasting time. I'm not sure I want to step out of the bathroom yet.

As I'm washing my hands, I notice how bad they're shaking. I take several calming breaths while I stare at my reflection in the mirror. Looking in the mirror now is a lot different than it was before I met Ben. I don't obsess over my flaws like I used to. The occasional insecurities are still there, but thanks to Ben, I've learned to accept myself for who I am and be grateful that I'm alive. Part of me hates that he gets some of the credit for my confidence, because I want to hate him. My life would be so much easier if I could hate him, but the guy is hard to hate when he's had such a positive impact on my life. It's the negative impact he's had on my life for the past year that makes me appreciate Amber for forcing me to make an effort tonight with my appearance. I'm wearing a slinky purple top that brings out the green in my eyes, and my hair has grown a few inches since last year. At least Ben is seeing this version of me rather than the version of me that was moping on the couch two hours ago. I don't want to exact revenge on the guy, but it would be nice if, when he looks at me, he feels as though he missed out. I would feel a little vindicated that he fell in love with another girl if I knew he was experiencing a few pangs of regret.

So many questions run through my mind as I finish up at the sink. Why isn't he here with Jordyn? Did they break up? Why is he even here? How did he know *I'd* be here?

Or did he just show up by chance? And what was he expecting when he went to that restaurant today, hoping I'd be there?

My reflection reveals no answers, so I make the brave journey to the bathroom exit, knowing he's probably out there somewhere. Waiting.

No sooner than I have the bathroom door open, a hand grips my arm and pulls me further down the hallway, away from the crowd. I don't even have to look at him to know it's him. My whole body feels the familiar hum of electricity that moves between us anytime we're together.

My back is against a wall, hands are beside my head, his eyes are boring into mine. "How serious is it with *Whale Pants* back there?"

Dammit if he doesn't make me laugh right off the bat. I groan. "I hate those pants."

A crooked, smug grin spreads across his face, but as soon as it appears, it disappears, replaced by a flicker of disappointment. "Why didn't you show up today?" he asks.

I can no longer tell a difference between the beat of my heart and the base of the music. They're in perfect sync, one no louder than the other, thanks to Ben's proximity.

"I told you last year I wasn't going to show

up today." I glance down the hallway, toward the club. It's dark back here, past the bathrooms, past the people. Somehow, in a building full of warm bodies, we have complete privacy. "How did you know I'd be here tonight?"

He gives his head a dismissive shake. "The answer to that question isn't nearly as significant as the answer to mine. How serious is it with this guy?"

His voice is low, his face close to mine. I can feel warmth radiating from his skin. It's hard to concentrate in this kind of distracting environment.

"I forgot what question you just asked me." I sway a little bit, but his fingers splay out against my hip and he steadies me.

He narrows his eyes. "Are you drunk?"

"Tipsy. Big difference. How's *Jordyn*?" I don't know why I say her name with spite. I don't harbor any resentment toward her. Okay, maybe just a little bit. But not much, because Oliver is such a cute kid and it's hard to be mad at someone who can make such a cute kid.

Ben sighs, glancing away for a split second. "Jordyn is fine. They're good."

Good. Good for them. Good for him and Oliver and their adorable fucking little family.

"That's nice, Ben. I need to get back to my date." I try to push past him, but he leans in closer, sandwiching me against the wall. His forehead meets the side of my head. He lets out a sigh and feeling the breath fall from his lips and rush through my hair forces me to squeeze my eyes shut.

"Don't be like that," he whispers into my ear. "I've been through hell today trying to find you."

I cringe from the way his words twist my stomach into knots. He slides his arms around me and pulls me into him. He feels stronger. More defined. Even more like a man this year. I'm stiff against him as I ask my next question. "Are you still with her?"

He looks crestfallen as he says, "You know me better than that, Fallon. If I had a girlfriend, I certainly wouldn't be standing here trying to convince you to come home with me." He studies my face for a reaction, scrolling over each of my features with desire-filled eyes. I try not to notice, but he's pressed against me, my thigh firm between both of his legs. It's obvious by the scorching hardness pressed against my thigh that the look in his eyes is genuine.

Feeling him like this again — his mouth dangerously close to mine — reminds me of the night I spent with him. The only night

I've ever allowed a man to completely consume me, heart, body, and soul — and the thought of what he was able to do to me that night almost forces me to whimper.

But I'm stronger than my hormones. I have to be. I can't go through another heartbreak like the one I'm still healing from. The wounds are still so fresh, it's as if he's clawing them open with his bare hands.

"Come home with me," he whispers.

No. No, no, no, Fallon.

I shake my head back and forth with immense effort in order to ensure I don't accidentally nod. "No, Ben. *No.* This past year has been the hardest year of my life. You can't expect me to just fall back into step with you because you showed up here tonight."

He runs the backs of his fingers across my cheekbone. "I don't expect that, Fallon. But I do pray for it. Every night, down on my knees, to any God who will listen."

His words feel like they penetrate the walls of my chest and all the air is let out of my lungs. I close my eyes when his breath grazes my jaw. He's taking advantage of the privacy and my weakness and I want to punch him for it, but first I just need to know if he tastes the same. If his tongue still moves the same way. If he still touches me like it's a privilege.

I'm being supported by a wall behind me and Ben in front of me, but still, when his hand drops to my thigh and his fingers begin slowly raking up my skirt, I feel like I'm about to crash straight to the floor. There's so much that needs to be discussed between us, but for whatever reason, my body wants my mouth to stay shut so his hand will continue moving. I've missed his touch so much, and even though I've made the effort to go out and try to get over Ben, I'm not sure I could ever find this kind of physical connection with another person. No one makes me feel as desirable as Ben does. I've missed it. The way he looks at me, the way he touches me, the way he makes it feel as if my scars are an improvement rather than a flaw. It's hard to say no to this feeling, no matter how hurt I've been over what transpired last year.

"Ben," I whisper, not so much in protest as I intended for his name to sound. He buries his face against my neck and breathes me in, and I forget everything I was about to protest. My head drops back against the wall, and then his hand slides around to the back of my thigh. His fingers graze the edge of my panties and when I feel them slip just beneath the hem, my whole body shudders.

I'm forced to bury my face against his shoulder and grip the back of his shirt just to keep myself upright. All he did was touch my ass and I feel like I can't even stand upright anymore. I should be embarrassed.

He pulls back, just a little bit, so that he can glance over his shoulder. I don't know who or what he's looking for, but when he sees no one is behind us, he reaches to the right of me — to a door. He pulls on the handle and it relents. Ben doesn't waste a second. He grabs me by the waist and pushes me toward the door, into the dark room, and then the door closes behind us, muffling the sound of the music.

Now I can hear how hard I'm breathing. Panting, really. But so is he. I can hear him right in front of me, but I can't see him. I hear him feeling around the room. It's pitch black, and the absence of the wall behind me and him in front of me makes me feel empty.

But then his hands are back on my waist. "Storage room," he says, pushing me until my back is to the door. "Perfect." And then I feel his breath against my lips, followed closely by his mouth as it brushes against mine. As soon as I feel it — the surge of electricity that shoots from his mouth to every nerve in my body — I push against his chest.

I open my mouth to protest, but I'm met with heat and tongue and lips that know just how to make it all work together. Instead of the word *stop* coming at him, all he gets is a moan and a hand in his hair, pulling, pushing, indecisive.

He pushes against me, his leg between both of mine. He's kissing me so hard, my mind is still wrapped around all the ways his tongue can move before I even notice his hand has moved around to the front of my thigh. And I know I should stop him. I should push him away and make him explain himself, but his hand feels too good for that right now. My legs tense and I grip the sleeve of his shirt with one hand while I pull on his hair with the other hand, tearing him away from my mouth so I can breathe. I take in one deep breath before he's back on my mouth, even hungrier than before.

And his hand. Oh, God, his fingers are slowly tracing up the front of my panties. I moan again. Twice. He puts just enough space between our mouths so that he can listen to me gasp as he slides his hand down the front of my panties.

My knees grow weak. I'm not sure I knew my body was capable of feeling these kinds of things. I think I just fell in love with my body a little bit more.

"Jesus, Fallon," Ben says, stroking me, breathing heavily against my mouth. "You're so wet."

As delicious as it feels to hear that, I can't help but laugh out loud. When I do, I quickly slap my hand over my mouth, but it's already too late. He heard my laughter in the midst of the most mind-blowing act of seduction I've ever been a part of.

He drops his forehead to the side of my head and I hear him laughing quietly. His mouth rests against my ear and I swear I can hear the smile in his voice when he says, "God, I've missed you so damn much."

That one sentence affects me more than anything he's said all night, and I don't know if it's because it felt like the old Fallon and Ben for a second, or if it's because he removes his hand and wraps his arms around me, pulling me into one of his soul-crushing embraces. His forehead rests against mine, and I almost wish he would have kept going with the physical stuff, because that's way easier than the emotional stuff.

As good as it feels to be back in his arms again, I'm scared I'm screwing up. I don't know what to do. I don't know if I should let him back into my life so easily, because the getting together part should be just as hard as the letting go part and this feels way too easy for him. I need time, I think. I don't know. I don't feel capable of making this kind of decision right now.

"Fallon," he says, his voice low.

"Yeah?" I breathe out.

"Come home with me. I want to talk to you, but I don't want to do it here."

We're back to this again. It makes me wonder if he's being so persistent because there's only a few hours left of November 9th and he wants to make the most of it, or if he wants me on all the other days, too.

I feel behind me for the door handle. When I find it, I push against Ben's chest and pull the door open. When I slip outside, his hand is on my right elbow and someone else grasps my left elbow. I gasp, just as my eyes meet Amber's.

"I was looking for you," she says. "What are you doing in . . ." Her question comes to a halt when she sees Ben walk out behind me. And then, "Sorry to interrupt this reunion, but Teddy is worried about you."

She's looking at me like she's disappointed in my decision to be making out in a dark closet with Ben while my date is in the same building, and *Oh, my God,* now that I think about it, that's a really shit thing to do.

"Crap!" I say. "I have to get back to the table."

Ben makes a face like that's the last thing he expected to come out of my mouth.

"Good choice," Amber says, eyeing Ben.

He can find me later. I have to get back to the table before Theodore realizes how pathetic I am. I follow Amber back to the booth, but luckily it's loud enough that I can't understand anything she's saying. I can tell she's lecturing me, though. We no more than slide back into our booth when Ben pulls up a chair and plops it down at the end of the table. He takes a seat and folds his arms in front of him.

Theodore puts his arm around my shoulders and leans in. "You okay?"

I force a quick smile and a nod, but I give him nothing more, considering Ben looks like he's about to crawl over the table and rip Theodore's arm away from my body.

I adjust myself so that Theodore doesn't think I'm reciprocating his affection. I lean forward, away from his arm, as if I have something I want to say to Amber. Just as I open my mouth, Ben's hand strokes my knee beneath the table. My eyes swing to Ben's and he shoots me an innocent look.

Luckily, Glenn steals Theodore's attention, so he doesn't notice when my entire body tenses. Ben begins to rake his fingers up my thigh, so I reach beneath the table and flick his hand away. He smiles and leans back in his seat.

"So," Amber says, turning her attention toward Ben. "Since we all just met you fifteen minutes ago and know absolutely nothing about you, since we've never been around you before, because we're all complete strangers, why don't you tell us about yourself? What do you do? Theodore says you're a writer? Are you writing anything interesting? A love story, maybe? How's that going?"

I kick Amber under the table. Could she be more obvious?

Ben laughs, and now that Amber just spat out the most random question in the world, Theodore and Glenn are both staring at Ben, waiting for him to answer.

"Well," Ben says, straightening up in his seat. "As a matter of fact, yes. I am a writer. I've had a really bad case of writer's block this year, though. Really terrible. Haven't written a single word in 365 days. But oddly enough, I think I just had a major breakthrough a few minutes ago."

"Imagine that," Amber says, rolling her eyes.

I lean forward, deciding to join in on this

cryptic conversation. "You know, Ben. Writer's block can be a tricky thing. Just because you had a breakthrough a few minutes ago doesn't mean it's permanent."

He pretends to give my comment a moment of thought, but then he shakes his head. "No. No, I know a breakthrough when I have one. And I'm certain that what I experienced a few minutes ago was one of the most mind-blowing breakthroughs known to man."

I raise an eyebrow. "There's a fine line between confidence and cockiness."

Ben matches my expression as his hand returns to my leg under the table, causing me to stiffen. "Well then, I'm straddling that line like it's the thigh of a long-legged brunette."

Oh, dear God those words.

Glenn laughs, but Theodore leans forward to get Ben's attention. "I have an uncle back in Nantucket who had a book published. It's a pretty hard thing to —"

"Theodore," Ben says, interrupting him. "You seem like a . . . nice guy."

"Thanks," Theodore says, smiling.

"Let me finish," Ben says, holding up a finger in warning. "Because you're about to hate me. I lied. I'm not writing a paper." He points at Glenn. "This guy told me earlier today where to show up tonight so that I could find the girl I'm supposed to spend the rest of my life with. And I'm sorry, but that girl just so happens to be your date. And I'm in love with her. Like, *really* in love with her. Crippling, debilitating, paralyzing love. So please accept my sincerest apologies, because she's coming home with me tonight. I hope. I pray." Ben shoots me an endearing look. "Please? Otherwise this speech will make me look like a complete fool and that won't be good when we tell our grandkids about this." He holds out his hand for me to take, but I'm as frozen in place as poor Theodore is.

Glenn covers his mouth, trying to hide his drunken laughter. Amber is actually speechless for once.

"What the *fuck*?" Theodore says. Before I can move out of his way, Theodore is reaching over me, grabbing the collar of Ben's shirt, pulling him closer so that he can choke him or punch him or . . . I'm not sure what he's doing, but I duck and crawl out of the booth so I'm not in the middle of it. When I turn around, Theodore is on his knees in the booth with Ben in a headlock over the table. Ben is grasping at Theodore's arm, trying to pull it away from his throat.

His eyes are wide and he's looking straight at me.

"You fucking prick!" Theodore yells.

Ben lets go of Theodore's arm with one hand and crooks his finger at me, wanting me to come closer. I take a hesitant step forward, not sure what to do to get him out of this mess. When I'm about two feet from them, Ben struggles to speak. "Fallon," he says, still clawing at the arm that's wrapped around his neck. "Are you . . . are you gonna come home with me or not?"

Oh, my God. He's relentless. And he's being pulled away from Theodore's chokehold by two bouncers who are intervening. But now both Ben and Theodore are being escorted outside, and Amber, Glenn, and I are following after them. Before we reach the door, Amber punches Glenn in the shoulder.

"You told Ben where we were gonna be tonight?" she hisses.

Glenn rubs his arm. "He showed up at our apartment today looking for Fallon."

Amber scoffs. "So you just told him where she would be? Why would you do that?"

"He's *funny*!" Glenn says, as if that's a legit defense.

Amber glances over her shoulder at me with an apologetic look. I don't tell her there's nothing to feel bad about. So far, I'm kind of glad Glenn told Ben where I'd be tonight. It makes me feel good to know that he waited at the restaurant for four hours and then went looking for me at my old apartment, hoping Amber and Glenn still lived there. It's a little bit flattering, even though it still doesn't make up for what he put me through.

As soon as we're outside, I immediately walk over to Theodore, who is pacing the pavement with a pissed-off look in his eye. He stops when he sees me standing in front of him and he points in Ben's direction. "Is that true?" he says. "Are the two of you like . . . fuck, I don't know. What are you? Dating? Exes? Do I even fit in the picture or am I wasting my goddamn time?"

I shake my head, completely at a loss. I don't know how to answer that, because I honestly don't know where I stand with Ben. But I do know where I stand with Theodore, so I guess I'll start there.

"I'm sorry," I say. "I swear, before tonight I haven't spoken to him in a year. I don't want you to think I was seeing both of you at the same time, but . . . I'm sorry. Maybe I just need some time to figure it out, I guess."

Theodore cocks his head, as if he's

shocked by what he just heard. "Figure it out?" He shakes his head. "I don't have time for this shit." He starts to walk in the opposite direction, but he's still within earshot when he mutters, "You aren't even that pretty."

I'm still processing the insult when I see Ben sprint past me. Before my eyes can even adjust, his fist is flying. I see Glenn rush to intervene, but . . . wait. No. Glenn *also* punches Theodore.

Luckily, the bouncers never even made it back inside and all three of them are separated before anyone is seriously injured. Theodore is struggling to break free from one of the bouncers and he's yelling obscenities at Ben the entire time. Meanwhile, Amber is standing next to me, steadying herself on a parking meter while she unfastens one of her heels.

"I want every one of you to leave the premises right now before we call the police!" one of the bouncers yells.

"Hold on," Amber says, holding up a finger while she pulls off her shoe. "I'm not finished." She takes her shoe in her hand and glowers at Theodore, then rears back and throws it across the sidewalk, hitting him square between the legs. "I hate your stupid pants, asshole!" she yells. "Fallon deserves better than you, and SO DOES NANTUCKET!"

Wow. Go, Amber.

The bouncer holding Theodore asks him where his car is parked. He escorts Theodore in that direction as Amber retrieves her shoe. Ben and Glenn aren't released until the bouncer returns without Theodore. "The four of you. Leave. Now."

As soon as the bouncer releases Ben's arms, he runs straight toward me, taking my face in his hands, inspecting me to see if I'm hurt. Or maybe he's checking my emotions, I don't know. Either way, he looks worried. "Are you okay?"

I can tell by the soothing sound of his voice that he's worried Theodore hurt my feelings. "I'm fine, Ben. That guy's insults about my appearance don't carry much weight when he willingly wears those pants."

I can see the relief in Ben's smile as he kisses me on the forehead.

"Did you bring a car?" Glenn asks, directing his question at Ben. Ben nods and says, "Yeah. I'll give the two of you a ride home."

"The *three* of you," I say to Ben, insinuating that just because he stood up for me doesn't mean I'm automatically going home to his place. "I'll need you to drop me off at my apartment."

Amber groans and then brushes my shoulder as she passes. "Just forgive him already," she says. "Glenn found a member of the male species he actually likes, and if you don't forgive Ben you'll break Glenn's heart."

Ben and Glenn are both quietly staring at me. Glenn is giving me puppy dog eyes and Ben's bottom lip is protruding.

I can't even. I shrug my shoulder in defeat. "Well, then. I guess if *Glenn* likes you, then that's that. I have to go home with you."

Ben doesn't even break eye contact with me when he holds out a stretched arm toward Glenn, his hand in a fist. Glenn bumps it and then they drop their arms, never saying a word.

As I pass Ben and head for the parking lot, I narrow my eyes at him and point. "You have a lot of explaining to do, though. *A lot.* And even more groveling."

"I'm very capable of both of those things," Ben says, following after me.

"And you have to cook me breakfast," I add. "I like well-done bacon and over-easy eggs."

"Got it," Ben says. "Explain myself, then grovel, then Nakey-nakey, eggs, and bakey." He puts his arm around my shoulder and redirects me to his car. He opens the passenger door for me, but before he climbs inside, he cups my face and presses his lips to mine. When he pulls back, I'm shocked by how much emotion is in his expression after the ridiculousness of the past fifteen minutes. "You won't regret this, Fallon. I promise."

I hope not.

He kisses me on the cheek and waits for me to climb inside his car.

Hands grasp my shoulders from behind and Glenn's face appears next to mine from the backseat. "I promise, too," he says, giving me a loud smack on the cheek.

As we pull out of the parking lot, I stare out my window because I don't want the three of them to see the tears in my eyes.

Because yes, hearing Theodore insult me didn't only hurt my feelings — it was easily one of the most embarrassing moments of my life. But knowing these three defended me without a second thought almost makes the insult worth it.

Ben

It's quiet after we drop Glenn and Amber off for at least a solid mile. She's been staring out the window the entire drive and I wish she would look at me. I know what I put her through last year hurt her more than I can probably imagine, and I hope she realizes that I'm going to make it right. If it takes me the rest of my life, I'll make it right. I reach over and grab her hand.

"I need to apologize," I say to her. "I shouldn't have said those things —"

She shakes her head, silently interrupting me. "Don't take it back. I thought it was admirable that you were honest with Theodore. Most men would be too chicken to say anything and would just steal the girl behind their friend's back."

She has no idea what I even feel bad about.

"I wasn't apologizing for that. I'm apologizing because I should have never said I was in love with you out loud like that, when the words weren't spoken directly to you. You deserve more than a secondhand I love you."

She regards me silently, but then she looks out her window again. I look back at the road, and then steal another glance in her direction. I can see her cheek lift in a smile as she squeezes my hand. "Maybe if the explaining and groveling go well tonight, you can give the *I love you* another shot before you cook me breakfast tomorrow."

I smile, because I know without a doubt the groveling and breakfast will be a piece of cake.

It's the explaining that I'm dreading. We still have at least a fifteen-minute drive, so I decide to go ahead and get started.

"I moved out right after Christmas last year. Ian and I let Jordyn and Oliver have the house."

I can feel the tensing of her hand in mine just at the mention of Jordyn's name. I hate that. I hate that I put that there and I hate that it's always going to be in the back of her head, for the rest of our lives. Because whether she wants it or not, Jordyn is Oliver's mother and Oliver is like a son to me. They'll always be in my life, no matter what.

"Would you believe me if I told you things

are great with us? With me and Jordyn?"

She gives me a sidelong glance. "Great in what way?"

I pull my hand from hers and grip the steering wheel so that I can squeeze the tension from my jaw with my other hand.

"I want you to hear me out before you speak up, okay? Because I might say some things you don't want to hear, but I need you to hear them."

She nods softly, so I inhale an encouraging breath. "Two years ago . . . when I made love to you . . . I gave everything to you. Heart and soul. But then that night when you made the choice to go an entire year without seeing me again, I couldn't understand what had happened. I didn't understand how I could have felt what I felt, when you felt nothing. And it fucking hurt, Fallon. You left and I was pissed and I can't even tell you how hard those next few months were. I wasn't just grieving Kyle's death, I was grieving the loss of you."

I stare straight ahead because I don't want to see what my words are doing to her. "When Oliver was born, it was the first time I felt happy since the moment you showed up unannounced at my front door. And it was the first time Jordyn smiled since Kyle died. So for the next few months, we spent every minute together with Oliver. Because he was the only bright spot in either of our lives. And when two people both love someone as much as we love him, it creates this bond that I can't even explain. Over the next few months, she and Oliver became the things that filled the massive voids that you and Kyle had left in my heart. And I guess in a way, I filled that void that Kyle had left in *her* heart. When things progressed between us, I don't even know if either of us gave it a prior thought before it happened. But it happened, and no one was there to tell me that I might regret it one day.

"I mean . . . there was even a part of me that believed you would be happy for me when we met up the following November. Because I thought maybe that's what you wanted, was for me to move on and stop holding on to what you viewed as this fictionalized relationship we created when we were eighteen.

"But then when I showed up that day . . . the last thing I expected was for you to be hurt like that. And the second you figured out that I had been seeing Jordyn, I could see in your eyes how much you really did love me and it was one of the worst moments of my life, Fallon. One of the worst fucking moments, and I can still feel the wounds your tears left in my chest every time I breathe."

I grip the steering wheel and blow out a steady breath. "As soon as Jordyn got home that night, she could see the heartache on my face. And she knew she wasn't the girl who put it there. And surprisingly, she wasn't that upset by it. We talked about it for probably two hours straight. About how I felt about you and about how she felt about Kyle and how we knew we were hurting ourselves by maintaining a relationship that would never equal what we'd both had with other people in the past. So we ended it. That day. I moved my stuff out of her room that night and back into mine until I was able to find a new place."

I dare a look in her direction, but she's still staring out the window. I can see her swipe a tear from her eye, and I'm hoping I didn't make her mad. "I'm not at all putting any of the blame on you, Fallon. Okay? I only brought up that year you walked away because I need you to know that it was always you who had my heart. And I would have never let anyone else borrow it if I knew there was a chance in hell you'd ever want it back."

I can see her shoulders shaking, and I hate

that I'm making her cry. I hate it. I don't want her to be sad. She looks at me with eyes spilling over with tears. "What about Oliver?" she asks. "You don't get to live with him anymore?" She swipes at another tear. "I feel *awful,* Ben. I feel like I took you away from your little boy."

She covers her face with her hands and breaks out into sobs and I can't take another second of it. I pull the car over to the side of the road and turn the hazards on. I unbuckle my seat belt and reach across the seat and pull her to me. "Baby, no," I whisper. "Please don't cry about that. Me and Oliver . . . we're perfect. I see him whenever I want, almost every single day. I don't have to live with his mom to love him the same."

I brush my hands through her hair and kiss the side of her head. "It's good. Things are great, Fallon. The only thing not going right in my life is the fact that you aren't a part of it every single day."

She pulls away from my shoulder and sniffs. "That's the only thing not right in *my* life, Ben. Everything else is perfect. I have two of the best friends in the world. I love school. I love my job. I have one and a half great parents." She says the last sentence with a laugh. "But the only thing that makes me sad — the biggest thing — is that I think about you every second of every day and I don't know how to get over you."

"Don't," I beg her. "Please don't get over me."

She shrugs with a half-hearted smile. "I can't. I tried, but I think I'd have to go to AA or something. You're just a part of my chemical makeup now, I think."

I laugh, relieved that she's . . . that she simply *exists.* And that we were lucky enough to exist in the same lifetime, in the same area of the world, in the same state. And that, after all these years, I surprisingly wouldn't change a single thing about what ultimately brought us together.

"Ben?" she says. "You look like you're about to be sick again."

I laugh and shake my head. "I'm not. I just really need to tell you I love you, but I feel like I should warn you before I do that."

"Okay," she says. "Warn me about what?"

"That by agreeing to love me back, you're taking on a huge responsibility. Because Oliver is going to be a part of my life forever. And I'm not talking like an uncle and a nephew, but like he's mine. Birthday parties and baseball games and —"

She puts her hand over my mouth to shut me up. "Loving someone doesn't just include that person, Ben. Loving someone means accepting all the things and people that person loves, too. And I will. I do. I promise."

I *really* don't deserve her. But I pull her to me and slide her between myself and the steering wheel. I pull her mouth to mine and I say, "I love you, Fallon. More than poetry, more than words, more than music, more than your boobs. Both of them. Do you have any idea how much that amounts to?"

She laughs and cries at the same time, and I press my lips to hers, wanting to remember this kiss more than any other kiss I've given her. Even though it only lasts two seconds, because she pulls back and says, "I love you, too. And I think that was a stellar explanation. One that doesn't even need much groveling, so I'd like to go back to your apartment now and make love to you."

I kiss her quick, and then push her back to her side of the car while I prepare to pull back out onto the highway. She puts her seat belt on and says, "But I still expect breakfast tomorrow."

"So technically, we've only spent about twenty-eight total hours together since we met," she says.

We're in my bed. She's draped across me, running her fingers up my chest. As soon as we got back to the apartment, I made love to her. Twice. And if she doesn't stop touching me like this, it's about to happen a third time.

"That's more than enough time to know if you love someone," I say.

We've been counting how much total time we've actually spent together over the course of four years. I honestly thought it would amount to more than that, because it sure does feel like it, but she was right when she said it wouldn't even equal two total days.

"Look at it this way," I say, breaking it down even more. "If we would have had a traditional relationship, we would have gone out on a few dates, maybe one or two a week, lasting a few hours each. That's an average of only twelve hours in the first month. Say you have a couple of overnight dates in the second month. Couples could easily be well into their third month of dating by the time they spend twenty-eight total hours together. And three months is the quintessential month for 'I love yous.' So technically, we're right on track."

She bites her lip to stop her grin. "I like your logic. You know how much I dislike insta-love."

"Oh, it was still insta-love," I tell her. "But ours is legit."

She lifts up onto her elbow, staring down at me. "When did you know? Like which second did you know for sure you were in love with me?"

I don't even hesitate. "Remember when we were kissing on the beach and I sat up and told you I wanted to get a tattoo?"

She smiles. "It was so random, how could I forget?"

"That's why I got the tattoo. Because I knew in that moment that I had fallen in love with a girl for the first time. Like *real* love. *Selfless* love. And my mother told me once that I would know the second I found selfless love, and that I should do something to remember that moment because it doesn't happen for everyone. So . . . yeah."

She picks up my wrist and looks down at my tattoo. She traces it with her index finger. "You got this because of me?" she asks, glancing back up at me. "But what does it mean? Why did you choose the word *poetic*? And a music staff?"

I glance down at my tattoo and wonder if I should really go into detail with her about why I picked it. But that moment would darken this one, and I don't want that.

"Personal reasons," I say, forcing a smile. "And I'll tell you about them one day, but right now I kind of want you to kiss me again."

It doesn't take ten seconds before I have her on her back and I'm buried deep inside her. I make love to her slowly this time — not in a wild rush like we did twice before. I kiss her, from her mouth to her breasts and back up again, softy pressing my lips against every inch of skin that I have the privilege of touching.

And this time when we finish, we don't talk afterward. We both close our eyes, and I know that when I wake up next to her tomorrow morning, I'm going to make it my mission to forgive myself for all the times I withheld the truth from her in the past.

After I make her breakfast.

Fallon

My stomach growls, reminding me that I never even ate dinner last night. I quietly roll out of bed and search for my clothes, but after locating my skirt, I come up empty. I don't want to turn on the light to find my shirt, so I walk to Ben's closet to search for a T-shirt or something to throw on while I go raid his refrigerator.

I feel like an idiot, searching blindly in his closet for a shirt with a smile on my face. But when I woke up this morning, I never expected the day to end this way. *Absolutely perfect.*

I decide to shut the door behind me and flip on the light so it doesn't disturb him. I locate a thin, soft T-shirt and pull it off the hanger. After I get it over my head, I go to flip off the light, but something catches my eye.

On the top shelf, next to a shoebox, is a

thick stack of pages. It looks like a manuscript.

Could it be . . .

My curiosity is piqued. I stretch on my tiptoes until I can reach it, but I only pull off the top page just to see what it is.

■ ■ ■ ■

November 9
by
Benton James Kessler

■ ■ ■ ■

I stare at the sheet for several seconds. Long enough to wage a full-on war with my conscience.

I shouldn't read this. I should put it back.

But I have a right to read it. *I think.* I mean, it's about my relationship with Ben. And I know he said he didn't want me to read it until it was finished, but now that he's no longer writing it, surely that cancels out his one and only rule.

I still haven't decided what to do when I take the entire manuscript off the shelf. I'll take it to the kitchen. I'll get something to eat. And *then* I'll decide what to do with it.

I flip off the light switch and slowly open the closet door. Ben is in the same position, breathing heavily, on the verge of what could be considered a snore.

I walk out of his bedroom and into his kitchen.

I carefully place the manuscript on the table in front of me. I don't know why my hands are shaking. Maybe because his true thoughts about me and us and everything we've been through is all right here in front of me. And what if I don't like his truth? People have a right to privacy, and what I'm about to do is violating every bit of his privacy. It's not a good way to start out a relationship.

What if I just read one scene? Just a couple of pages and then I'll put it back and he'll never know.

I already know what I want to read about. Since the moment it happened, it's been eating at me.

I want to know why Kyle punched him in the hallway during our second year together. It had nothing to do with me, so that should be a safe enough scene to read without feeling too guilty about it afterward.

I do my best to flip through the manuscript without absorbing any of the sentences. Ben makes it easy to find, considering he's divided up the chapters by his age. The fight happened the second year we were together, so I find the chapter labeled, "Age Nineteen" and I pull it in front of me. I skip through his internal dialogue while he waited at the restaurant for me to show up. Hopefully one day he'll let me read this, because I'm dying to know his true thoughts. But I refuse to read all of it. Compromising with my guilt by just reading a few pages still makes me feel like shit. I can imagine how I'd feel if I read the entire thing.

My eyes skim over the page until I see Kyle's name. I pull the page in front of me and begin reading in the middle of a paragraph.

"Everything will be fine, Jordyn. I promise."

The front door opens and she looks up. I can see by the excitement in her eyes that it's more than likely Kyle.

My stomach turns from the nerves that have just become heavier than rocks. *Fuck.* He said he wouldn't be home until after seven tonight.

"Is that Kyle?" I ask Jordyn.

She nods, pushing past me. "He took off early to help me," she says, walking to the sink. She grabs a napkin and dabs at her eyes. "Tell him I'll be right out. I don't want him to know how much I've been crying today, I feel like such a spaz."

Shit.

Maybe he won't remember. It's been so long now and we've never talked about it. I take a deep breath and head back into the living room, trying to hide the panic. He can't ruin this for me.

"All is well with Jordyn," I say as I reenter the living room, hoping to play off my nerves. I stop short when I see him, because the look on his face lets me know he definitely remembers. And he's pissed.

Kyle's jaw hardens. He tosses his keys onto the entry table and points at me. "We need to talk."

At least he's pulling me away from Fallon

to discuss it. That's a relief. It doesn't look like he'll be saying anything in front of her. I can deal with him in private, that's not an issue. I can fight my way out of the shit I've gotten myself into, but the last thing I want is for Fallon to be brought into it.

I smile at Fallon because I can tell by the look on her face that she's aware something is off with Kyle. I want to reassure her that everything is okay, even though it's so far from it. "Be right back." She nods, so I follow Kyle down the hallway. He stops just outside his bedroom door.

He points in the direction of the living room. "Can you please explain to me what the fuck is happening?"

I glance back to the living room, wondering how I can possibly talk my way out of this. But I know there's nothing he'll believe other than the truth.

I put my hands on my hips and look down at the floor. The disappointment in his eyes is hard to see. "We're friends," I tell him. "I met her last year. At a restaurant."

Kyle releases a disbelieving laugh. "Friends?" he says. "Because Ian just introduced her as your fucking *girlfriend,* Ben."

Shit.

I do what I can to diffuse his temper. I've never seen him this angry. "I swear, it's not like that. I just . . ." Dammit, this is so fucked up. I throw my hands up in defeat. "I like her, okay? I can't help it. It's not like that's what I set out to do."

Kyle looks away, running his hands down his face in frustration. When he turns around again, I'm not prepared for what happens. He pushes me, hard, and I slam into the wall behind me. His hands are pressed against my shoulders and he's pinning me against the wall. "Does she know, Ben? Does she have any idea that you're the one who started that fire? That you're the reason she almost *died*?"

I feel my jaw tighten. *He can't do this. Not today. Not to her.* "Shut *up,*" I say through clenched teeth. "*Please.* She's in the other room, for Christ's sake!" I try to push him off me, but he shoves his arm against my throat.

"What kind of fucked-up situation did you get yourself in, Ben? Are you an idiot?"

Just as the question leaves his mouth, I see her walk around the corner. She stops short as she takes in the scene, and the shock that appears on her face reassures me that she didn't hear anything else.

FALLON

I slam the pages back on top of the others.

He's fucked up.

Ben is a twisted, fucked-up writer. How dare he take something real . . . something that I suffered through . . . and turn it into fiction with a ridiculous plotline.

I'm pissed. *How could he do this?* But then again, he didn't finish it, so am I even allowed to be angry?

But *why* would he do this? Doesn't he know how personal that story is to me? I can't believe he would try to capitalize on such an awful tragedy.

I'd almost like it better if he *was* telling the truth and he really *did* start the fire. At least then I wouldn't feel like he was taking advantage of my story.

Why would he make up part of the fight when everything else surrounding the fight between him and Kyle actually happened? Did he even make up any of it at all?

I laugh at myself. It's not true. He didn't meet me until two years after the fire. There was no way he could have been there. Besides, what are the chances he would run into me on the anniversary of the fire, exactly two years later? He would have had to have been following me.

He wasn't following me.

Was he?

I need water.

I get water.

I need to sit down again.

I sit down.

Spin, spin, spin. The web of possible lies is spinning, my mind is spinning, my stomach is spinning. It even feels like the blood in my veins is spinning. I stack the pages of the manuscript back into a neat and tidy pile, just as I found them.

Why would you write this, Ben?

I look at the cover and run my fingers over the title. *November 9.*

He needed a good plot. Is that what he's done? He just fabricated his plotline?

There's no way he could be responsible for the fire. It makes absolutely no sense. My father is to blame. He knows, the police know and I know it.

I find myself lifting the cover page off the stack. I stare down at the first page of the manuscript, and I do the only thing I can to find more answers.

I read.

NOVEMBER 9
BY
BENTON JAMES KESSLER

"To begin, at the beginning."

— Dylan Thomas

Prologue

Every life begins with a mother. Mine is no different.

She was a writer. I'm told my father was a psychiatrist, but I wouldn't know for sure since I never had the chance to ask him. He died when I was three. I have no memory of him, but I suppose it's for the best. It's hard to grieve people you don't remember.

My mother had a master's degree in poetry and completed her thesis on the Welsh poet Dylan Thomas. She quoted him often, although her most favorite quotes weren't from his world-famous poetry, but rather from his everyday dialogue. I never could tell if she respected Dylan Thomas as a poet or a person. Because from what I've learned about him in my research, there wasn't much to respect about his character. Or maybe that's what is to be respected — the fact that Dylan Thomas did little to gain popularity as a person and everything to gain it as a poet.

I suppose I should get on with how my mother died. I should probably also get on with how a girl who inspired me to write this book relates to a story that begins with my mother. And I suppose if I get on with both of those things, I should also get on with how Dylan Thomas relates to my mother's life, most importantly her death, and how both led me to Fallon.

It seems so complicated, when in fact, it's very simple.

Everything relates.

Everything is connected.

And it all begins on November 9th. Two years before I came face to face with Fallon O'Neil for the very first time.

November 9th.

The first and last time my mother would die.

November 9th.

The night I intentionally started the fire that almost claimed the life of the girl who would one day save mine.

FALLON

I stare at the pages in front of me in complete disbelief. Bile rushes up the back of my throat.

What have I done?

I swallow hard to force it back down and it stings.

What kind of monster did I give my heart to?

My hands are shaking. I'm unable to move. I can't decide if I need to read more — to get to the next page where it's obviously going to state that everything I read is a work of Ben's magnificent yet twisted imagination. That he's found a way to make our story marketable by mixing fact and fiction. Do I read more?

Or do I run?

How can I run from someone I've slowly given myself to over the course of four years?

Or is it six?

Has he known me since I was sixteen?

Did he know me the day we met in the restaurant?

Was he there *because* of me?

So much blood, all of it, every drop is rushing through my head, even my ears begin to ache from the pressure. Fear grips my body like I'm a cliff and it's dangling from my ledge. It grips every part of me.

I need to get out of here. I grab my phone and quietly call for a cab.

They say there's one down the street and it will arrive in a few minutes.

I'm consumed by so much fear. Fear of these pages in my hands. Fear of deception. Fear of the man asleep in the next room who I just promised all of my tomorrows to.

I scoot the chair back to get my stuff together, but before I stand, I hear his bedroom door open. On high alert, I swing my head over my shoulder. He's paused in his doorway, wiping sleep from his eyes.

If I could freeze this moment, I would take full advantage so that I could study him. I would run my fingers over his lips to see if they really were as soft as the words that come from them. I would pick up his hands and brush my thumbs over his palms to see if they really felt capable of caressing the scars they were responsible for. I would wrap my arms around him and stand on my tiptoes to whisper in his ear, *"Why didn't you tell me that the foundation you taught me to stand on is made from quicksand?"*

I see his gaze flicker to the pages of his manuscript that are gripped tightly in my hand. In a matter of seconds, every thought he has flashes across his face.

He's wondering how I found it.

He's wondering how much I've read.

Ben the Writer.

I want to laugh, because Benton James Kessler isn't a writer. He's an *actor.* A master of deception who just completed a four-year-long performance.

For the first time, I don't see him as the Ben I fell in love with. The Ben who single-handedly changed my life.

Right now, I see him only as a stranger.

Someone I know absolutely nothing about.

"What are you doing, Fallon?"

His voice makes me flinch. It sounds exactly the same as the voice that said, "I love you," just an hour ago.

Only now, his voice fills me with panic. Terror consumes me as a rush of unease takes over.

I have no idea who he is.

I have no idea what his motive has been these past few years.

I have no idea what he's capable of.

He begins to advance toward me, so I do the only thing I can think to do. I run to the other side of the table, hoping to put a safe distance between myself and this man.

Hurt washes over his face when he sees my reaction, but I have no idea if it's genuine or rehearsed. I have no idea if I should believe everything I just read . . . or if he made it all up for the sake of having a plotline.

I've cried for lots of reasons in my life. Mostly from sadness, sometimes out of frustration or anger. But this is the first time a tear has ever escaped because of fear.

Ben watches the tear roll down my cheek and he holds up a reassuring hand. "Fallon." His eyes are wide, and they hold almost as much fear as mine. But I have no idea anymore if what I see on his face is real. "Fallon, please. Let me explain."

He seems so concerned. So genuine. Maybe it's fiction. Maybe he turned our story into fiction. Surely he didn't do this to me. I point at the manuscript, hoping he doesn't notice the trembling of my hand. "Is that true, Ben?"

He glances to the manuscript, but then he looks back up at me, as if he can't stomach seeing the pages on the table. *Shake your head, Ben. Deny it. Please.*

He does nothing.

His lack of denial hits me hard and I gasp.

"Let me explain. Please. Just . . ." He begins to move toward me, so I stumble backward until I meet the wall.

I need out of here. I need to get away from him.

He moves right instead of left, which puts him further away from the front door than me. I can make it. If I move fast enough, I can make it to the door before him.

But why is he allowing that to happen? Why would he allow me the chance to run?

"I want to leave," I tell him. "Please."

He nods, but he's still holding a hand up in the air, palm facing me. His nod tells me one thing, but his hand is asking me to stay put. I know he wants to give me an explanation . . . but unless he's going to tell me that what I just read isn't true, then I don't want to stay and listen to anything else he has to say.

I just need him to tell me it's not true.

"Ben," I whisper, my hands pressed flat against the wall behind me. "Please tell me what I read isn't true. Please tell me I'm not your fucking *plot* twist."

My words pull out the one expression I was hoping I wouldn't see. *Regret.*

I taste the bile again.

I clench my stomach.

"Oh, God."

I want out. I need out of here before I'm too sick and weak to leave. The next few seconds are a hazy blur as I mutter, "Oh, God," again and rush toward the couch. I need my purse. My shoes. I want out, I want out, I want out. I reach the door and slide the dead bolt to the left, but his hand cups mine and his chest meets my back, pressing me against the door.

I squeeze my eyes shut when I feel his breath against the back of my neck. "I'm sorry. I'm sorry, I'm sorry, I'm sorry." His words are as desperate as the grip he has on me when he spins me around to face him. He's wiping away my tears and his own begin to form in his eyes. "I'm so sorry. Please don't go."

I won't fall for this. I won't let him fool me again. I push against him, but he grips my wrists, holding them to his chest as he presses his forehead against mine. "I love you, Fallon. God, I love you so much. Please don't leave. Please."

And that's when everything inside of me morphs from one extreme to the next. I'm no longer scared.

I'm angry.

Pissed.

Because hearing those words come out of his mouth make me reflect on the difference I feel hearing them now than from just an hour ago. How dare he lie to me. Use me for the purpose of a book. Make me believe he saw the real me — not the scars on my face.

The scars he's responsible for.

"Benton James Kessler. You do *not* love me. Never speak those words again. Not to me — not to anyone. Those three words are a disgrace when they fall from your mouth."

His eyes widen and he stumbles backward when I shove my hands into his chest. I don't give him time to spit out more lies and false apologies.

I slam his door and fumble with the strap of my purse, putting it over my shoulder. My bare feet meet the pavement and I take off in a sprint toward the cab I see pulling into his complex. I hear him calling my name.

No.

I won't listen. I owe him nothing.

I swing open the door and climb inside. I tell the driver my address, but by the time the driver enters it into the GPS, Ben is at the car. Before I notice the window is down, he reaches his hand inside and covers the button that rolls it up. His eyes are pleading.

"Here," he says, shoving pages at me. They fall in my lap, some slide to the floor. "If you won't let me explain, then read it. All of it. Please, just —"

I grab a handful of pages from my lap and throw them toward the seat next to me. I grab what's left in my lap and I try to toss them out the window, but he catches them and shoves them back inside the car.

I'm rolling up my window when I hear him mutter under his breath, "Please don't hate me."

But I'm scared it's already too late.

I tell the driver to leave, and when I'm a safe distance across the parking lot, the cab pauses before pulling out onto the road. I glance back at him. He's standing in front of his apartment door, his hands gripping the back of his head. He's watching me leave. I grab as many pages of the manuscript as I can reach and I toss them out the window. Before the cab pulls away, I turn just in time to see him fall to his knees on the pavement in defeat.

It took four years for me to fall in love with him.

It only took four pages to stop.

■ ■ ■ ■

Sixth November 9th

■ ■ ■ ■

Fate.
A word meaning destiny.
Fate.
A word meaning doom.
— Benton James Kessler

Fallon

I just lived through the longest minute of my life.

Sitting on my couch, watching the second hand on my clock move at a snail's pace as it processed the date from November 8th to November 9th.

Although there was no sound when the second hand struck midnight, my whole body jerked as if every chime from every clock on every wall in every house just rang inside my head.

My phone lights up at ten seconds after midnight. It's a text from Amber.

It's just a date on a calendar, like any other. I love you, but my offer still stands. If you want me to spend the day with you, just text.

I also notice a missed text from my mother that came in two hours ago.

I'm bringing you breakfast tomorrow. I'll let myself in when I get there, so no need to set an alarm.

Crap.

I really don't want company when I wake up. Not from Amber, not from my mom, not from anyone. At least I know my dad won't remember the anniversary. That's a plus side to our sporadic relationship.

I click the button on the side of my cell phone to lock it, and then I wrap my arms back around my knees. I'm sitting on my couch, dressed in pajamas that I don't plan to take off until November 10th. I'm not leaving this house for the next twenty-four hours. I'm not speaking to a single person. Well, except to my mom when she brings me breakfast, but after that, I'm taking the day off from the world.

I decided after what I went through last year with Ben, that this date is cursed. From now on, no matter how old or married I am, I will never leave my home on November 9th.

I've also reserved it as the only day I'll allow myself to think about the fire. To think about Ben. To think about all the things I wasted on him. Because no one is worth that much heartache. No excuse is good enough to justify what he did to me.

Which is why, when I left his apartment last year, I drove straight to the police station and filed a restraining order against him.

It's been exactly one year and I haven't heard from him since the night I drove away.

I never told anyone what happened. Not my father, not Amber, not my mother. Not because I didn't want him to get in trouble, because I do believe he deserves to pay for what he did to me.

But because I was embarrassed.

I trusted this man. I loved him. I believed whole-heartedly that the connection between us was rare and real and that we were one of a lucky few who found love like ours.

Finding out that he was lying throughout our entire relationship is something I'm still trying to process. Every day I wake up and force myself to push thoughts of him out of my head. I went on with my life as if Benton James Kessler had never entered it. Sometimes it works, sometimes it doesn't. Most of the time it doesn't.

I thought about seeing a therapist. I thought about telling my mom about him and his responsibility for the fire. I even thought about talking to my dad about him. But it's hard to bring him up when most of the time I'm trying to pretend he never existed.

I keep telling myself it will get easier. That

I'll meet someone someday who will be able to blind me to thoughts of Ben, but so far I won't even bring myself to trust someone enough to flirt with them.

It's one thing to experience trust issues with men due to infidelity. But Ben lied to me on such a large scale that I have no idea what was true, what was a lie and what was fabricated for his book. The only thing I know to be accurate is that he was somehow responsible for the fire that almost took my life. And I don't care if it was intentional or an accident, that isn't the part that infuriates me the most.

I'm the most devastated when I think about all the times he made my scars feel beautiful, while never once admitting that he was actually the one who put them there.

No excuse will ever justify those lies. So there isn't even a point in hearing them.

In fact, there isn't even a point in allowing myself to think about it any more than I already have. I should just go to bed. Maybe by some miracle, I'll sleep through most of tomorrow.

I reach over and turn off the lamp next to my couch. As I'm making my way toward the bedroom, there's a knock on my front door.

Amber.

She's done well not to bring up today's date until yesterday. She pretended she wanted to have a sleepover out of the blue a few hours ago, but I declined. I know she just doesn't want me to be alone tonight, but it's a lot easier to mope when there's no one to judge you.

I unlock my apartment door and open it.

No one is here.

Chills run up my arms. Amber wouldn't do something like this. She wouldn't find humor in pranking a girl who lives alone this late at night.

I immediately step back inside the apartment to slam the door shut, but right before I go to close it, I glance down at the ground and see a cardboard box. It isn't wrapped, but there's an envelope on it with my name sprawled across the top.

I look around, but there's no one near my door. There is a car pulling away, though, and I wish it wasn't so dark so I could see if I recognized the vehicle.

I glance back down at the package and then quickly scoop it up and rush inside, locking the door behind me.

It looks like one of the cardboard gift boxes that department stores use to package shirts, but the contents are much heavier than a shirt. I set it on the kitchen counter and peel the envelope off the top of it.

It isn't sealed. The flap is just tucked into the back of the envelope, so I pull the piece of paper out and unfold it.

Fallon,

I've spent most of my life preparing to write something as important as this letter. But for the first time, I don't feel like the English language has developed enough letters in the alphabet to adequately express the words I want to say to you.

When you left last year, you left with my soul in your hands and my heart in your teeth, and I knew I would never get either of them back. You can keep them, I don't really need them anymore.

I'm not writing this letter in hopes that you will forgive me. You deserve better. You always have. Nothing I can say would ever make my feet worthy enough to walk on the same ground you walk upon. Nothing I can do would ever make my heart worthy enough to share a love with yours.

I'm not asking you to seek me out. I'm just asking that you read the words on the pages in this box in hopes that it can allow you, and maybe even me, to walk away from this with as little damage as possible.

You may not believe me, but all I want is

for you to be happy. That's all I've ever wanted. And I'll do anything to make that happen for you, even if it means helping you to forget me.

The words you're about to read have never been read by anyone but you, nor will they ever be read by anyone but you. This is the only copy. You can do whatever you want with it when you're finished. And I know you owe me nothing, but I'm not asking you to read this manuscript for me. I want you to read it for yourself. Because when you love someone, you owe it to them to help them be the best version of themselves that they can be. And as much as it crushes me to admit this, the best version of you doesn't include me.

Ben

I lay the pages carefully on the table next to the box.

I bring a hand to my cheek, checking for tears, because I can't believe there aren't any. I thought surely if I'd heard from him again, I would be an emotional wreck.

But I'm not. My hands aren't shaking. My heart isn't aching.

I bring my fingers to my throat to see if I even have a pulse. Because surely I haven't spent so much of this past year building up an emotional wall so high, that even words like the ones he just wrote can't penetrate it.

But I'm scared that's exactly what's happened. Not only will Ben never break these walls back down, but I'm afraid he's forced me to build them so thick and high that I'll be hiding behind them forever.

He's right about one thing, though. I owe him nothing.

I walk to my bedroom and crawl into bed, leaving every single page unread on the kitchen counter.

It's 11:15.

I'm squinting, so that means there's sun. Which means it's 11:15 a.m.

I bring my hand to my face and I cover my eyes. I wait a few seconds and then I pick up my cell phone.

It's November 9th.

Shit.

I mean, it's no surprise I didn't sleep for twenty-four hours straight, so I don't know why I'm upset. Especially considering the eleven hours of sleep I *did* get. I'm not sure I've slept this much since I was a teenager. And I especially haven't slept this much on today's anniversary. I normally don't sleep at all.

I stand in the middle of my bedroom and debate how to proceed with today. Behind door number one lies my bathroom, my toothbrush, and my shower.

Behind door number two lies a couch, a television, and a refrigerator.

I choose door number two.

When I open it, I suddenly wish I had chosen door number one.

My mother is sitting on my couch.

Shit. I forgot she was bringing me breakfast. Now she'll think I do nothing but sleep every day, all day.

"Hey," I say to her as I walk out of my bedroom. She glances up, and I'm immediately confused by her expression.

She's crying.

My first thought is what happened and who did it happen to? My father? My grandmother? Cousins? Aunts? Uncles? Boddle, my mom's dog?

"What's wrong?" I ask her.

But then I look down at her lap and realize that *everything* is wrong. She's reading the manuscript.

Ben's manuscript.

Our story.

Since when did she start invading privacy? I point at it and shoot her an offended look. "What are you doing?"

She picks up a discarded tissue and wipes at her eyes. "I'm sorry," she says, sniffling. "I saw the letter. And I would never read your personal things, but it was open this morning when I brought breakfast and I just . . . I'm sorry. But then" — she picks up some of the pages of the manuscript and flops them back and forth — "I read the first page and I've been sitting here for four hours now and haven't been able to stop."

She's been reading it for four hours?

I walk over to her and grab the stack of pages from her lap. "How much did you read?" I pick the manuscript up and walk it back to the kitchen. "And why? You have no business reading this, Mom. Jesus, I can't believe you would do that." I shove the lid back on the cardboard box and I walk it to the trash can. I step on the lever to open the lid, and my mother is moving faster than I've ever seen her move before.

"Fallon, don't you dare throw that away!" she says. She grabs the box from my hands and hugs it to her chest. "Why would you do that?" She sets the box on the counter, smoothing her hand over the top of it like it's a prized possession I almost just broke.

I'm confused why she's reacting this way to something that should infuriate her.

She releases a quick breath and then looks

me firmly in the eye. "Sweetie," she says. "Is any of this true? Did these things really happen?"

I don't even know what to tell her, because I have no idea which "things" she's referring to. I shrug. "I don't know. I haven't read it yet." I pass her and walk toward the couch. "But if you're referring to Benton James Kessler and the fact that he allowed me to completely fall in love with a fictitious version of himself, then yes. That happened." I lift one of the couch cushions in search of my remote control. "And if you're referring to the fact that I found out he was somehow responsible for a fire that almost killed me, but failed to point out that minor detail as I was falling in love with him, then yes, that happened, too." I find my remote.

I sit on the couch and cross my legs, preparing for a twelve-hour binge of reality TV. Now would be the perfect time for my mother to leave, but instead, she walks over to the couch and sits next to me.

"You haven't read any of this?" she asks, placing the box on the coffee table in front of us.

"I read the prologue last year. That was enough for me."

I feel the warmth of her hand encase mine. I slowly turn my head to find that she's looking at me with an endearing smile. "Sweetheart . . ."

My head falls against the back of the couch. "Can your advice *please* wait until tomorrow?"

She sighs. "Fallon, look at me."

I do, because she's my mother and I love her and for some reason, even though I'm twenty-three, I still do what she says.

She lifts a hand to my face and tucks my hair behind my left ear. Her thumb brushes the scars on my cheek, and I flinch because it's the first time she's ever purposefully touched them. Other than Ben, I've never allowed anyone to touch them.

"Did you love him?" she asks.

I don't do anything for a few seconds. My throat feels like it's burning, so rather than say yes, I just nod.

Her mouth twitches and she blinks fast, twice, like she's trying not to cry. She's still brushing her thumb across my cheek. Her eyes deviate from mine and she scrolls over the scars on my face and neck. "I'm not going to pretend that I know what you've gone through. But after reading those pages, I can assure you that you aren't the only one who was scarred in that fire. Just because he chose not to show you his scars doesn't mean they don't exist." She picks up the box and sets it on my lap. "Here they are. He's put his scars on full display for you, and you need to show him the respect he showed you by not turning away from them."

The first tear of the day escapes my eyes. I should have known I wouldn't get away with not crying today.

She stands and gathers her things. She leaves my apartment without another word.

I open the box, because she's my mother and I love her and for some reason, even though I'm twenty-three, I still do what she says.

I skim through the prologue I read last year. Nothing has changed. I flip to the first chapter and start from the beginning.

BEN'S NOVEL — CHAPTER ONE
NOVEMBER 9TH
AGE 16

"Break in the sun till the sun breaks down, And death shall have no dominion."
— Dylan Thomas

Most people don't know what death sounds like.

I do.

Death sounds like the absence of footsteps down the hallway. It sounds like a morning shower not being taken. Death sounds like the lack of the voice that should be yelling my name from the kitchen, telling me to get out of bed. Death sounds like the absence of the knock on my door that usually comes moments before my alarm goes off.

Some people say they get this feeling in the pit of their stomach when they have a premonition that something bad is about to happen.

I don't have that feeling in the pit of my stomach right now.

I have that feeling in my whole goddamn body, from the hairs on my arms, to my skin, down to my bones. And with each second that passes without a single sound coming from outside my bedroom door, that feeling grows heavier, and slowly begins to seep into my soul.

I lie in my bed for several more minutes, waiting to hear the slam of a kitchen cabinet or the music she always turns on from the television in the living room. Nothing happens, even after my alarm buzzes.

I reach over to turn it off, my fingers shaking as I try to remember how to silence the same damn alarm I've silenced with ease since I got it for Christmas two years earlier. When the screeching comes to a halt, I force myself to get dressed. I pick up my cell phone from the dresser, but I only have one text message from Abitha.

Cheer practice after school today. See you at 5?

I slip the phone in my pocket, but then I pull it out again and grip it in my hands. Don't ask me how I know, but I might need it. And the time it takes to pull my phone out of my pocket may be precious time wasted.

Her room is downstairs. I go there and I stand outside the door. I listen, but all I hear is silence. As loud as silence can be heard.

I swallow the fear lodged in my throat. I tell myself I'll laugh about this a few minutes from now. After I open her door and find that she's already left for work. She might have gotten called in early and she just didn't want to wake me.

Beads of sweat begin to line my forehead. I wipe them away with the sleeve of my shirt.

I lift my hand and knock on the door, but my hand is already on the doorknob before I wait for her to answer me.

But she can't answer me. When I open the door, she isn't here.

She's gone.

The only thing I find is her lifeless body lying on the floor of her bedroom, blood pooled around her head.

But she isn't here.

No. My mother is *gone.*

It was three hours from the moment I found her to the moment they walked out of the house with her body. There was a lot they had to do, from photographing everything in her bedroom, outside her bedroom, and in the entire house to questioning me, to looking through her belongings for evidence.

Three hours isn't a very long time if you think about it. If they thought foul play was involved, they would have cased off the house. They would have told me I needed to find somewhere else to stay while they conducted their investigation. They would have treated this way more seriously than they did.

After all, when a woman is found dead in her bedroom floor with a gun in her hand and a suicide letter on her bed, three hours is really all it takes to determine she was at fault.

It takes Kyle three and a half hours to get here from his dorm, so he'll be here in thirty minutes.

Thirty minutes is a long time to sit and stare at the bloodstain that remains in the carpet. If I tilt my head to the left, it looks like a hippo with its mouth wide open, about to devour prey. But if I tilt my head to the right, it looks like Gary Busey's mug shot.

I wonder if she'd have still gone through with it if she knew her blood stain would resemble Gary Busey?

I didn't spend much time in the room with her body. Just the time it took me to dial 911 and for the first responders to arrive, which, despite feeling like an eternity, was probably only a few minutes. But in those few minutes, I learned more about my mother than I thought would be possible in such a short span.

She had been lying on her stomach when

I found her, and she was wearing a tank top that revealed the end words of a tattoo she got several months ago. I knew it was a quote about love, but that's all I really knew. Probably Dylan Thomas, but I never even asked her.

I reached over and pulled the edge of her shirt aside so I could read the entire quote.

Though Lovers be lost, love shall not.

I stood up and walked a few steps away from her, hoping the chills would go as fast as they arrived. The quote never meant anything until now. When she first got it, I assumed it meant that just because two people stopped loving one another didn't mean their love never existed. I couldn't relate to it before, but now it feels like the tattoo was a premonition. Like she got it because she wanted me to see that even though she's gone, her love isn't.

And it pisses me off that I didn't know how to relate to words on her body until her body was nothing more than just a body.

Then I notice the tattoo on her left wrist — the one that's been there since before I was born. It's the word *poetic* written across a music staff. I know the meaning behind this one because she explained it to me a few years ago when we were in the car together, just the two of us. We were talking about love and I had asked her how you know if you're really in love with someone. At first, she gave the quintessential answer, *"You just know."* But when she glanced over at me and saw that answer didn't satisfy me, her expression grew serious.

"Oh," she said. *"You're asking for real this time? Not as a curious kid, but as someone who needs advice? Well then, let me give you the real answer."*

I could feel my face flush, because I didn't want her to know I thought I might be in love. I was only thirteen and these feelings were new to me, but I was sure Brynn Fellows was going to be my first real girlfriend.

My mother looked back at the road and I saw a smile spread across her face. *"When I say you just know, it's because you will. You won't question it. You don't wonder if what you feel is actually love, because when it is, you'll be absolutely terrified that you're in it. And when that happens, your priorities will change. You won't think about yourself and your own happiness. You'll only think about that person, and how you would do anything to see them happy. Even if it meant walking away from them and sacrificing your own happiness for theirs."*

She gave me a sidelong glance. *"That's what love is, Ben. Love is sacrifice."* She tapped her finger against the tattoo on her left wrist — the tattoo that had been there since before I was born. *"I got this tattoo the day I felt that kind of love for your father. And I chose it because if I had to describe love that day, I would say it felt like my two favorite things, amplified and thrown together. Like my favorite poetic line mixed into the lyrics of my favorite song."* She looked at me again, very seriously. *"You'll know, Ben. When you're willing to give up the things that mean the most to you just to see someone else happy, that's real love."*

I stared at her tattoo for a bit, wondering if I could ever love anyone like that. I wasn't sure I would want to give up the things I loved the most if it meant I wouldn't get anything out of it in return. I thought Brynn Fellows was beautiful, but I wasn't even sure I'd give her my lunch if I were hungry enough. I certainly wouldn't get a tattoo because of her.

"Why did you get the tattoo, though?" I asked her. *"So my father would know you loved him?"*

She shakes her head. *"I didn't get it for your father, or even because of your father. I got it mostly for myself, because I knew with one hundred percent certainty I had learned how to love selflessly. It was the first time I wanted more happiness for the person I was with than I wanted for myself. And a mixture of my two favorite things was the only way I could think to describe the way that kind of love feels. I wanted to remember it forever, in case I never felt it again."*

I didn't get to read the suicide letter she left, but I was curious if she had changed her mind about selfless love. Or if maybe she only loved my father selflessly, but never her own children. Because suicide is the most selfish thing a person can do.

After I found her, I checked to make sure she really was gone and then I called 911. I had to stay on the phone with the operator until the police arrived, so I didn't have a chance to case her bedroom for a suicide note. The police found it and picked it up with a pair of tweezers and put it in a Ziploc bag. Once they sealed it up as evidence, I just didn't have the balls to ask them if I could read it.

One of my neighbors, Mr. Mitchell, was here when they left. He told the officer that he would watch over me until my brothers arrived, so I was left in his care. But as soon as they drove away, I told him I would be okay and that I needed to make some phone calls to family members. He told me he needed to run to the post office anyway and that he'd be back to check on me later today.

It was like my puppy had died and he was wanting to tell me it would be okay, that I could get a new one.

I'd get a Yorkie, because that's exactly what the bloodstain looks like if I cover my right eye and squint.

I wonder if I'm in shock. Is that why I'm not crying?

My mother would be pissed that I'm not crying right now. I'm sure attention played at least a small role in her decision. She loved attention, and not in a bad way. It's just a fact. And I'm not sure that I'm giving her death enough attention if I'm not even crying yet.

I think I'm mostly just confused. She seemed happy most of my life. Sure, there were days she was sad. Relationships that went south. My mother loved to love, and up until the moment she blew her face off, she was an attractive woman. Lots of men thought so.

But my mother was also smart. And even though a relationship she thought had promise ended a few days ago, she just didn't seem like the type who would take her life to prove to a man that he should have stuck with her. And she's never loved a man enough to feel as though she couldn't live without him. That kind of love isn't real, anyway. If parents have been able to survive the loss of children, then men and women can easily live with the loss of a relationship.

Fifteen minutes have passed since I began contemplating why she would do this and I'm no closer to an answer than I was before.

I decide to investigate. I feel a little guilty, because she's my mother and she deserves her privacy. But if a person has time to write out a suicide note, surely they have time to destroy things they would never want their children to find. I spend the next half hour (why isn't Kyle here yet?) snooping through her stuff.

I scroll through her phone and email. Several text messages and emails later, I'm convinced I know exactly why my mother killed herself.

His name is Donovan O'Neil.

FALLON

I drop the page with my father's name on it. It flutters to the floor with some of the other pages I just read.

I push the manuscript off my lap and quickly stand up. I rush to my bedroom and opt for door number one. I take a shower, hoping to calm down enough to continue reading, but I cry the entire time. No sixteen-year-old should have to go through what Ben went through, but it still doesn't answer all the questions I have about how this relates to me. But now that I know my father was involved with Ben's mother at some point, I have a feeling I'm getting closer. And I'm not so sure I want to keep reading, but now that I've started, I can't stop. Despite the fact that I feel nauseous, my hands have been trembling for fifteen minutes straight, and I'm too scared to read what my father has to do with any of this, I force myself to forge ahead.

It's at least an hour later before I have the courage to return to the manuscript. I sit back down on the couch and pick up right where I left off.

Ben's novel — Chapter Two
Age 16

"When one burns one's bridges, what a very nice fire it makes."

— Dylan Thomas

Kyle finally made it to the house. So did Ian. We sit around the kitchen table and talk about anything except why our mother hated her life more than she loved us. Kyle tells me I was brave today. He treats me like I'm still twelve, even though I've been the man of this house since he left home six months ago.

Ian calls one of those companies that provide cleanup service after a death. One of the officers must have left their business card on the counter, knowing we would need it. I didn't even know those existed, but Ian mentioned some movie he watched called *Sunshine Cleaning* a few years back about a couple of women who did it for a living.

The company sends two men. One man who doesn't speak English and one man who doesn't speak at all. He writes everything down on a pad that he keeps in his front pocket.

When they're finished, they find me in the

kitchen and hand me a note.

Stay out of the bedroom for at least four hours so the carpet can dry. Your total comes to $200.

I find Kyle in the living room. "It costs $200."

We both look for Ian, but we can't find him. His car is gone and he's the only one with that kind of cash. I find my mother's purse on the kitchen counter. "She has enough cash in her wallet. You think it's okay if we use it?"

Kyle snatches the money out of my hands and leaves the room to pay the guys.

Ian returns later that afternoon. He and Kyle argue about whether or not he informed us he was going to the police station, because Kyle doesn't remember Ian leaving and Ian says Kyle just wasn't paying attention.

No one asks why he went to the police station in the first place. I think maybe he wanted to see the suicide letter, but I don't ask him about it. After reading how in love she was with this guy Donovan, the last thing I want to read is how she couldn't live without him. It pisses me off that my mother would allow the breakup over a man to devastate her more than the thought of never seeing her sons again. It shouldn't even be a tossup.

I can almost see how her decision played out. I imagine her sitting on her bed last night, crying over the pathetic bastard. I imagine her holding a picture of him in her right hand and a picture of me, Kyle, and Ian in the left. She looks back and forth between the pictures, focusing on Donovan. *Do I just end it now so I don't have to live without this man for one more day?* And then she looks at the picture of us. *Or do I stick out the heartache in order to spend the rest of my life with three men who are grateful to have me as their mother?*

What I *can't* imagine is what would motivate her to choose the picture in her right hand over the picture in her left.

I know that if I don't see for myself what was so special about this man that it will eat at me. A slow, painful gnawing that will chip away at my bones until I feel as worthless as she felt when she circled her lips around the tip of that gun.

I wait a few hours until Kyle and Ian have gone to their bedrooms and then I walk into her room. I search through all the things I read earlier, the love notes, the arguments, the proof that their relationship was as tumultuous as a hurricane. When I finally locate something with enough information about him on it to Google his address, I leave the house.

I feel odd taking her car. I just turned sixteen four months ago. She was saving up to help me buy my first car, but we hadn't gotten there yet, so I just used hers when it was available.

It's a nice car. A Cadillac. I sometimes wondered why she didn't just sell it so she could afford two cheaper cars, but I felt guilty thinking that. I was a sixteen-year-old kid and she was a single mom who worked hard to get where she was in her career. It wasn't fair of me to think we even remotely deserved equal things.

It's after ten p.m. when I pull into Donovan's neighborhood. It's a much nicer neighborhood than the one we live in. Not that our neighborhood isn't nice, but this one has a privacy gate. It's not that private though, because the gate is stuck in the open position. I debate whether or not to turn around, but then I remember what I'm here to do, which is nothing illegal. All I'm doing is scoping out the house of the man responsible for my mother's suicide.

At first, it's hard to see the houses. They're all really long driveways with lots of space between lots. But the further down I drive, the more sparse the trees become. When I close in on the address, my pulse begins to thump in my ears. I feel pathetic that I'm nervous to see a house, but my hand slips on the steering wheel from the sweat on my palm.

When I finally reach the house, I'm instantly unimpressed. It's just like all the others. Pitched, pointy roofs. Two car garages. Manicured lawns and mailboxes encased in stone that match the houses.

I expected more from Donovan.

I'm impressed with my own bravery when I drive past the house, turn around, and then pull the car over a few houses down so that I can stare at it. I kill the engine and then manually switch off the headlights.

I wonder if he knows?

I'm not sure how he would, unless they have mutual friends.

He probably knows. I'm sure my mother had a multitude of friends and coworkers and a side to her personality I never saw.

I wonder if he cried when he found out. I wonder if he had any regrets. I wonder if he had the choice to go back and unbreak her heart, would he do it?

And now I'm humming Toni Braxton. Fuck you, Donovan O'Neil.

My cell phone vibrates on the seat. It's a text message from Kyle.

Kyle: Where are you?

Me: I had to run to the store.

Kyle: It's late. Get back ASAP. We have to be at the funeral home by nine tomorrow morning.

Me: What are you, my mother?

I wait for him to respond with something like *too soon, man.* But he doesn't. I stare at the phone a little longer, wishing he would respond. I don't know why I sent that text. I feel bad now. There should be an unsend button.

Great. Now I'm singing the words *unsend my text* to the tune of unbreak my heart.

Fuck you, Toni Braxton.

I sink down into my seat when I notice headlights coming toward me. I sink even further when I see them pull into Donovan's house.

I stop singing and I bite the inside of my cheek as I wait for him to get out of the car. I hate that it's so dark. I want to see if he's good-looking, at least. Not that his level of attractiveness should have played any part in my mother's decision to depart this world.

One of his garage doors opens. As he pulls in, the other garage door also begins to open. Fluorescent lights are beaming down on both vehicles in the garage. He kills the engine to the Audi he's driving and then steps out of the car.

He's tall.

That's it. That's the only thing I gather from this far away. He might have dark brown hair, but I'm not even sure about that.

He pulls the other car out of the driveway. Some kind of classic car, but I know nothing about cars. It's red and sleek and when he gets out of it, he pops the hood.

I observe him as he toys under the hood for the next several minutes. I make all kinds of observations about him. I know that I don't like him, that's a given. I also know that he probably isn't married. Both cars seem to be cars a man would own and there isn't room for another car in the garage, so he probably lives alone.

He's more than likely divorced. My mother probably liked the appeal of his neighborhood and the prospect of moving us in with him so that I could have a father figure in my life. She probably had their lives mapped out and was waiting for him to propose, when instead, he broke her heart.

He spends the next several minutes washing and waxing his car, which I find odd since it's so late at night. Maybe he's always gone during the day. That has to be irritating for the neighbors, although the neighboring homes are far enough apart that no one even has to notice what goes on next door if they don't want to.

He retrieves a gas can from the garage and fills the car with gas. I wonder if it takes a special kind of gas, since he's not filling it at a fuel station.

He sets the gas can down next to the car in a hurry, and then fishes out his cell phone. He looks at the screen and then brings his phone to his ear.

I wonder who he's talking to. I wonder if it's another woman — if that's why he left my mother.

But then I see it — in the way his hand grips the back of his neck. The way his shoulders droop and the way his head shakes back and forth. He begins pacing, worried, upset.

Whoever is on the other end of that line just told him my mother was dead.

I grip my steering wheel and lean forward, soaking in his every movement. Will he cry? Was she worth dropping to his knees over? Will I be able to hear him scream in agony from here?

He leans against his precious car and ends the call. He stares at the phone for seventeen seconds. Yes, I counted.

He slides the phone back into his pocket and then, in a glorious display of grief, he punches the air.

Don't punch the air, Donovan. Punch your car, it'll feel much better.

He grabs the rag he used to dry off his car and he tosses it at the ground.

No, Donovan. Not the rag. Punch your car. Show me you loved her more than you love your car and then maybe I won't have to hate you as much.

He pulls his foot back and kicks at the gas can, sending it several feet across the grass.

Punch your fucking car, Donovan. She might be watching you right now. Show her that your heart is so broken, you don't even care about your own life anymore.

Donovan lets us both down when he storms inside his house, never once laying a finger on his car. I feel bad for my mother that he didn't throw more of a fit. I'm not even sure if he cried, I was too far away to see.

The fluorescent lights go out in the garage.

The garage doors begin to lower.

At least he's too upset to pull the car inside.

I watch the house for a few more minutes, wondering if he'll ever come back outside. When he doesn't, I begin to grow restless.

A huge part of me wants to drive away and never think about this man again, but there's a small part of me that's growing more and more curious with every second I sit here.

What is so fucking special about that damn car?

Anyone who just received news as devastating as he did would want to lash out at the thing closest to them. Any normal man in love would have bashed their fist onto the hood of the car. Or, depending on how much you loved the woman, maybe even bashed their fist through a windshield. But this asshole grabs a rag to throw on the ground. He chose to get his aggression out on an old, weightless rag.

He should be embarrassed.

I should help him grieve properly.

I should punch the hood of the car *for* him. And even though I know nothing good will come of this, I'm already out of my car and halfway across the road before I tell myself it's not a good idea. But when it comes to a battle between your adrenaline and your conscience, adrenaline always wins.

I reach the car and don't even bother looking around me to see if anyone is outside. I know they aren't. It's after eleven at night by now. No one is probably even awake on this street, and even if they were, I wouldn't care.

I pick up the rag and inspect it, hoping there's something special about it. There isn't, but I decide to use it to open the car door. Don't want to leave fingerprints behind if I accidentally scratch up his car.

The inside of the car is even nicer than the outside. Pristine condition. Cherry-red leather seats. Wood grain trim. There's a pack of cigarettes and some matches on the console, and it disappoints me that my mother would love a smoker.

I look back at the house and then I look back down at the matches. Who uses matches anymore? I swear I keep finding more and more reasons to hate him.

Go back to your car, Ben. There's been enough excitement for one day.

Adrenaline beats down my conscience yet again. I glance back at the gas can.

I wonder . . .

Would Donovan be more upset over his precious little classic car going up in flames than he was over my mother's death?

I guess we'll soon find out, because my adrenaline is picking up the gas can and pouring the liquid over the tire and up the side of the car. At least my conscience is still alert enough to know to set the can back right where he kicked it. I strike one and only one of the matches, and then I flick it out of my fingers — just like they do in the movies — as I walk back to my car.

The air makes a quick *whoosh* sound behind me. The night lights up like someone just turned on Christmas lights.

When I reach my car, I'm smiling. It's the first time I've smiled today.

I crank my car and patiently drive away, feeling somewhat justified for what she did to herself. For what she did to me.

And finally, for the first time since finding her body this morning, a tear falls out of my eye.

And then another.

And another.

I begin to cry so hard that it's too hard to see the road in front of me. I pull over on a hill. I lean across the steering wheel and my cries turn to sobs, because I miss her. It hasn't even been a day and I miss her so fucking much and I have no idea why she would do this to me. It feels so personal, and I hate that I'm selfish enough to believe that it had anything to do with me, but didn't it? I lived with her. I was the only one left still in that house. She knew I would be the one to find her. She knew what this would do to me and she still did it and I've never loved someone I hate so much, and I've never hated someone I love so much.

I cry for so long that the muscles in my stomach begin to ache. My jaw hurts from the tension. My ears hurt from the blare of the sirens as they pass.

I glance in my rearview mirror and watch as the fire truck makes its way down the hill.

I see the orange glow against the dark sky behind me and it's much brighter than I expect it to be.

The flames are way higher than they should be.

My pulse is pounding way harder than I want it to be.

What did I do?

What have I done?

My hands are shaking so hard, I can't get the ignition to switch back into drive. I can't catch my breath. My foot slips on the brake.

What did I do?

I drive. I keep driving. I try to suck in air, but my lungs feel like they're filled with thick, black smoke. I grab my phone. I want to tell Kyle that I might be having a panic attack, but I can't calm my hand long enough to dial his number. The phone slips from my hands and lands in the floorboard.

I only have two miles left. I can make it.

I count to seventeen exactly seventeen times and then I'm pulling into my driveway.

I stumble into the house, thankful Kyle is still awake and in the kitchen. I don't have to try to make it upstairs to his room.

He puts his hands on my shoulders and ushers me to a chair. I expect him to start panicking with me when he sees the wide-eyed, tear-filled look on my face, but instead, he gets me water. He speaks calmly to me, but I have no idea what he's saying. He keeps telling me to focus on his eyes, focus on his eyes, focus on his eyes.

"Focus on my eyes," he says. It's the first sound I process.

"Breathe, Ben."

His voice becomes louder.

"Breathe."

My pulse gradually begins to find a rhythm again.

"Breathe."

My lungs begin to bring in air and dispel it like they're supposed to do.

I breathe in and out and in and out and take another sip of water and then as soon as I can speak, I want nothing more than to get this secret out of me before I explode.

"I fucked up, Kyle." I stand up and begin

pacing. I can feel the tears on my cheeks and I hear the tremor in my voice. I squeeze my head with my hands. "I didn't mean to do it, I swear, I don't know why I did it."

Kyle cuts me off mid-pace. He grips my shoulders and dips his head, looking me hard in the eyes. "What did you do, Ben?"

I suck in another huge breath and I release it as I pull away from him. And then I tell him everything. I tell him about how her bloodstain looked like Gary Busey's head and how I read all the letters Donovan wrote to her and how I just wanted to see why she cared about that man more than us and how he didn't get angry enough when he found out she died and how I didn't mean to catch his house on fire, I didn't even mean to catch his *car* on fire, that's not why I went there.

We're sitting now. At the kitchen table. Kyle hasn't said very many things, but the next thing he says terrifies me more than anything has ever terrified me in my life.

"Was anyone hurt, Ben?"

I want to shake my head no, but it won't move. My answer won't come, because I don't know. Of course no one was hurt. Donovan was awake, he would have gotten out in time.

Right?

I gasp for another breath when I see worry in Kyle's eyes. He quickly pushes away from the table and stalks toward the living room. I hear the TV click on and, for a second, I have the thought that this is probably the last time that TV will ever click on to the Bravo channel now that my mother won't be watching it anymore.

And then I hear the stations change and change again. But then I hear the words "fire" and "Hyacinth Court," and "one injured."

Injured. He probably tripped running out of the house and cut his finger or something. That's not so bad. I'm sure he had house insurance.

"Ben."

I stand up to join Kyle in the living room. I'm sure he's summoning me to tell me it's okay, that everything is okay and I should go to bed.

When I reach the entryway to the living room, my feet stop moving forward. There's a picture on the TV in the top right-hand corner. A girl. She looks familiar, and I can't place her right away, but I don't have to because the reporter does it for me.

"Latest reports indicate that Fallon O'Neil, sixteen-year-old lead actress in the hit TV show *Gumshoe,* has been airlifted from the scene. No word as to her condition, but we'll keep you updated as reports come in."

Kyle doesn't tell me it'll be okay.

He doesn't say anything at all.

We stand in front of the TV, soaking up news reports that break in between infomercials. At a little after one in the morning, we learn that the girl was taken to a burn center in South Bay. Ten minutes later, we learn she's in critical condition. At one thirty in the morning, we learn she has suffered fourth-degree burns over thirty percent of her body. At one forty-five, we learn that she is expected to survive, but will undergo extensive reconstructive surgery and rehabilitation. At one fifty, reporters state that the owner of the home admitted to spilling fuel near a car parked outside his garage. Investigators state they have no reason to believe the fire was caused intentionally, but a complete investigation will follow up to corroborate the homeowner's claims.

One reporter insinuates that the victim's career may be put on hold indefinitely. Another says producers will have a huge decision to make when it comes to either recasting the role or putting production on hold while the victim recovers. The news reports transition from updates on the victim to how many Emmy Awards Donovan O'Neil was nominated for during the height of his career.

Kyle turns off the television at approximately 2 a.m. He sets the remote down carefully — quietly — on the arm of the couch.

"Did anyone witness what happened?" His eyes lock with mine, and I immediately shake my head.

"Did you leave behind anything? Any possible evidence?"

"No," I whisper. I clear my throat. "He's right. He kicked over his gas can and then went inside the house. No one saw what I did after that."

Kyle nods and then squeezes the tension out of the back of his neck. He takes a step closer. "So *no one* knows you were there?"

"Only you."

He then closes the distance between us. I think he might want to hit me. I don't know for sure, but the anger in the set of his jaw indicates he might want to. I wouldn't blame him.

"I want you to listen to me, Ben." His voice is low and firm. I nod. "Take off every item of clothing you're wearing right now and put them in the washing machine. Go take a shower. And then you're going to go to bed and forget this happened, okay?"

I nod again. I might be sick in a second, I'm not sure.

"You are never to leave the slightest traceable connection to what happened tonight. Never look those people up online. Never drive by their house again. Stay away from anything that can trace you to them. And never, ever speak another word of this. Not to me . . . not to Ian . . . not to anyone. Do you hear me?"

I'm definitely about to be sick, but I still manage to nod.

He studies my face for a minute, making sure he can trust me. I don't dare move. I want him to know he can trust me.

"We have a lot to do tomorrow to prepare for her funeral. Try to get some sleep."

I don't nod again, because he walks away, turning out the lights as he goes.

I stand in the dark for several minutes. Quiet . . . still . . . alone.

I should probably be worried that I'll get caught. I should probably be upset that from this point forward, I'll always feel a sense of guilt whenever Kyle looks at me. I should probably be worried that this night — coupled with this morning and finding my mother — will screw me up in some way. If maybe I'll suffer from PTSD or depression.

But none of that matters.

Because as I run up the stairs, swing open my bathroom door and expel all the contents of my stomach into the toilet, the only thing my thoughts surround is that girl and how I've just completely ruined her life.

I drop my forehead to my arm as I sit here with a death grip on porcelain.

I don't deserve to live.

I don't deserve to live.

I wonder if my bloodstain will look like Gary Busey.

Fallon

I barely make it to the toilet before I throw up.

Beads of sweat trickle down my forehead.

I can't do this.

I can't read anymore.

There's too much. Too much and it's too hard and I'm too sick now to keep reading.

I somehow pull myself off the floor and make it to the sink. I wash my hands. I cup them under the stream of water and bring my hands to my mouth, swishing the water around. I do this several times, washing the taste of bile out of my mouth.

I look in the mirror at the scars that run from my cheek to my neck. I pull my shirt off and look at the scars on my arm, my breast, my waist. I run the fingers of my right hand up my arm and neck, over my cheek, and back down again. I run them over my breast and down my waist.

I lean forward until I'm flush against the

counter . . . as close to the mirror as I can get. And I really look at them. I look at them with more concentration than I've ever looked at them before, because what I'm feeling is confusing me.

It's the first time I've ever looked at them without at least a trace of anger following close behind.

Until I read Ben's words, I never knew how much I blamed my father for what happened to me. For so long, I've hated him. I made it difficult for him to grieve with me over what happened. I found fault in everything he said. Every conversation we had turned into a fight.

I'm not excusing that he can be an insensitive jerk. He's *always* been an insensitive jerk. But he's also always loved me, and now that I have a clearer picture of what happened that night, I shouldn't blame him for forgetting about me anymore.

I only stayed at his house once a week, and he had just found out someone he loved had died. His mind must have been wrecked. And then for me to expect him to react with perfect precision when he sees his house is on fire is way more than I should expect of him. In a matter of minutes, he was grieving and then angry and then panicking because of the fire. To expect him to immediately remember that I had texted him twelve hours earlier to let him know I was sleeping at his house that night is completely unrealistic. I didn't live there. It wasn't like living at home with my mom and me being the first thing she would think about in a panic. My father's situation was completely different, and I should treat it as such. And even though we've kept in touch over the past few years, our relationship isn't what it used to be. I take half the blame for that. We don't get to choose our parents, and parents don't get to choose their children. But we do get to choose how hard we're willing to work in order to make the best of what we're given.

I pull my cell phone out of my pocket and open a text to my father.

Me: Hey, Dad. Want to have breakfast tomorrow? Miss you.

After I hit send, I pull my shirt back on and walk back into the living room. I stare down at the manuscript, wondering how much more I'll be able to endure. It's so hard to read, I can't imagine Ben and his brothers having to live through this.

I say a quick prayer for the Kessler boys, as if what I'm reading is happening now and Kyle is even still around to be prayed for.

And then I pick up right where I left off.

BEN'S NOVEL — CHAPTER THREE
AGE 16

"Great is the hand that holds dominion over man by a scribbled name."

— Dylan Thomas

You know what's worse than the day your mother kills herself?

The day *after* your mother kills herself.

When a person is in a lot of physical pain — say they accidentally slice off their hand — the human body produces endorphins. These endorphins act similarly to drugs such as morphine or codeine. So it's normal not to feel very much pain right after an accident.

Emotional pain must work in a similar way, because today hurts so much worse than yesterday did. Yesterday I was in some kind of dreamlike state, as if my conscience wouldn't fully allow me to believe she was actually gone. In my mind, I was holding on to that thin thread of hope that somehow, the entire day wasn't really happening.

That thread isn't there anymore, no matter how hard I try to grasp it.

She's dead.

And if I had money and connections, I'd

numb this pain with whatever drugs I could find.

I refused to get out of bed this morning. Ian and Kyle both tried to fight me into going to the funeral home with them, but I won. I've been winning all day, actually.

Eat something, Kyle said at lunch.

I didn't eat. I won.

Aunt Chele and Uncle Andrew are here, Ian said around two o'clock this afternoon.

But they're gone now and I'm still in bed, so I won.

Ben, come eat dinner. There's lots to eat, people have been bringing food by all day, Kyle said when he stuck his head in my bedroom around six o'clock.

But I chose to stay in bed and not touch those sympathetic casseroles, making me the winner yet again.

Talk to me, Ian said.

I'd like to say I won this round, but he's still sitting on my bed, refusing to leave.

I pull the covers over my head. He pulls them back down. "Ben. If you don't get out of bed I'll start overreacting. You don't want to force me to call a psychiatrist, do you?"

Jesus *Fucking* Christ!

I sit up in bed and punch the pillow. "Just let me fucking *sleep,* Ian! *Dammit!*"

He doesn't react to the fact that I'm yelling. He just stares at me complacently. "I *have* been letting you sleep. For almost twenty-four hours now. You need to get out of bed and brush your teeth or shower or eat or *something.*"

I lie back down. Ian pushes off the bed and groans. "Benton, look at me!"

Ian never yells at me, which is the only reason I pull the covers from over my head and look up at him. "You aren't the only one hurting, Ben! We have shit to figure out! You're sixteen years old and you can't live here alone and if you don't come downstairs and prove to me and Kyle that this didn't completely fuck you up, then we're probably going to make the wrong decision for you!"

His jaw is twitching, he's so mad.

I think about this for a second. About how neither of them lives here. Ian is in flight school. Ben just started college. My mother is dead.

One of them is going to have to move back home because I'm a minor.

"Do you think mom thought of that?" I ask, sitting up on the bed again.

Ian shakes his head in frustration. His hands drop to his hips. "Thought about *what?*"

"That her decision to kill herself would

force one of you to give up your dream? That you'd have to move back home to take care of your brother?"

Ian shakes his head, confused. "Of *course* she thought about that."

I laugh. "No, she didn't. She's a selfish fucking bitch."

His jaw hardens. "Stop."

"I hate her, Ian. I'm *glad* she's dead. And I'm glad I was the one who found her, because now I'll always have the visual of how the black hole in her face matched the black hole in her heart."

He closes the gap between us and grabs the collar of my shirt, shoving me back down on the bed. He brings his face close to mine and talks through tightly gritted teeth. "You shut your fucking mouth, Ben. She loved you. She was a good mother to us and you'll respect her, do you hear me? I don't care if she can see you right now or not, you'll respect her in this house until the day you die."

My eyes rim with tears and I'm suffocating with hatred. How could he defend her?

I guess it's easy when his memory of her isn't tarnished by the visual I got when I walked into her room.

A tear falls from Ian's eye and lands on my cheek.

His grip loosens from around my neck and he turns around and buries his head in his hands. "I'm sorry," he says, his voice tearful. "I'm sorry, Ben."

I'm not.

He turns around and looks at me, not even attempting to hide his tears. "I just . . . how can you say that? Knowing what she was going through . . ."

I chuckle under my breath. "She broke up with her boyfriend, Ian. That hardly constitutes misery."

He turns until he's facing me on the bed. He tilts his head. "Ben . . . did you not read it?"

I shrug. "Read what?"

He sighs heavily, and then stands. "Her note. Did you not read the letter she left before the police took it?"

I swallow hard. I knew that's where he went yesterday. I knew it.

He runs his hands through his hair. "Oh, my God. I thought you read it." He walks out of my bedroom. "I'll be back in half an hour."

He's not lying. It's exactly thirty-three minutes when he walks back through my bedroom door. I spent the entire time wondering what could be in that letter that would make the difference between me hating her and Ian feeling sorry for her.

He pulls a piece of paper out of his pocket. "They can't release the actual letter yet. They took a photo and printed it out, but you can still read it." He hands me the piece of paper.

He walks out of my bedroom and closes my door.

I sit back on my bed and read the last words my mother will ever say to me.

To my boys,

I've spent my entire life studying writing. No writing course . . . no amount of college . . . no life experience could ever prepare a person to write an adequate suicide note for their children. But I'm sure as hell going to try.

First, I want to explain why I've done this. I know you don't understand it. And Ben, you're probably the first one reading this, since I'm sure you were the first to find me. So please read this letter in its entirety before you decide to hate me.

I found out four months ago that I have ovarian cancer. Brutal, unbeatable, silent cancer that spread before I even developed symptoms. And before you get angry and say I gave up, that's the last thing I would do. If my illness was something I could fight, you boys know I would have fought it with everything I have. But that's the thing about cancer. They call it the fight, as if the stronger ones win and the weaker ones lose, but that's not what cancer is at all.

Cancer isn't one of the players in the game. Cancer is the game.

It doesn't matter how much endurance you have. It doesn't matter how much you've practiced. Cancer is the be-all and end-all of the sport, and the only thing you can do is show up to the game with your jersey on. Because you never know . . . you might be forced to sit the bench for the entire game. You may not even be given the chance to compete.

That's me. I'm being forced to sit the bench until the game is over, because there's nothing more that can be done for me. I could go into all the details, but the fact of the matter is, they caught it too late.

So now comes the tricky part.

Do I wait it out? Do I allow the cancer to slowly rob me of everything I have? You boys remember Grandpa Dwight, and how cancer completely swallowed him up, but refused to spit him out for months. Grandma had to alter her entire life to care for him. She lost her job, the home medical bills piled up, and they eventually lost their house. She was evicted two weeks after he finally died. All because the cancer took its precious time with him.

I don't want that. I can't bear the thought of you boys having to take care of me. I know if I don't end my own life, I might be lucky enough to live on this earth for another six months. Maybe nine. But those months will rob each of you of the mother you knew. And then, when my dignity and my cells aren't enough to satisfy it anymore, the cancer will take everything else it can get, too. The house. Savings. Your college funds. All the happy memories we've shared together.

I know as much as I try and justify my decision, it's still going to hurt the three of you more than you've ever hurt in your life. But I knew if I spoke to you about this prior to doing it, you would have talked me out of it.

I'm especially sorry to you, Ben. My sweet, sweet baby boy. I'm so sorry. I'm sure I could have done it a better way, because no child should have to see their mother in that condition. But I know if I don't do it tonight before you come home, I might never do it. And to me, that would be an even more selfish decision than this one. I know you'll find me in the morning, and I know it will gut you because it's gutting me just thinking about it. But either way, I'm going to be dead before you turn seventeen. At least this way, it will be quick and easy. You can call 911, they'll take away my body, and it'll be over in less than a few hours. A few hours for me to die and be removed from the house is so much better than the several months it could potentially take for the cancer to do its job.

I know this will be difficult for you to deal with, so I've tried to make it as easy as possible. Someone will need to clean up after they take my body, so I've left a card on the kitchen counter for who you should call. There's plenty of cash in my purse. I've left it in the kitchen, on the counter.

If you look in my office, third drawer down on the right, you'll find that I've prepared all the necessary paperwork to file for survivor benefits. Make sure you do this right away. Once the paperwork is filed, you'll get a check in a matter of weeks. There's still a mortgage on the house, but there will be enough left to cover tuition for each of you. I've set all that up through our lawyer.

Please keep the house until you're all grown and settled. It's a good house and despite this one thing, we had a lot of good memories here.

Please know that you three boys made every second of my life worth living. And if I could take away this cancer, I would do it. I would be so selfish about it; I'd probably give it to someone else to suffer through just so I could spend more time with each of you. That's how much I love you.

Please forgive me. I had two poor choices to choose from, neither of which I wanted. I just went with what would be more beneficial to all of us in the end. I hope one day you can understand. And I hope that by choosing to do this, I don't ruin this date for you. November 9th is significant to me, in that it's the same day Dylan Thomas died. And you boys know how much his poetry means to me. It's gotten me through a lot in life, especially your father's death. But my hope for you is that this date will just be a date for you in the future with little significance and little excuse to mourn.

And please don't worry about me. My suffering is over. In the wise words of Dylan Thomas . . . After the first death, there is no other.

With all my love,
Mom

I can barely read my mother's signature

through my tears. Ian walks back into the room several minutes later and sits beside me.

I want to thank him for making me read it, but I'm so mad I can't even speak. If I had just read the letter before the police took it, I would have known everything right then. The last two days would have turned out so different. I may not have been in such a state of shock had I been able to read the letter then. I also wouldn't have misconstrued everything and assumed a man had to do with her decision.

And I would have actually stayed home last night, rather than make the choice to get in her car, drive to a stranger's house, and start a fire that went out of control.

When I double over from the sobs, Ian puts his arm around me and pulls me in for a hug. I know he thinks I'm crying because of everything I just read, and he's partly right. He also probably assumes I'm crying for saying such hateful things about my mother, and he's partly right about that, too.

But what he doesn't know is that most of these tears aren't tears of grief.

They're tears of guilt for being responsible for ruining the life of an innocent girl.

Fallon

I set the page down and pick up another tissue. I don't think I've stopped crying since I started reading.

I check my phone and there's a response from my father.

Dad: Hey! I'd love to, I miss you, too. Tell me when and where and I'll be there.

I try not to cry when I read his text, but I can't help but feel my bitterness has wasted a lot of good memories that could have been made with him. We'll just have to make up for it over the next few years.

I've taken breaks to eat. To think. To breathe. It's almost 7:00 p.m. now and I've only made it through half of the manuscript. I usually get through books in a matter of a few hours, but this has been the hardest thing I've ever had to read in my life. I can't imagine how hard it must have been for Ben to write.

I glance at the next page, trying to decide

if I need another break before beginning. When I see that this next chapter is the day we met in the restaurant, I decide to continue reading. I need to know what motivated him to show up there that day. And more so, why he made the choice to enter my life.

I sit back on the couch and take in a deep breath. And then I start reading chapter four of Ben's manuscript.

BEN'S NOVEL — CHAPTER FOUR
AGE 18

"Somebody's boring me. I think it's me."
— Dylan Thomas

My arm dangles over the side of the bed, and I can tell by the way my hand lies across the carpet that the bed doesn't have a frame or box springs. It's just a mattress on the floor.

I'm on my stomach. There's a sheet draped halfway over me and I'm facedown on the pillow.

I hate these moments. When I wake up too discombobulated to know where I am or who might be on the bed next to me. I usually lie still long enough to get a grip on my surroundings before moving in hopes I don't wake up whoever might be in the room with me. But this morning is different, because whoever was on this bed with me is already awake. I can hear a shower running.

I try to count how many times this has happened — when I've gotten so drunk that I can barely remember anything the next day. I'm guessing at least five times this year, but this is by far the worst. I can usually at least remember which party I was at.

Which friend I was with. Which girl I was flirting with before everything went black. But right now, I've got nothing.

My heart begins to beat as hard as the pounding in my head. I know I'm about to have to stand up and find my clothes. I'll have to look around to try and figure out where I am. I'll have to figure out where I might have left my car. I might even be forced to call Kyle again. But he'll be my absolute last resort, because I'm not in the mood for another lecture today.

To say he's been disappointed in how I've turned out is an understatement. Things haven't been the same at home since the day our mother died two years ago.

Well . . . *I* haven't been the same. Kyle and Ian are hoping my downward spiral will find an uphill slope soon. They were hoping once I graduated high school that I would get serious with college, but that hasn't happened in the way they maybe think it has. In fact, my grades are so bad due to absences, I'm not even sure I'll make it through the semester.

And I try. *God* do I try. Every day I wake up and I tell myself that today will be better. Today will be the day I resolve myself of guilt. But then something will happen that will trigger that feeling that I want to drown faster than it appeared. And that's exactly what I do. I drown out everything with alcohol, friends, and girls. And at least for the rest of that night, I don't have to think about the mistakes I made. The life I ruined.

That thought forces my eyes to open and face the sunlight beaming into the room. I squint and cover my eyes with my hand. I wait a moment before attempting to stand up and find my clothes. When I can finally stand upright, I locate my pants. I find the T-shirt I remember putting on before class yesterday.

But after that? Nothing. I remember absolutely nothing.

I find my shoes and slip those on. When I'm fully dressed, I take a second to look around the room. It doesn't look familiar at all. I walk to the window and look outside and see that I'm in an apartment building. Nothing looks familiar though, but that could be because I can't open my eyes wide enough to see very far. Everything hurts.

I'm about to find out where I am though, because the door to the bathroom is opening up behind me. I squeeze my eyes shut, because I have no idea who she is or what she'll expect.

"Morning, sunshine!"

Her familiar voice flies across the room at

the speed of a torpedo and goes straight through my heart. My knees feel like they're about to buckle beneath me. In fact, I think they are. I reach for a nearby chair and I take a quick seat, dropping my head into my hands. I can't even look at her.

How could she do this to Kyle?

How could she let *me* do this to Kyle?

Jordyn walks closer to me, but I still refuse to look at her. "If you're about to puke, you better do it in the bathroom."

I shake my head, wanting her voice to go away, wanting her apartment to go away, wanting the second-worst thing I've ever done to go away. "Jordyn." When I hear the weakness in my voice, I can tell why she thinks I'm on the verge of being sick. "How did this happen?"

I hear the dip of her mattress as she plops down on the bed a few feet in front of me. "Well . . ." she says. "I'm sure it started with a shot or two. A few beers. Some pretty girls. And then it ended with you calling me crying at midnight last night, rambling about the date and how you need to go home but you were too drunk and you didn't want to call Kyle because he'd be mad at you." She stands and walks toward her closet. "And believe me, he would have been pissed. And if you tell him I let you sleep it off here so that he wouldn't find out, he'll be pissed at *me.* So you better not rat me out, Ben. I'll kill you."

My mind is trying to catch up, but she talks too fast.

So I called her? For help?

We didn't . . .

God, no. She wouldn't do that. I, on the other hand, seem to have no control over the things I do when I get in that state. But at least I called her before I did something stupid. She and Kyle have been together long enough that she's like a sister to me, and I would trust her not to tell Kyle. But the question still remains . . . *why was I naked? In her bed?*

She walks back out of the closet and it's the first time I've looked at her today. She looks normal. Not guilty at all. A little bit tired, maybe, but smiley as usual.

"I saw your ass this morning," she says, laughing. "What the hell did you do? I told you to use my shower, but you could have put your clothes back on afterward." She makes a face. "Now I have to wash my sheets."

She begins to pull her sheets off her mattress. "I hope when I move in with Kyle you start wearing boxers or something. And I can't believe I was forced to sleep on my own couch while your drunk ass stole my bed." I want to tell her to slow down, but every time she talks, I feel more and more relieved. "You owe me big-time."

She loses the smile on her face as she takes a seat on the mattress across from me again. She leans forward and looks at me sincerely. "I don't want to pry into your life. But I love your brother and as soon as my lease is up, we're all going to be living together. So I'm only going to say this once. Are you listening?"

I nod.

"We're only given one mind and body at birth. And they're the only ones we get, so it's up to us to take care of ourselves. I hate to say this, Ben, but right now, you are the absolute *worst* version of yourself that you could possibly be. You're depressed. You're moody. You're only eighteen, and I don't even know where you're getting your alcohol, but you drink way too much. And as much as your brothers have tried to help you, no one can force you to want to be a better person. Only you can do that, Ben. So if you have any hope left in you at all, I suggest you dig deep for it, because if you don't find it, you'll never be the best version of yourself. And you're going to bring your brothers down with you, because they love you that much."

She stares at me just as long as it takes for her words to make sense in my head. She sounds like my mother, and that thought hits me hard.

I stand up. "Are you finished? Because I'd like to go find my car now."

She sighs with disappointment and it makes me feel bad, but I refuse to let her see that all I can think about now is my mother and how, if she saw me today, what would she think of me?

After a few texts to friends, I discovered where my car was. As Jordyn drops me off, I debate apologizing to her. I stall at the car with the door halfway shut, wondering what to say. Finally, I lean down and look at her.

"Sorry for the attitude earlier. I appreciate you helping me last night, and thanks for the ride." I go to shut the door, but she calls my name and steps out of the car. She looks at me over the hood.

"Last night . . . when you called? You kept saying something about the date today, and . . . I don't want to pry. But I know it's the anniversary of what happened with your mom. And I think maybe it would be good for you if you went to see her." She looks down and taps her fingers on the hood.

"Think about it, okay?"

I stare at her for a moment and then I give her one quick nod before getting into my car.

I know it's been two years. I don't need a reminder. Every single day I wake up and take my first breath, I'm reminded of that day.

I grip the steering wheel, unsure if I'm going to get out of my car. It's bad enough that I drove out to the cemetery in the first place. I've never visited her gravesite before. I just don't feel the need to because I don't feel like she's really there. I talk to my mother sometimes. Of course the conversations are one-sided, but I still talk to her. I don't feel like I need to stare at a headstone in order to do that.

So why am I here?

Maybe I was hoping it would help. But the fact of the matter is, I've accepted my mother's death. I understand why she did it. And I know that if she didn't make the choice to take her own life, the cancer would have taken her soon after. But everyone in my family seems to think I can't move on. That I miss her so much it's affecting my life.

I do miss her, but I've moved on from

that. What I haven't moved on from is what I did that night.

I listened to Kyle when he said not to mention Fallon or her father ever again. I don't look them up online. I don't drive by whatever houses they may live in now. Hell, I don't even know where they live. And I don't plan to find out. Kyle was right in that I need to keep my distance from that. They chalked it up as accidental, and the last thing I need is someone growing suspicious of that night.

But I still think about that girl every single day. She lost her career because of me. A *good* career. One lots of people only dream about. And my actions from that night are going to follow her for the rest of her life.

Sometimes I wonder how she's doing now. There have been several times I've wanted to research her — maybe even see her up close — just to see how badly she was injured in the fire. I don't know why. Maybe I think it'll help me move on in some way if I see that she's living a good life. But the one thing that prevents me from looking her up is the fact that she may not be. Her life could be so much worse than I expected, and I'm afraid of how I'll take it if that's the case.

Just as I'm about to crank my car, another

car pulls into the parking lot beside me. The driver's side door opens and before he even steps out, I can feel the dryness creep into my throat.

What is he doing here?

I can tell it's him by the back of his neck, his height, the way he carries himself. Donovan O'Neil has a very recognizable presence about him, and considering I saw him plastered all over the TV the night of the fire, I'll never get his face out of my head.

I look around me, wondering if I should crank my car and back away before he notices me. But he's not even aware of his surroundings. In his right hand, he's holding a bundle of hydrangeas. He's heading toward her gravesite.

He's here to see my mother.

I'm suddenly brought back to the night I was sitting in this same car, watching him from across his street. This feels like that, only now I'm watching out of curiosity rather than hatred. He doesn't stay at her gravesite long. He replaces the wilted flowers with the new ones. He stares at her headstone for a moment, and then he walks back to his car.

He's familiar with this routine, like he does it all the time. And for a moment, I feel guilty for thinking he never cared about her. Because it's obvious he did, if he's still visiting her gravesite two years later.

He looks at his watch on his way back to his car, and then he picks up his pace. He's late for something. And I wonder if, by some miracle, that something has to do with his daughter. I tell myself to stop when I reach for the ignition. I say, "Don't do this, Ben," out loud, hoping I listen to myself.

But curiosity wins today, because I'm following his car out of the cemetery and I have absolutely no idea why I'm doing it.

I park a few cars down from his at the restaurant he pulled into. I watch him as he goes inside the restaurant. I see someone stand up to hug him — *a girl* — and I clench my jaw so tight it hurts.

That has to be her.

My palms begin to sweat. I don't know if I actually want to see her. But I know there's no way I'm leaving here with her so close without at least going inside and walking past their table. I have to know. I need to know what I've done to her.

I grab my laptop before walking inside so I can have something to focus on while I'm sitting alone. Or at least pretend I'm focusing on it. When I walk inside, I can't see her face to even know for sure if she's Fallon.

Her back is to me. I try not to stare because I don't want her father seeing me paying them any attention.

"Table or booth?" the waitress asks.

I nod at the booth behind theirs. "Can I get that one?"

She smiles and grabs a menu. "Just one today?"

I nod and she leads me to the booth. My heart is pounding so fast, I can't even find the courage to glance at her when I walk by. I take a seat so that I'm facing the opposite direction. I'll work up the courage in a few minutes. There's nothing wrong with me being here. I don't know why it feels like I'm breaking the law when all I'm doing is sitting down for a meal.

My hands are threaded together on the table in front of me. I try to come up with a multitude of reasons to turn around and glance over my shoulder, but I'm afraid when I do I may not be able to stop staring. I have no idea what kind of damage I've done to her, and I'm scared if I look in her eyes, I'll see that she's sad.

But I'm scared if I *don't* look in her eyes, I'll miss the fact that she could be happy.

"I'm only half an hour late, Fallon. Cut me some slack," her father says.

He said her name. That's definitely her. In

the next few minutes, I could be coming face-to-face with the girl whose life I almost took.

Luckily, a waiter comes up and takes my order, distracting me from myself. I'm not at all hungry, but I order something anyway, because what kind of guy comes into a restaurant and doesn't order any food? I don't want to draw attention to myself.

The waiter tries to strike up a conversation with me about the fact that the guy behind us looks just like Donovan O'Neil, the actor who played Max Epcott. I pretend I don't know who that is and he's wildly unimpressed. I just want him to go away. Finally, he does. I lean back in the booth so I can hear more of their conversation.

"So, yeah. I'm a little shocked, but it's happening," her father says.

I wait for her to respond. I missed whatever he just said to her, thanks to nosey McWaiter, but her silence proves it wasn't something she wanted to hear.

"Fallon? Are you going to say anything?"

"What am I supposed to say?" *She doesn't sound happy.* "Do you want me to *congratulate* you?"

I feel her father fall against the back of his booth. "Well, I thought you'd be happy for me," he says.

"*Happy* for you?"

Okay. Whatever he told her has pissed her off. She's got spunk, I've got to give her that.

"I didn't know I had it in me to become a father again."

I don't know how I feel about that. For a second, I'm reminded that this man used to be in love with my mother, and this could have possibly been a situation he got himself into with her, had the cancer not taken her first.

I mean . . . I know the cancer didn't take her. The gun did. But either way, the cancer was at fault.

"Releasing sperm into the vagina of a twenty-four-year-old does not a father make," Fallon says.

I laugh quietly. I don't know why, but just hearing the way she talks to him eases some of my guilt. Maybe because I'd always pictured her to be this meek, quiet girl, wallowing in self-pity. But she sounds like a firecracker.

But still . . . this is insane. I shouldn't be here. Kyle would kill me if he found out what I was doing.

"You don't think I have the right to call myself a father? What does that make me to you, then?"

I shouldn't be listening in on their private

conversation. I spend the next few moments trying to focus on the laptop I brought with me, but I'm just scrolling through screens, pretending to work, all the while listening to what an inconsiderate prick her father is.

I can hear her sigh from where I'm seated. "You're impossible. Now I understand why Mom left you."

"Your mother left me because I slept with her best friend. My personality had nothing to do with it."

How could my mother have ever loved this man?

Now that I think about it, I'm not so sure she did. He seemed to be the one sending all the letters and texts. I never saw anything she sent him, so maybe this was a short-lived, one-sided relationship that he can't get over.

That makes me feel better, anyway. I shudder to think my mother was just a regular woman who sometimes made bad relationship choices, and not the all-knowing heroine I've probably made her out to be in my memory.

The waiter interrupts their conversation to deliver their lunch. I roll my eyes when he pretends to just now notice that Donovan O'Neil is sitting there. I hear him ask Fallon if she'll take a picture of the two of them. I stiffen in my seat, wondering if she'll stand up and come into my view. I'm not so sure I'm ready to see what she looks like.

But it doesn't matter if I'm ready or not, because she just told them to take a selfie and that she's heading to the bathroom. She begins to walk past me, and the second she comes into view, my breath hitches.

She's walking in the opposite direction, so I don't see her face. What I do see is hair. Lots of it, long and thick and straight, chestnut brown, just like the shoes she has on, and it falls all the way down her back.

And her jeans. They fit her so perfectly, it looks like they were custom made, molding to every curve, from her hips, all the way down to her ankles. They move with her so well, I find myself wondering what kind of panties she has on under them. Because I can't see a panty line. She could be wearing a thong, but she could also be going . . . *what the hell, Ben? How in the hell did your brain move in this direction?*

My pulse speeds up because I know I need to leave. I need to get up and walk away and accept that she seems to be okay. Her father may be an asshole, but she's able to hold her own pretty well, so my being this close to either of them isn't good for anyone.

But dammit if the waiter isn't eating up

the fact that Donovan O'Neil is giving him the time of day. I don't even care about my food, if he would just bring me the check I could pay it and get the hell out of here.

I start to bounce my knee up and down in nervousness. She's been in there a really long time. I know she's going to walk out any second, and I don't know if I should look at her or look away or smile or run or *fuck what do I do?* She's walking out.

She's looking down and I still can't see her face, but her body is even more perfect from the front than it was from the back.

When she glances up at me, my stomach drops. My heart feels like it melts, right in the confines of its chamber. For the first time in two years, I'm seeing exactly what I did to her.

From the top of her left cheek, near her eye, all the way down to her neck, there are scars. Scars that are there because of me. Some more faded than others, but they're very prominent with the way the skin is pinkish in hue, brighter, and much more fragile looking than the parts of her that were unharmed. But it's not even the scars that stand out the most. It's her green eyes that are staring back at me now. The lack of confidence behind them speaks volumes of just how much damage I've caused to her life.

She lifts a hand and pulls a piece of hair in her mouth, covering some of the scars. At the same time, she darts her eyes to the floor, allowing her hair to fall over her cheek and hide more of the scars. I keep watching her, because it hurts not to. I think about what that night must have been like for her. How scared she must have been. How much agony she must have gone through in the months afterward.

I clench my hands in fists, because I've never felt more of a need to make things right. I want to drop to my knees right here in front of her and tell her how sorry I am for causing her so much pain. For ruining her career. For making her think it's necessary to have to hide her face with her hair when she's this fucking beautiful.

She has no idea. She has no idea she's lifting her eyes and looking into the eyes of the guy who ruined her life. She has no idea that I would give anything to press my lips to that cheek — to kiss the scars I gave her, to tell her how incredibly sorry I am.

She has no idea that I'm on the verge of tears just seeing her face, because it's equal parts exquisite and excruciating. I'm afraid if I don't smile at her right now, I'll cry for her.

And then this thing happens when she passes me, where everything inside my chest constricts. Because I'm worried that what just passed between us — that one tiny smile — is all that will ever pass between us. And I don't know why that worries me, because before today, I wasn't even sure I ever wanted to see her.

But now that I've seen her, I don't know that I want to stop. And the fact that her father is behind me right now, beating her down, telling her she's not pretty enough to act anymore, makes me want to climb over this booth and strangle him. Or at least climb into the booth next to her and defend her.

This is the exact moment the waiter decides to bring me my food. I try to eat. Really, I do, but I'm still reeling from hearing the way her father speaks to her. I slowly down French fries as I listen to her father grow more and more insincere. At first, I'm relieved when I hear she has plans to move away.

Good for you, I think.

Knowing she's brave enough to move across the country and pursue acting again fills me with more respect for her than I've ever had for anyone. But hearing her father continuously try to tell her she's not good enough fills me with more disrespect than I've ever had for anyone.

I hear her father clear his throat. "You know that's not what I meant. I'm not saying you've reduced yourself to audiobooks. What I'm saying is that you can find a better career to fall back on now that you can't act anymore. There isn't enough money in narration. Or Broadway, for that matter."

I don't hear what she says next, because all I see is red. I can't believe this man — a father who is supposed to defend and support his daughter in the wake of a challenge — is saying these things to her. Maybe he's practicing tough love, but the girl has been through enough.

The conversation ceases for a moment. Long enough for her father to request a refill. Long enough for the waiter to bring me my own refill, and long enough for me to get up and go to the bathroom, try to calm myself down and then return to my seat without strangling the man behind me.

"You make me want to swear off men forever," she says.

Hell, her father makes *me* want her to swear off men forever. If men are really as shallow as this one, *all* women should swear off men forever.

"That shouldn't be a problem," her father says. "I've only known you to go on one date, and that was over two years ago."

And that's when all reason goes out the window.

Does he not have any idea what today is? Does he not have one single fucking clue what his daughter has been through emotionally in the past two years? I'm sure she spent a good year recovering, and I can tell just by the few seconds I looked in her eyes that she doesn't have a single ounce of confidence in her. And here he is commenting on the fact that she hasn't dated since her accident?

My hands are shaking, I'm so pissed. I think I might even be angrier than the night I caught his car on fire.

"Well, Dad," she says, her voice strained. "I don't really get the same attention from guys that I used to get."

I'm sliding out of the booth, unable to stop myself. But I'll be damned if I allow this girl to spend one more second without someone defending her in a proper way.

I'm sliding into the seat next to her.

"Sorry I'm late, babe," I say, wrapping my arm around her shoulders.

She stiffens beneath my arm, but I keep

going. I press my lips to the side of her head, unintentionally taking in the floral scent of her shampoo. "Damn L.A, traffic," I mutter.

I reach for her father's hand and before I say my name, I wonder if he'll recognize it somehow, having known my mother. She changed back to her maiden name a few years after my father's death, so he may have no idea who I am. I hope. "I'm Ben. Benton James Kessler. Your daughter's boyfriend."

Not a single flash of recognition registers in his expression. He has no idea who I am.

Her father's hand falls into mine and I want to yank him across the table and punch his teeth in. I probably would if I didn't feel her grow even more tense beside me. I lean back and pull her against me, whispering in her ear. "Just go with it."

It's as if a lightbulb goes off in her head at this very second, because the confusion on her face turns into delight. She smiles affectionately at me, leaning into me, and she says, "I didn't think you'd make it."

Yeah, I want to say. *I didn't think I'd be sitting here, either. But since I can't possibly make your life worse on this date, the least I can do is try to make it a little bit better.*

Fallon

I make a new pile with the pages I've already read. I stare down at the manuscript in disbelief. I know I should be angry that he's lied to me for so long, but being in his head is somehow justifying his behavior to me. And not only that, but it's also justifying my father's behavior.

Ben is right. Now that I look back on that day, I can see that my father wasn't entirely to blame. He was expressing his opinion over my career, which every parent has the right to do. And even though I disagreed with him and the way he delivered it, he never was the best at communication. Besides, I obviously had it out for him as soon as he sat down at the booth. He went into defense mode, I was in attack mode, and things just went south from there.

I need to remember that there's more than one way people show love. And even though his way and my way are completely opposite, it's still love.

I go to flip to the next chapter, but a few pieces of notebook paper fall out of the section between chapters five and six. I set the pages of the manuscript down and pick up the letter. It's another note written by Ben.

Fallon,

You know everything that happens after this point in the manuscript. It's all here. Every day we spent together and even a few days we didn't. Every thought I've ever had in your presence . . . or close to it.

As you can tell from the chapter you just finished, I wasn't in a good place when we met. The two years of my life since the fire had been hell, and I was doing everything I could to drown out the guilt I felt. But that first day I spent with you was the first day in a very long time that I felt happy. And I could tell that I made you happy, and that's something I never thought possible. And even though you were moving away, I knew that if there was a way we could each start looking forward to November 9th, it could make a huge difference in both of our lives. So I swore to myself that on the days I spent with you, I would allow myself to enjoy it. I wouldn't think about the fire — I wouldn't think about what I did to you. For one day each year, I wanted to be this guy who was falling for this girl, because everything about you captivated me. And I knew if I allowed my past to eat me up in your presence, that I would somehow slip. That you would find out what I'd done to you. I knew that if you ever found out the truth, there was no way you could forgive me for all I had taken.

Even though I should probably feel a world of guilt, I don't regret a single minute I spent with you. Of course I wish I had handled things differently. Maybe if I had walked up to you and your father that day and explained the truth, I would have saved you a lot of heartache. But I can't dwell on all the things I should have done differently, when to me this was our fate. We were drawn to each other. We made each other happy. And I know without a doubt there were several times during the past few years that we were madly in love with each other at the same time. Not everyone experiences that Fallon, and I'd be lying if I said I regretted it.

And that's one of my biggest fears — that you've spent the past year assuming I've told you more than one lie, but I haven't. The only lie I've ever told you is the one I omitted — the part where I was responsible for the fire. Every word that came out of my mouth in your presence beyond that was the absolute truth. When I said you were beautiful, I meant it.

If you take one thing from this manuscript, let it be this one simple paragraph. Absorb these words. I want them to stain your soul, because these words are the most important. I'm terrified that my lies have resulted in a loss of the confidence you gained during the times we were together. Because while I did withhold a huge truth from you, the one thing I couldn't have been more honest about was your beauty. And yes, you have scars. But anyone who sees your scars before they see you doesn't deserve you. I hope you remember that and believe that. A body is simply a package for the true gifts inside. And you are full of gifts. Selflessness, kindness, compassion. All the things that matter.

Youth and beauty fade. Human decency doesn't.

I know I said in my previous letter that I didn't write this for your forgiveness. While that's the truth, I'm not going to pretend that I'm not praying on my knees for your forgiveness, hoping for a miracle. I'm not going to act like I won't be sitting at the restaurant for hours upon end, hoping you walk through those doors. Because that's exactly where I'll be. And if you don't show up today, I'll be there next year. And the next. Every November 9th I'll wait for you, hoping one day you'll be able to find enough forgiveness to love me again. But if that doesn't happen and you never show, I'll still be grateful to you until the day that I die.

You saved me the day we met, Fallon. I know I was only eighteen, but my life would have turned out so different had we not spent that time together. The first night we had to say goodbye, I drove straight home and started writing this book. It became my new life goal. My new passion. I took college more seriously. I took life more seriously. And because of you and the impact you had on my life, the last two years I spent with Kyle were great ones. When he died, he was proud of me. And that means more to me than you will ever know.

So whether or not you can find it in your heart to love me again, I needed to thank you for saving me. And if there is any part of you capable of forgiving me, you know where I'll be. Tonight, next year, the next, for eternity.

The choice is yours. You can continue reading this manuscript, and hopefully it will help you find closure. Or you can stop reading now and come forgive me.

Ben

■ ■ ■ ■

Last November 9th

■ ■ ■ ■

If lies were written, I would erase them
But they are spoken; etched within
With convalesced truth, I scream out my
atonement
Let me repent against your skin.

— Benton James Kessler

Ben

There were 83,456 words in the manuscript I dropped off at her front door last night. There are roughly 23,000 words in the first five chapters, before she would have gotten to the note. She could have easily read 23,000 words in three hours. If she started the manuscript right after I dropped it off, she would have finished the first section by 3 a.m.

But it's almost midnight. It's been almost twenty-four hours since I saw her pick up the manuscript and close her door. Which means she's had twenty-one hours to spare and she's still not here.

Which means, obviously, she isn't coming.

Most of me believed she wouldn't show up today, but a small part of me still held out hope. I can't say that her choice has broken my heart, because that would mean my heart was still whole to be broken.

I've been heartbroken for a solid year, so her not showing up feels just as crippling as the last 365 days have felt.

I'm surprised the restaurant has let me wait it out here in this booth for so long. I've been here since the crack of dawn this morning in hopes that she stayed up and read the manuscript last night. Now that it's almost midnight, that's a good eighteen hours I've spent occupying this booth. That's gonna be one big tip.

At 11:55 p.m., I leave the tip. I don't want to be here when the clock strikes November 10th. I'd rather wait out the last five minutes in my car.

When I open the door to leave the restaurant, the waitress shoots me a pitiful look. I'm sure she's never seen anyone wait so long after being stood up, but at least it'll give her a good story to tell.

It's 11:56 p.m. when I reach the parking lot.

It's 11:56 p.m. when I see her open her door and step out of her car.

It's still 11:56 p.m. when I clasp my hands behind my head and suck in a rush of cool November air just to see if my lungs are working.

She's standing by her car, the wind blowing strands of hair across her face as she looks at me from across the parking lot. I feel like if I take a step toward her, the earth would crumble beneath my feet from the weight of my heart. We both stand still for several long seconds.

She glances down at the phone in her hands, and then she looks back up at me. "It's 11:57, Ben. We only have three minutes to do this."

I stare at her, wondering what she means by that. Is she leaving in three minutes? Is she only giving me three minutes to plead my case with her? Questions are bouncing around in my head when I see the corner of her mouth lift into a smile.

She's smiling.

As soon as I realize she's smiling, I'm running. I make it across the parking lot in a matter of seconds. I wrap my arms around her and pull her against me and when I feel her arms go around me, I do the most non-alpha thing I can possibly do.

I cry like a fucking baby.

My arms are squeezing her tight, my hands are wrapped around the back of her head, my face is pressed into her hair. And I hold her for so long, I have no idea if it's still November 9th anymore or if it's the 10th now. But the date doesn't matter, because I'm going to love her through every single one of them.

She loosens her grip and pulls away from my shoulder to look up at me. We're both smiling now, and I can't believe this girl found it in her heart to forgive me. But she did, I can see it all over her face. I can see it in her eyes, in her smile, in the way she holds herself. And I can feel it in the way her thumbs brush over my cheeks, wiping my tears away.

"Do fictional boyfriends cry as much as I do?" I ask her.

She laughs. "Only the really great ones."

I drop my forehead to hers and I squeeze my eyes shut. I want to soak this moment up for as long as I can. Just because she's here and just because she has forgiven me doesn't mean she's here to love me forever. And I have to be prepared to accept that.

"Ben, I have something I want to say."

I pull back and look down at her. Now there are tears in *her* eyes, so I don't feel so pathetic. She reaches up and puts her hands on my face, gently stroking my cheek. "I didn't come here to forgive you."

I can feel the hardening of my jaw, but I try to relax. I knew this was a possibility. And I have to respect her decision, no matter how hard it will be for me.

"You were sixteen," she says. "You had

been through one of the worst things a child could ever experience. Your actions from that night weren't because you were a bad person, Ben. It was because you were a scared teenage boy and sometimes people make mistakes. You've carried so much guilt for what you did, and for so long. You can't ask for my forgiveness, because there's nothing to forgive. If anything, I'm here for *your* forgiveness. Because I know your heart, Ben, and your heart is only capable of love. I should have recognized that last year when I doubted you. I should have given you the chance to explain it then. If I had just listened to you, then we could have avoided an entire year of heartache. So for that . . . I'm sorry. I'm *so* sorry. And I hope you can forgive me."

She's looking up at me with genuine hope — like she honestly believes she's partly at fault for anything we've ever been through.

"You aren't allowed to apologize to me, Fallon."

She lets out a rush of air and nods. "Then you aren't allowed to apologize to me."

"Fine," I say. "I forgive myself."

She laughs. "And I forgive *my*self."

She brings her hands up to my hair and runs her fingers through it, smiling up at me. My eyes fall to a bandage on her left wrist and she notices. "Oh. I almost forgot the most important part. It's why I'm so late." She begins to unwrap the bandage from around her wrist. "I got a tattoo." She holds up her wrist, and there's a small tattoo of an open book. On each of the two open pages lie a comedy and a tragedy mask. "Books and theater," she says, explaining the tattoo. "My two favorite things. I just got it about two hours ago when I realized how selflessly in love with you I am." She looks back up at me, her eyes glistening.

I blow out a quick breath, taking her wrist in my hand. I pick it up and I kiss it. "Fallon," I say. "Come home with me. I want to make love to you and fall asleep with you. And then in the morning, I want to cook you the breakfast I promised you last year. Well-done bacon and over-easy eggs."

She smiles, but doesn't agree to the breakfast. "Actually, I'm having breakfast with my father tomorrow."

Hearing her say that she's having breakfast with her father makes me even happier than if she would have agreed to have breakfast with me. I know her father isn't the ideal parent, but he's still her father. And I've felt so much guilt over the fact that I'm responsible for a lot of the strain in their relationship.

"But I'll still come home with you," she says.

"Good," I tell her. "Tonight you're mine. I'll just wait to cook you breakfast until the day *after* tomorrow. And every day after that, until next November 9th when I get down on one knee and give you the most book-worthy marriage proposal in history."

She slaps me in the chest. "That was a *huge* spoiler, Ben! Did you not learn about spoiler alerts during your reading binge?"

I grin as I lower my mouth to hers. "Spoiler alert. They lived happily ever after."

And then I kiss her.

And it's a twelve.

Not the end.

Far from it.

ACKNOWLEDGMENTS

First, I want to thank everyone who had a hand in this book. My beta-readers and best friends. In no particular order: Tarryn Fisher, Mollie Kay Harper (my sex-scene guru), Kay Miles, Vannoy Fite, Misha Robinson, Marion Archer, Kathryn Perez, Karen Lawson, Vilma Gonzalez, Kaci Blue-Buckley, Stephanie Cohen, Chelle Lagoski Northcutt, Jennifer Stiltner, Natasha Tomic, Aestas, and Kristin Delcambre.

To the women who help run my chaotic life, from making sure my bills are paid or helping out in my online reader groups: Stephanie Cohen, Brenda Perez, Murphy Hopkins, Chelle Lagoski Northcutt, Pamela Carrion, and Kristin Delcambre.

And even though The Bookworm Box isn't related to this book, the volunteers have absolutely had a hand in making sure this book was finished. So to all who have helped pack boxes, print labels, and who have donated books, I thank you! But mostly Lin Reynolds, who has dang near single-handedly kept this charity up and running despite our many obstacles.

To my parents, my sisters, Heath and the boys. All of you. I know our lives have changed drastically over the last few years. It means the world to me that every single one of you has been open and receptive to these changes. You don't argue when I forget to call you back, you don't get mad when I travel too much and you don't burn my clothes when I fail to unpack them from my suitcases for weeks at a time. Your patience and understanding is appreciated. You are my foundation, my backbone, my heart. All of you.

To Johanna Castillo, my wonderful, beautiful editor with the killer legs. My happiness comes first for you, and that's all I could ever ask for.

TO MY PUBLICIST, ARIELE STEWART FREDMAN! I'M PUTTING THIS IN CAPS BECAUSE I'M STILL SO EXCITED I FINALLY GOT YOU! NOT ONLY AS MY PUBLICIST, BUT AS A GREAT, AWESOME FRIEND!

To my publisher, Judith Curr, and the rest of the team at Atria Books, I can't thank you enough for the support you have given me. From nailing the cover on your first attempt, to inviting me to be a part of this crazy app idea. I can't wait to see what my future holds with you.

To my agent, Jane Dystel, and the entire Dystel & Goderich Literary Team. I can't thank you enough for being such a huge part of my career. My dream. My life goal. It wouldn't be possible without your help.

To X Ambassadors, one of the greatest bands of our time. Thank you for inspiring so much of this book. Thank you for creating music that feeds our souls.

And last but not least, thank you to Cynthia Capshaw, for giving birth to my soul mate.

If I forgot anyone, it's all Murphy's fault. Even though she moved on to her own career in editing and is no longer my assistant, I'm still going to blame her for everything that goes wrong. Because she'll always be my sister.

To listen to music created specifically for this novel, visit: https://www.colleenhoover.com/portfolio/november-9/.

ABOUT THE AUTHOR

Colleen Hoover is the #1 *New York Times* bestselling author of *Slammed, Hopeless, Maybe Someday, Maybe Not, Ugly Love, Confess, November 9, It Ends with Us, Without Merit,* and *All Your Perfects.* She has won the Goodreads Choice Award for Best Romance three years in a row — for Confess (2015), *It Ends with Us* (2016), and *Without Merit* (2017). *Confess* was adapted into a seven-episode online series. In 2015, Colleen and her family founded The Bookworm Box, a bookstore and monthly subscription service offering signed novels donated by authors. All profits are given to various charities each month to help those in need. Colleen lives in Texas with her husband and their three boys. Visit ColleenHoover.com.

The employees of Thorndike Press hope you have enjoyed this Large Print book. All our Thorndike, Wheeler, and Kennebec Large Print titles are designed for easy reading, and all our books are made to last. Other Thorndike Press Large Print books are available at your library, through selected bookstores, or directly from us.

For information about titles, please call:
(800) 223-1244

or visit our website at:
gale.com/thorndike

To share your comments, please write:
Publisher
Thorndike Press
10 Water St., Suite 310
Waterville, ME 04901

CPSIA information can be obtained
at www.ICGtesting.com
Printed in the USA
BVHW052042210622
640349BV00001B/13